Hot & Cold

Tegan Phillips was diagnosed with Fibromyalgia at 16-years-old, and has used her lived experiences to convey character's struggles in fiction. After a school trip to the States, she discovered her love for ice hockey and wrote her debut novel, *Melting For You*, in the years following.

Also by Tegan Phillips

The Spears Players Series

Melting For You
Hot & Cold

Hot & Cold

TEGAN PHILLIPS

hera

First published in the United Kingdom in 2026 by

Hera Books, an imprint of
Canelo Digital Publishing Limited,
20 Vauxhall Bridge Road,
London SW1V 2SA
United Kingdom

A Penguin Random House Company
The authorised representative in the EEA is Dorling Kindersley Verlag GmbH.
Arnulfstr. 124, 80636 Munich, Germany

Copyright © Tegan Phillips 2026

The moral right of Tegan Phillips to be identified as the creator of this work has been asserted in accordance with the Copyright, Designs and Patents Act, 1988.
All rights reserved. No part of this publication may be reproduced or transmitted in any form or by any means, electronic or mechanical, including photocopy, recording, or any information storage and retrieval system, without permission in writing from the publisher.
No part of this book may be used or reproduced in any manner for the purpose of training artificial intelligence technologies or systems. In accordance with Article 4(3) of the DSM Directive 2019/790, Canelo expressly reserves this work from the text and data mining exception.

A CIP catalogue record for this book is available from the British Library.

Print ISBN 978 1 83598 139 9
Ebook ISBN 978 1 83598 140 5

This book is a work of fiction. Names, characters, businesses, organizations, places and events are either the product of the author's imagination or are used fictitiously. Any resemblance to actual persons, living or dead, events or locales is entirely coincidental.

Printed and bound in Great Britain by Clays Ltd, Elcograf S.p.A.

Look for more great books at
www.herabooks.com | www.dk.com

Chapter One

Lyndsey

March

Bees. That's all I can hear when I come into consciousness. Bees buzzing around inside my head. Who let all these bees into my goddamn hotel room? That is the only explanation for the ringing in my ears.

There is always a moment before you wake up when everything in life is right and just. That lasts for a second before the reality of life sinks in. Sometimes it comes in waves and sometimes it's a tsunami of memories thrashing against you. This morning is the former, a slow, soft trickle slowly bringing me back to the now.

Sunlight flitters in through the blinds and I take the moment to bask in the feeling of its rays warming my face. As I lie here with my eyes closed, I feel like I'm sunning on a beach. Soft sand under my warm skin and a hangover from all the sunset-coloured cocktails I drank lounging on a cabana instead of shots on the Vegas strip. Coming to Vegas to celebrate the end of the Seattle Spears hockey team's season was supposed to be a fun weekend with my best friend and boss Ellis, her fiancé and his teammates; but I might have taken *fun* a little far.

I'm not the type of person who parties all night long, not any more anyway. Back in my early twenties drinking more nights a week than not was the norm in the circles I ran. I thought I had found people who were going to be by my side forever, people who understood me and the struggle I had growing up. I was wrong. Not only did those friends not understand, they didn't care.

Looking back it's not surprising that a bunch of party-central twenty-year-olds didn't actually care about me or my problems, they cared about which bar to go to next.

That's not to say I stopped drinking altogether: I didn't have a problem with drinking; I had problems I was trying to hide from with alcohol. Last night I drank, and drank and drank some more. Ellis left the kids with Liam's parents, Tracy and Alek, and she wanted to let loose. I'm the master at getting loose. I just wanted her to enjoy her first time in a different state to her two beautiful kids. Plus I wanted to get my ex out of my head. For weeks Kayla has been texting me begging to have me back and no matter how much I ask her to stop, she just keeps going. Once the plane touched down, I threw my phone into my bag and was determined not to check it, to get out of the funk Kayla has put me in. I wanted to spend time with my friend and show her a good time on the strip.

Now I'm suffering for her enjoyment. Luckily, Liam 'Ruin' Ruinsky has just finished his final season with the Seattle Spears hockey team, so that means we all got the best rooms in the best hotel on the strip. Another pro to having a handful of six-foot-tall hockey men around meant both of us felt incredibly safe to get sloppy because we knew we had protection. I used that to its highest degree.

I find myself wearing a mask around everyone, even on this trip, and I don't even know why. I'm the fun, sassy, flirty best friend in Ellis' life. I flirt because it is how I like people to see me. I'm fun because I don't want them to look at me differently, like I'm a disappointment for not being perfect. I've seen that look before, when my parents found out I was not the perfect religious daughter they raised.

I wouldn't be able to bear seeing that disappointment reflected in the eyes of my new friends, my found family. I worry they would be disappointed if they knew that I'm not the fun, bubbly me all of the time. Is that irrational? Yes, but nobody ever thinks their family would turn their back on them and, when that has happened once, you will do everything in your power to make sure it doesn't happen again.

So I laugh, I smile, I dance and make jokes at my own expense because that is how I know how to let people get close to me. So last night I did just that. Made sure everyone around me was comfortable and having a good time, even if it meant I drank more than I would have liked to make sure Ellis didn't feel alone.

Stretching out on the bed, I hear my bones clicking into place and I definitely don't want to risk making the impending headache worse by prying my eyes open just yet. Instead, I turn over to bury my face into the pillow and pull the blankets up to tuck under my chin, trying to remember if I washed my make-up off before falling into bed. I'm inhaling deeply when the first inkling that something strange is afoot enters the recesses of my mind. Something more than just *hangxiety*.

Like lightning striking, I realise what is wrong, and it's just as painful. My bed smells just like *him*. But surely not. My mind must be playing tricks on me. We were in a big group last night, of course some remnants of aftershave are expected to hang in the air – the players certainly wear enough of it. But *this* feels more familiar to me. I recognise it too well.

My body tingles with embarrassing realisation. It could only be one person.

Aiden Anders.

The bachelor captain for the Seattle Spears, Seattle's very own cowboy hailing from the lone-star state. He's suddenly everywhere – I can smell him all over my sheets. My senses are overwhelmed by his cologne and the smell of his damn body wash, the exact same woodsy smell that follows him around like a cloud. *Shit*.

While my eyes still adjust to the foreign bedroom, I find the second and most damning evidence of Aiden: his damn tattooed arm wrapped over my waist. He isn't covered in tattoos the way that his offence player Jay 'Edge' Brink is. No, Aiden picks his art more sparingly. Each one kills me, especially the snake wrapped around his forearm. The one whose stark black ink is currently standing out against my pale skin. I try my hardest not to wake him but he is holding me tight. Very tight.

Almost like he knew when it was time for me to wake up and I was going to want to escape. If I can do it without waking him up, even better. We have hardly spoken since New Year's Eve when our strange relationship reached a disastrous peak and I don't want to deal with his questions when my head is pounding like a drum.

Just as I slide a little bit out of his grip, he somehow manages to band around me even tighter still. His nose now burrows against my neck; my movements must have woken him slightly because his warm lips meet the skin of my shoulder, kissing lightly.

"Five more minutes," he mumbles sleepily against me. His voice is gravelly and his southern accent is so much stronger when he is still half asleep. A strong reminder of why Anders is the team player I've crushed for over a year – if we are only going on when I met him, and not the posters from my teenage wall.

Then I snap. Instead of going slow, which clearly wasn't working in my favour, I jump out of the bed instead. Maybe speed will be the best way to escape without any backlash. In an instant I'm on my feet and scrambling for any clothes within reach. Which there are none, the room is surprisingly clean, no trail of clothes hanging on lampshades. One saving grace is that I'm not naked, I have at least my underwear to preserve my decency.

Admittedly, this isn't the first time I've woken up from a one-night stand. But I'm usually a lot more naked and smell a lot less like Aiden. Also, I'm no expert in his anatomy, but I have a sneaking suspicion that if we had slept together, I might be more touch-tender, which I'm not now. *Maybe we didn't have sex?*

When we met last year as Ellis and her partner Liam started dating, I flirted with Aiden when I could. It was harmless. And hell, I'm a woman, I wasn't the first and I won't be the last. He helped me at work when Ellis was pregnant and on bed rest. He made me laugh when I was overwhelmed. Plus he's handsome. So damn handsome. His short blond hair with some darker pieces glow in the morning sunlight. Stormy grey eyes that are flecked with blue when you look at them long enough. And that damn southern drawl that he uses like the weapon it is.

Of course I flirted with him, *of course* I got butterflies whenever he gave me a helping hand. That doesn't mean I'm a fool. I know I was nothing but a way to pass the time between games, I won't begrudge him putting me off to the side when he got bored, that wouldn't be fair of me. I got his attention for a while and I took that for the fun time it was, until last night apparently. Now I'm near naked in a hotel room with him, that doesn't feel like the carefully crafted bubble I placed him in.

My head protests the sudden movements from lying to suddenly running around the room but the only clear thought I can hear over the incessant pounding is the need to know how I got here. How *we* got here.

Beams of sunlight shining through the blinds are not enough to illuminate the room fully but one thing is for sure and that is that this is definitely not my hotel room. My room this weekend is posher than anything I've stayed in before but this is a step above even that, avocado-coloured panel walls and solid wood underfoot cushioned by a sage-green rug. They say lightning doesn't strike twice but that doesn't feel very true right now as the memories of the prior night cloud my vision.

Drinking.

Dancing.

Aiden.

Dancing with Aiden.

Shots with Aiden.

Then blackness. And the buzzing in my head every time I move.

I can feel Aiden's eyes on me but I ignore that for now. Once I have something over my underwear, I can meet his gaze. Or not. Hopefully not. Maybe he will grant me the decency to let me escape with my pride and without sharing a word. That would be nice, I know it's not going to happen but it would be a dream. His eyes rake over my exposed skin as I eventually find my travel bag thrown under a chair in the corner.

Looks like I had the forethought to stop at my own room to grab my stuff before coming up here. *Yay drunk me*. Drunk me should have gone to her own room, but this is better than nothing.

As I throw on a summer dress, I hear Aiden cough. But still, neither of us breaks the precious silence. Once the dress comes down over my head, I finally see he's awake, and my heart skips a beat. For the first time since I jumped from the bed Aiden isn't buried in the sheets. He's looking at his hand. His left hand. And the ring staring back at him.

I stifle a laugh. How cliché and unrealistic. A wedding ring in Vegas, Something I suppose he or the other players would find funny. I want to crack a joke, ask who the lucky girl is. Until a new weight on my hand stops me.

It's suddenly the only thing I can feel. A tight heavy band around my left fourth finger. I look down, and it all becomes real. A simple gold band with a small red stone. Maybe a garnet, a ruby? Why is that what my brain is focusing on? Jesus Christ, it looks like I'm married and I'm trying to guess gemstones.

Then I start laughing. No, not laughing, I start *cackling*.

"Darlin', take a breath for me," Aiden says as he slides out of the bed. I'm so distracted by my new jewels that I barely look at his naked chest. Just barely.

"Oh sure, *husband*, I will get right on that," I snap sarcastically. "This can't be real, can it? It's just a messed-up joke – right?" I practically plead.

At this point I'm borderline hyperventilating in between bursts of booming laughter. My eyes dart around the room trying to find some clue to tell me this is all fake. It wouldn't be my first panic attack, and I think if it was ever socially acceptable to have a panic attack it would be waking up next to the Spears hockey captain with matching wedding bands after dodging him for the past few months. When my eyes settle on what appears to be a legal document my hands start to shake even harder. My steps feel heavy as I edge over to the nightstand. There, looking up at me, is a goddamn marriage certificate signed by both of us.

"Okay, how about we keep calm." He walks closer in what I think is an attempt to soothe me, eyeing the paper himself.

"Has my brain broken or did you just tell me to calm down… WHEN WE JUST WOKE UP MARRIED!" I'm glad we are in his suite right now because the chances for a noise complaint are slim to none. In a normal room someone would be banging on the wall with how loud I yell. He just earned it, who tells a woman to calm down in a situation like this?

Actually he seems remarkably calm right now. Way too calm for this situation. Maybe he has taken too many pucks to the head and has fewer brain cells than necessary, because there is no way he is relaxing right now after waking up with me wrapped in his arms. Apart from casting a glance at my body in front of him, he has barely twitched. Yes, he is a professional captain and that means he is cool under pressure; but this isn't a game and I'm not one of his damn teammates.

"Fuck, Aiden!" I rip the ring from my finger, launching it at his chest, and storm into the bathroom, slamming the door on my way.

What have I done?

Chapter Two

Aiden

With the way my head is pounding, silence would be welcomed right now. Lyndsey and I might not be talking, but the elevator music as we descend from my suite to the hotel restaurant for a group breakfast sounds so loud mixed with the tension. It's one of those sounds that, unless your attention is drawn to it, you can ignore, it ticks along almost the same in every elevator: a simple background to conversation for busy people.

When it is the only sound around, that is quite different. No, then it is incredibly loud, it drones on like a soundtrack to our misery. I may be exaggerating but then that might be the effects of the leftover alcohol in my system.

Lyndsey doesn't seem comfortable in the silence per se but she also isn't trying to break it. I think after she called me an array of colourful expletives from inside the suite she has run out of things to call me. Or she is just taking her time finding more to hurl at me. It's not like I planned this. I didn't sit on the flight here plotting ways to get Lyndsey Stone into my bed. Did I watch her on the flight? Yes, but that is only because it is near impossible not to watch her. Her elegant curves highlighted in the form-fitting lounge suit she was wearing, she looked like a dream, of course I was looking.

Drunk me obviously had other ideas that ended with rings on our fingers. I've imagined being married in the future, not seriously, but I've pictured it. Standing at the front of the aisle waiting for the woman I love to walk towards me. I've never put much thought into what that woman would be like. Now I have a wife and she looks like she stepped out of every one of my wet dreams, even with the scowl that currently mars her face.

I push my brain to remember last night, our wedding, but I draw a blank every time. I long to see her walking towards me, did she have flowers? Did she smile up at me so wide her eyes squinted? I'd like to believe she did, that she was just as caught in the moment, that she was excited to meet me at the end of the aisle no matter what she thinks now. I think last night we were in love, or an illusion of it.

As I watch her now in the mirrored wall of the elevator I don't dare break the silence. Every time I try, her frown deepens between her brows. If she wants our current indiscretions to be unnoticed she is going to have to put on a better game face than that. Ellis is an observant woman, I don't know if it has something to do with being a parent but she can sniff a lie a mile away and, if Lyndsey isn't careful, we won't be able to hide it through one meal, never mind long enough to get an annulment.

"You're going to have to talk to me eventually," I dare to speak into the canyon between us.

"No the fuck I don't," Lyndsey huffs through clenched teeth. I think if I listened closely enough over the music around us, I would be able to hear them grinding together. "Look, this is El and Liam's weekend and you are gonna keep your pretty mouth shut until it is over okay, cowboy?"

"You think I'm pretty?" I make a bad attempt at lightening the mood.

"Oh shut it! Now isn't the time for your jokes. Last night was a mistake and we are going to forget this nightmare as soon as possible." The finality in her words is punctuated by the elevator doors finally sliding open and her breezing through them slipping on a perfect mask as she goes.

It is selfish of me but I'll admit that I don't regret what happened. Waking up with my arms wrapped around Lyndsey felt like a waking dream. Her skin buttery soft and her curves felt perfect under my callused palms. While I was slipping in and out of dreams, I wasn't sure which was real and which was still inside my head.

It wouldn't have been the first time I've dreamed of Lyndsey. I've dreamed about her dozens of time since I first met her through Ellis. Shockingly, they aren't just sexual either. Some of them are. Others are just like this morning, waking up, the sun streaming through the windows highlighting the gold in her red hair, the green of her eyes stark against her pale skin and even paler bed sheets. Lyndsey's arms and sweet voice wrapped around me as she whispers sweet nothings against me. I always wake up and try to forget about them. Try to remember that what Lyndsey and I did was harmless, casual flirting while our friends are the ones in the serious, grown-up relationship. I try to push away the coffees we drank together and how she made me laugh.

This morning there were no sweet words. And nothing about this feels harmless any more. There was anger and an urgency that my dreams never have. That was when

I knew I was awake, feeling her fury bounce off of me instead of her fingers running through my hair.

I want to fix this. It's what I'm told to do, I'm the oldest brother and I'm the captain. I haven't always been straight-cut – hell, I'm still not quite – but if I want to ever begin shaking my old reputation as a wild southern bull, I'm going to have to start by fixing this. That is if I can think of a place to start.

Getting married in Vegas is not the best start to proving myself a capable leader.

My mind runs through every possibility. I'm sure there is a way to annul this marriage without much fuss, but there is more to us than there would be a normal drunken mishap. I'm a recognisable face – not to everyone, of course, there are millions of people who have never watched a game of hockey in their life but the truth is I'm known.

It would take one person to hear about this to want to use it against me, against Lyndsey. That is something I couldn't forgive: if she was caught in the crossfire because a hockey fan in some divorce office told a sports news outlet about what they perceived as an indiscretion.

Fuck, I'm too hungover to think clearly. I must be because the only solution my drunk and selfish brain can think of is to ignore this in the hope it will all just go away. As though that would ever happen. I want to fix this in a way that causes the least amount of pain to both of us.

I'm not selfish, no matter what my thoughts are trying to convince me of now. No. I'll go to the Spears PR manager, Cassie, as soon as we land tonight. She will help, she will see what I can't right now but above all she will be discreet. She is always discreet.

By the time we make it to the table Lyndsey has shrouded herself in a cloak of happiness and is not the angry wolf-woman I was stood in a metal box with ten seconds ago. Nobody notices that we arrive together. Nobody notices we arrive at all because every single one of them looks worse for wear. Even my enforcer, Jay 'Edge' Brink, looks slightly green, a sight I've never seen. He is normally a brooding shadow in a bar or club, hugging the walls so he doesn't attract the attention of women who might think they stand a chance. I don't remember if that was the case for him last night but he must have drunk more than usual if the dark bags under his eyes are anything to go by.

Ellis, bless her heart, looks like a combination of every sleepless night as a parent and every hangover she has suffered rolled into one very grumpy-looking woman. Her blond hair hangs low over her face. Well, what little face I can see behind the world's largest sunglasses. Her fiancé and my old teammate Ruin has his arm strung over her shoulder but he looks seconds away from falling asleep in his porridge.

Finn 'Rook' Jonas, on the other hand, might still be drunk. The rowdiest Spears player sways lightly in his seat, and when Lyndsey darts over to the open seat on Ellis' left I'm forced to sit beside him. Rook is a good kid, he is passionate and fun, but in Vegas there is a thin line between fun and dangerous. A line I apparently toed the wrong side of last night.

"Morning, Cap," he slurs before pouring us both a coffee from the jug on the table. There are two already empty. Looks like they were busy trying to clean themselves up before we got here. There are plates of food, some half eaten and some still completely full, as though whoever ordered them underestimated how much they could handle.

Nobody pays any mind as my head spins, they must assume I look as bad as them because of the drink. I probably am but the bigger part is still spiralling how to make this right. I sip the coffee Rook hands me but I don't indulge in any food, I'm too nauseous to deal with it right now – how Liam is eating so freely I don't understand. The guy looks like he is on autopilot.

"Ruin's only said one word since sitting down, eh. Porridge. He looked pretty scary, I'm surprised the waitress wasn't more worried." Rook is nodding over at Liam as he speaks, chewing through his own plate of food.

"We're in Vegas, Rook, it's the most normal thing in the world to her." I sip more at my coffee, hiding my grimace behind the ceramic.

"Probably, I think if I had the energy, I could make it up to her, if you know what I mean," he jokes, his Canadian accent so different from my Texan one. I try to laugh. I really do but it just doesn't come out.

I had the nerve to warn Lyndsey about her game face, with a poker face as bad as mine seems to be right now I would lose every cent to my name. I look like a deer caught in the cross hairs of the rifles I saw as a kid. If my team were even an ounce less drunk I know they would be questioning me. I thank my lucky stars for tequila. And vodka. And rum. If the smell of alcohol on their breaths is anything to go by they drank much more than that. Hell, I must have drunk more than ever before, blacking out is new even to me.

It's why I'm trying so hard to remember what happened last night, there must be something in the recess of my brain that remembers my own damn wedding. Even if I could remember where the hell we did it, I wonder if my wedding was officiated by Elvis? Most of all though, I wish I remembered our vows. What did drunk me say to her as we slipped those rings on? Did I joke around? Was I serious for a change?

And most of all, what would my parents think if they could see me now?

Chapter Three

Aiden

A baseball cap isn't the best disguise, but my brain was too busy this morning to think any further than that. I pull it tight over my head, letting the brim shade my face as I shuffle down the aisle of the plane. Technically I don't have to hide, I have flown on a lot of planes and have not been recognised, but then I have also been on many flights where I have had to sign napkins and pose for pictures. Today I want to stay under the radar. The fewer people who speak to me, the better.

I'm like a swan. On the surface I'm calm and collected but under the waterline I'm floundering. I'm not an amateur when it comes to waking up next to a woman but *being married to one* is new to me. As soon as we land back in Seattle, I'm going to have to put on my captain hat, rally all the right people to make sure this is dealt with swiftly. As much as I love being the Spears captain, I like being able to leave that version of me at the rink. When I'm at home, I don't want to have to be in control of everything, I just want to relax and have a good time. Looks like the good times went too far this weekend.

The whole team are sat together on the plane as I slide down the aisle to where I'm supposed to be sat next to Liam. When I pause by the seat, I find his fiancée, Ellis, asleep on his shoulder and Rook asleep on the other side. Even without my brain firing on all cylinders I know what that means. Lyndsey is sat alone and the only open chair will be next to her. Not knowing the drama it might cause, Liam silently nods towards where Lyndsey is sat fiddling with her phone. Not wanting to wake Ellis, he mouths a "sorry". I stifle my annoyance at the situation, instead sending him a wink before turning my back on him as quickly as I came.

My eyes fall closed in exhaustion, preparing for the headache that is already starting to build in my temples. I know we are going to need to talk about our next steps, but I was really hoping for a quiet few hours to cure my hangover and come up with some kind of plan before she starts hounding me. I know that her biggest priority is sweeping this under the rug so we can pretend it never happened, and I'm right there with her. But truthfully, I'm a bit less frantic about the whole thing. I know it will work out. Things always work out in the end. That's what my mom always said.

"Hey, wife," I jibe at her quietly, settling into the open seat, my long legs cramped into the space in front of me. I can't help but smirk as an almost wolfish growl rumbles in her chest. Even now that I know I shouldn't push her, I can't help it to see the fire in her green eyes.

"What are you doing? You should be over there," she whispers in a stern tone, looking around for an open seat, but when she realises there is nowhere else her eyes snap back to me.

"Ellis abandoned you for her man so you get me. Sorry." I shrug, not bothering to hide my smile. That just makes her madder.

"You're not sorry, you're enjoying this," Lyndsey accuses. I can't help but laugh as she puts her attention back on her phone. Despite the tension in my shoulders, I don't let her see me sweat.

"You're right, I'm not sorry," I tell her, pulling her phone out of her hands so she can't hide from this conversation. "But not because I'm enjoying this but because this gives us time to talk."

"What is there to talk about? We are getting divorced, end of story." She stretches over me trying to snatch back her phone, but my long arms hold it far out of her reach.

I try to ignore the way her breasts push against my shoulder but even now, when I know I should keep my distance, she is hard to keep away from. Drunk me has good taste in women. Plus sober me would have never made a move after so much has happened between us over the past year.

From strangers, to friends, to flirting, back to whatever the hell we were before I married her.

"Do you have a lawyer?" I ask, breaking the heavy silence between us as she continues to scramble for her phone.

"Do you?" Her teeth are grinding together.

"The Spears do," I sigh, handing her phone back over. I wore a damn cap to hide my identity and now here I'm causing a scene by having a beautiful woman all but sprawled over me.

I need to get a hold of myself.

"Oh, great. That means they are all going to find out." She nods her head in the direction of the other players, but I shake my head subtly.

"No, just Cassie. Which is probably worse." I rest my head back against the uncomfortable plane seat, dreading my conversation with the Spears PR manager. Over the past few years as captain I have managed to keep my image intact enough that Cassie doesn't get frustrated with me any more. Not the way she does with Edge and his angry-on-ice antics anyway. I'm good at keeping my reputation clean with a well-placed wink and some of my southern charm. Still, every once in a while, Cassie will get pissed at me for not being reasonable enough.

"At least she will keep it on the down-low, nobody can find out about this." Lyndsey copies my movements, throwing herself back in her chair.

"Aw, are you embarrassed of me, darlin'?" I nudge her ribs with my elbow, making her squirm away from me, glaring as her body turns towards the window, trying to shut me out.

"Very. The smell of your aftershave is making me nauseous so leave me alone, I'm going to get some sleep." She throws the words over her shoulder as the flight attendants start their safety briefing. Too focused on myself to pay attention, I watch Lyndsey throw her jacket over her body as a makeshift blanket and tuck her arms under her neck.

"Good luck with that." I snigger at how stubborn she is, trying too hard to ignore me that she would rather be uncomfortable for hours instead of talking to me. I could do with some shut-eye too but I'm suddenly feeling pretty keyed up.

"By the way," she flops back over to me again, "I want to be there when you talk to Cassie." She gives me a pointed glare, I wish it would make me mad but there is something about having her mossy eyes on me that makes me want to keep them there.

"Why?" I ask, even though I know why. She wants some kind of control over this mess. I just want to hear her talk before she goes back to ignoring me like she has over the past few months.

"Because I want to make sure this is done right." She raises her eyebrows as though asking me to question her. And still I do. I must be a glutton for punishment.

"And you don't think I can do that?" I pout dramatically, acting as if I'm really offended.

"If you want something done properly, do it yourself and all that." She shrugs, not at all put out by my display. Instead of waiting for a reply she turns back over into her uncomfortable solace.

As the plane speeds down the runway for take-off I shift in my seat, coming to an uncomfortable realisation. For at least a few days, if not weeks, I'm a married man. It reminds me of my dad. He always said meeting Mom was what made him a man. Her influence is what settled him and helped him become a better person because he wanted to be worthy of her.

I wonder what they would think if they could see me now. Married to a woman I barely know with no recollection of how we got here. I remember drinking and dancing for hours, sweat dripping down my back in my shirt, but at some point it goes black. Then I'm waking up with Lyndsey flying out of my bed like her ass is on fire. Even in all my escapades over the years I haven't got to a place of blacking out. I wish I could remember more than that but no matter how hard I try nothing comes to the surface. My parents must be turning in their graves to see their only son still being so irresponsible at twenty-eight. And even knowing that I still can't find it in me to pretend to be something I'm not. Hopefully they are up there looking over my sisters for a few weeks instead of me while I get this sorted out.

Chapter Four

Lyndsey

It's a few days later by the time we sit outside of Cassie's office in the Spears arena. Now that my phone is back on, Kayla has been drunk-texting me again most days and Aiden has tried to text me since we got back but I have done my best to ignore them both. Hopefully, she will move on to her next true love soon and leave me alone. And when it comes to Aiden, I don't need to talk to him, I need to talk to a lawyer and wipe what happened from existence. That is why even though he is sat in the seat next to me I'm trying my hardest to ignore him.

"This is very immature, darlin', I expected more from you." I know he is just trying to get under my skin and I hate that it is working. There was a time when his sharp words and grey eyes would render me speechless, but now I have to battle to bite my tongue.

Last year when he would bring me coffee, his flirting words would make me laugh and blush. I longed for him to make a move but when he asked me out, I said no. A part of me deep down must have known he would bring me nothing but trouble. Case in point: the ring hidden in my bedside drawer, tucked under some sexy underwear I never get to wear any more. Still, I wish I had been firmer with him, maybe then we wouldn't be in this damn position. I think back to some distinct memories I have from all those months ago. Times when I should have done better to push him away.

The dinging of the bell on the flower-shop door has my attention snapping there. When my eyes drift up to welcome the customer, my eyes lock with familiar deep eyes. Eyes that I used to see on the billboard near Washington University when I was dating Kayla. Eyes I saw up close in Liam's kitchen a few weeks ago when Ellis introduced me to the team. Aiden Anders.

"Mornin', darlin'." *His sweet southern drawl makes my knees weak. Something about that accent is my kryptonite.*

"Cowboy." *I nod, acknowledging his presence while keeping my aloof, unaffected mask in place.* "What can I help you with?"

Instead of answering straight away he places three cups onto the counter between us. Two hot coffees and one ice latte. Digging into his pocket he pulls out a selection of sugar and sweetener as well as those little milk containers. Looking between him and the coffee I'm honestly confused.

"So, I didn't know how you like it. I panicked so I got a plain black hot coffee and an iced coffee so you can pick whichever," *he explains, picking up the third cup and taking a big gulp, like he is trying to keep his mouth occupied.*

"Thank you." *I know I'm blushing. I can feel the heat of it on my chest but I can only hope it doesn't spread over my cheeks and it will stay hidden behind my jumper. I busy myself mixing some milk into the hot coffee, leaving the iced one over on the side.*

"So milk, no sugar. I'll remember that." *He sweeps up the sugars and shoves them back into his pocket, leaning his hip against the counter. I'm praying for a customer to come in. Aiden is basically a stranger. Yes, I know more about him than he knows about me because of Ellis and because of* Hot Hockey News. *It isn't the most reliable news source but it's a fun read.*

"I'm sweet enough," I say after realising we have been in silence for a while.

"Ain't that the truth." He winks. With his hand resting on the counter I can see the way his arm muscles bunch under his blue T-shirt.

"Need a bouquet for a hot date?" Ignoring his comment and the way his skin ripples over his muscles I take a small step away from the counter, straightening my spine. I was almost leaning over into his space inspecting his tanned arms. I need to put space between us. Physically and mentally. I have been blinded by a pretty exterior before and I'm not doing that again. Aiden could have any woman with a pulse, as if he would want to date me. I need to get a hold of myself.

"No, I just wanted to see you." Oh. He smiles brightly at me. His straight white teeth look like something from a dentistry ad. I bet he usually flashes that smile and every woman in a five-mile radius loses their panties.

"Oh. Why?" I cough. I pick up the coffee and take a huge gulp, needing something to distract me from his direct attention. I have never had anyone look at me as intently as he is.

"Well, I was wondering if you would grab dinner with me," he asks, putting both hands on the desk between us and leaning forward into my space a little. Not in an overbearing way, but it's definitely intense. Having his undivided attention on me makes me blush harder, but I won't be swept up in his allure.

"Like a date?" He could just mean as friends, right? I mean, our friends are having a baby, we are going to be around each other a lot. He probably just means as friends, maybe even a meal with the rest of the team.

"Yes, darlin', a date." Oh. He laughs at my wide eyes. His smile quirks up on the left as he smirks at me.

"I don't think that's a good idea."

So I stuck to it, I didn't go on a date with him. After a while he got bored anyway. The day Ellis passed out and Aiden came to check on me was the last day things felt normal between us. After I sobbed into his chest in an adrenalin drop, he put distance between us. A typical man, unable to handle emotion. I know it was a good thing to put walls between us but maybe if I had gone on the date and things had faded more naturally, I wouldn't have still had some lingering feeling for him that led me up the aisle.

The door to Cassie's office swings open to reveal her stood in a grey pinstripe pencil skirt with matching jacket and a white high-neck top underneath. Her white patent leather pumps make her short legs look great and her black bob finishes her look. I don't know how she always looks so put together but I wish she would share some tips. I'm good at putting outfits together but I have never looked this professional a day in my life.

"Come in, what the hell is the matter with you?" she asks Aiden, crossing her arms over her chest as we shuffle past her. A man in a suit is sat at her desk, I'm assuming it is one of the Spears lawyers.

"Look, Cas, I didn't mean for this to happen." For the first time Aiden actually seems sheepish. It's a new sound but I think he is just trying to soften her up. It doesn't work.

"Sit down!" She rolls her eyes, moving her attention to me as she sits at her desk across from us. "Other than the obvious, how are you?"

"I'm doing okay, just want to get this wrapped up," I admit, clasping my hands together on my knee to keep my leg from bouncing. Cassie's eyes shift between Aiden and me and under normal circumstances I would probably squirm under her scrutiny, but right now I have too much going on to care.

"Looks like I missed a real party, next time I'll move some meetings around so I can come." She laughs lightly.

"I wish you were there," I sigh. "You'd have kept us in line. Cas, we need to keep this quiet."

"I'm good at quiet." A strange smile spreads across her face. A mixture of determination and a small excitement at getting to do the thing she loves. Her job.

"Really?" I ask, a little sceptical. I mean, there hasn't been a lot of drama around the Spears from what I can remember. Other than Edge's on-ice aggression and Ellis' pregnancy stirring up a little bit of trouble last year, everything is usually calm.

"Do you remember when an ex-Spears player got a DUI? Or when a girl claimed Felix was going to be the father of her baby, even though she wasn't pregnant?" she asks, tapping her fingers on the desk, clearly proud at the shocked look on my face.

"Did that really happen?" Aiden asks, and I'm even more shocked to know he was clueless. The team treat their captain like their personal therapist, always asking him to pick them up from nights out or to ask advice about family drama. He is a big part of what makes this team work, he is always willing to be a listening ear and has a special knack for making people feel at ease.

"Yeah, and I kept it quiet, and I can do it here too." She laughs, moving her attention to the suited man next to her. "Mr Collins here will be helping to get divorce papers written up."

"Divorce? What happened to an annulment?" My voice comes out a little shrill. Okay, a lot shrill, but I can't be blamed. I thought we would be signing a form today and this would be over.

"Your wedding was legally binding. The marriage is ironclad, the only way to end the wedded bliss is with a divorce." Mr Collins at least has the decency to look apologetic but that doesn't do much to soothe me right now.

"But that will take longer, won't it?" I ask, my hands wringing in my lap. My voice still comes out loud and a little aggressive but I can't seem to catch my breath enough to act normal.

"Unfortunately, it's the best we can do." He shifts in his chair, no longer looking me in the eye.

"How quickly will the papers be drafted?" My hand slams down on the desk between us. I need him to look me in the eyes and tell me the truth.

"Lyndsey, calm down," Aiden starts, making me swivel my head in his direction.

"Don't tell me to calm down, how are you okay with all of this?" I snarl, throwing my arms out, nowhere near close to calming down.

"I don't want to be married either but it's not his fault. We got married, just because we don't remember it that doesn't mean you can put the blame on everyone else." He leans forward, grabbing my hands in his, but I wiggle out of his hold, my anger growing into a borderline state of panic.

"Easy for you to say! You don't have a shitty family or a crazy ex you're trying to keep this from." My words come out somewhere between a growl and choked cry. Tears flood my eyes but I bite the inside of my cheek to keep them at bay.

"What?" he asks, his eyes widening and his voice reaching a low, dangerous tone. He looks like he does on the ice right now, that is not something I've ever seen, even between all of our moments alone during my shifts at Ellis' floral shop, Bloom and Blossom.

"Nothing, don't worry about it." I shake my head, reminding myself to keep my cool. I turn back to Mr Collins and ask, "So a few days? A few weeks?"

"Probably a week but as soon as..." The office door swinging open interrupts his explanation. All four of our heads snap to the intrusion to find Edge filling out the door frame.

"Jesus, Edge, just because you're a regular that doesn't mean you don't have to knock," Cassie snaps, and Edge looks between all of us, confused.

"Sorry, I thought... nobody would be here, it's an off day," he mumbles, properly chastised.

"Well, you're wrong so close the door," she says, but before he has the chance to do what she says I jump to my feet, wanting out of this room.

"Don't bother, Edge, are you busy or can you drop me off at home?" I ask, shrugging my handbag over my shoulder. I can't imagine how frazzled I must look but he doesn't mention it.

"Lyndsey?" Aiden takes a hold of my wrist, but not wanting to say anything else – he knows that if he says too much we will be caught.

"Yeah, of course I can, you okay?" Edge coughs, nodding slightly. His eyes still look between us all but he doesn't comment.

"I will be." I look back down at Aiden and where he has his fingers around my wrist. "Just let me know when everything's ready, okay? And maybe stay away from any booze for a while, you can't be trusted."

Without giving him time to reply, I pull my arm free and storm out of the office. Edge follows me without a word. It's one of the things I like most about the Spears offensive player, he minds his business. People see him as a brute just because he can get aggressive on the ice but when I see him holding Liam and Ellis' baby Charlotte in his huge arms, he is soft and calm.

After the past few days, it will be nice to spend some time in comfortable silence without prying questions. It will give me time to figure out what I'm going to do while I wait for Mr Collins to contact me about the papers being ready. As soon as that is done, I can go back to my regular life. I can go to work and laugh with Ellis without hiding stuff from her. I can go back to ignoring Kayla's texts begging to have me back. I can spend time in my apartment as far away from the Spears captain as I can get.

Chapter Five

Aiden

Hockey is a year-round sport. Yes, the season is only six to eight months depending on if you make it to the playoffs but even now during our off-season the Spears are holding an exhibition game. A way for us to show off our skills and to keep ourselves in winning shape. It's a double-edged sword though, because as much as this game is just for fun the stands will be filled with mostly Spears fans wanting to see us coming out on top and the players of our opposing team from Toronto will be gunning for the win. We are supposed to keep it fun and yet every year this is one of the games I tie myself up in knots about the most.

I feel like I always lose. Either I upset the fans by losing or I upset the Spears management by taking it too seriously. They want me to always be gracious and make friends with the other team but it feels so insincere. I'm usually a master at having that balance but tonight I can't find it. Tonight I'm on edge and I think I'm throwing the vibes off for all of my teammates.

My mind is still so filled with thoughts of how I have let my parents down and now here I am having to pick who I'm going to annoy. For the first time in my career I feel like I can't make my mind up. I'm always so sure of my opinion; that's what makes me a good captain. I pick something and stick to it good or bad, I stand by my decisions. That's why this thing with Lyndsey is niggling under my skin because I can't stand by that choice. I have to admit that I was wrong. And I'm not used to that.

I'm sure I've made a bunch of mistakes in my life. Hell, I have probably made a bunch of mistakes this year already and we are only halfway through the year. Yet I can usually roll with the punches and move on to the next thing without lingering, but not this time. All I can do is linger. Imagine every outcome and fill my head with what ifs. It's affecting my ability to play the game I love.

"Anders, what's crawled up your ass, eh?" Rook hollers from across the room and instantly I feel my blood heat. A spark to the gasoline that I try to smother before I take everyone up in flames.

"Leave it, Rook." My words are a lethal crack around the room, everyone hushes at the strange tone. They are used to me laughing everything off and bouncing back from anything. The mixture of every thought in my head multiplied by the fact I can't talk to anybody about it is a powder keg.

"Jesus, dude, you good?" He laughs awkwardly, unsure of how to take my mood. A part of him probably thinks I'm joking, but when I turn to face him, I see the light humour in his eyes fading.

"Rook, I'm telling you now, for once mind your own business, yeah?" I speak slowly, needing him to hear me because I can only hold the dam of rage back for so long. The sound of my locker slamming shut is like a bullet silencing the rest of the room.

"Damn." He rears back at the sound as though I have punched him. His eyes dart around looking for someone to take the heat off of him but nobody comes to his rescue.

It should be my job. I'm the one defusing the tension usually between Rook and Edge and that thought makes me feel like shit all over again. It's as though a bucket of ice-cold water is tossed over me seeing my teammate feel bad because of me.

"Fuck, that was... Rook, I'm sorry." I move across the locker room until I'm in front of him, putting my hand on his shoulder. This shit isn't his fault, it's my own.

"All good, Cap. We all have those days, eh, let's go play some hockey." I can hear some hesitation laced in his voice but I know he won't hold it against me. He reminds me a lot of myself when I was the young kid on the team, wanting to be everyone's friend while also thinking I was the best thing since sliced bread. I needed guidance and he does too, that is the job I'm supposed to have. I'm supposed to be the moral backbone of the team and still I find myself making stupid decision after stupid decision.

"Let's go *win* some hockey!" I correct, officially telling my team exactly what I want from them on the ice. We are going to give the fans what they want and if the higher-ups have a problem with it? Well, I'll cross that bridge when I come to it. Or just avoid them until they forget.

The lights in the arena flash white and red, matching our Spears jerseys, as we skate out to the ground-shaking roar of the crowd. Feet stomp and the glass around the rink vibrates as they knock on it to get our attention, but I try to block it out. At a normal game I might skate around, smile and wave at the fans, maybe even wink at a few women in the audience. An image pops into my mind, one of Lyndsey in the front row cheering for me. My name on her back and a wedding band on her finger.

The rage I have just managed to temper flares back up again. Never has a woman knocked me off my game and I won't let that start now. Still, as my eyes skim the crowd and the signs they are holding, every redhead draws my attention and a sick feeling comes over me that I'm disappointed she isn't here.

Now my anger is focused solely on myself. The women I have slept with have no right to invade my mind when I'm doing my job and I haven't even slept with Lyndsey. We woke up together but our underwear was intact, that means she has even less right to be in my mind right now.

Muscle memory kicks in as I skate to the centre of the ice for the puck drop. I'm barely even paying attention to the people around me. I'm trying so hard to focus but the harder I try the less attention I'm paying. The whistle blows at my side and the puck hits the ice, I swing my stick out but I'm too slow. The Toronto captain is three steps ahead as he hits the puck off to his players. Anger bubbles in my chest hearing the fans boo at me. All of their anger is focused on me, matching my own emotions.

I try to regroup but everything I try just seems to make things worse. By the time I'm called off for a line change I'm actually glad to be off the ice. I need to get myself together but, as we come closer to the end of the first period, we are two goals down and I know I'm to blame. I do what I can to put on the face of the calm, collected man my teammates know and, when I step back on the ice during the second period, I'm almost feral in need of a win.

For the first time since the whistle blew, I have a solid grip on the puck. I glide across the ice: the picture of a perfectly composed man ready to score a damn goal. My feet weave in between Toronto's players, my stick knocking away their advances. The net is in my sights as I skirt around another player. I can see Rook is open and as I go to slap the puck in his direction, I'm rocked into the boards.

It's a dirty check, he not only throws his body into my ribs but he uses his stick to bat against my kneecaps. The sound of the crowd is drowned out by the thumping of my heartbeat in my ears. The red haze of rage I have been pushing back all damn night overtakes my body.

Before his body even has a chance to pick its weight off me, I'm throwing my gloves on the ice and swinging my bare fists into his head, knocking his helmet off with the force. Pandemonium breaks out around us, but before I can get another hit in, Edge wedges himself in front of me, taking a hit from the asshole Canadian before using all of his force to push the asshole onto the ice and straddling his legs. I stand behind him, my chest puffing as the haze slowly dissipates to see the scene around me of all the refs trying to pull Edge from his knees and barely being able to move his weight.

The captain in me takes over and I jump back into motion. Hooking one hand in the neck of his jersey I pull him back far enough so my head is next to his.

"Let him go," I say slowly, and instantly Edge's fists drop to his sides and he stands himself up. The refs come between us, yelling about Edge going into the penalty box, but before he lets them guide him away, he catches my eye.

"Get your shit together!" he yells, and only then does he turn away and skate into the box for five minutes for roughing.

I know he is right. Right there on the ice I struggle to stay on my blades. Looking over at Coach Mitch he raises his eyebrows at me, asking if we are good, but I'm not. I shake my head, almost imperceptibly, but he sees.

Nodding once, he calls me over and subs me out of the game. I'm no use to anyone in this state.

My team deserve to have the best chance to win and the captain in me knows that to do that I need to cut the dead weight, it just happens that tonight the dead weight is me.

Everyone else on the bench gives me a wide berth as I stomp to an open space and drop myself down. This isn't the type of man I am. I don't even understand why I'm so affected? I need this divorce as soon as possible because I can't keep letting my team down like this just because of a woman. Hopefully in a few weeks' time I can go back to the man I like to be. The flirt. The uplifter. The positivity when things go wrong. Not the reason things go wrong.

Mr Collins can't file those papers quick enough if you ask me. I'm too wrapped up in my temporary wife that it is affecting my game, this is why I never wanted to get married in the first place. Marriage brings nothing but complications – just because my mom made my dad a better man, that isn't the norm.

I have only been a husband for a week and I can't wait for my life to go back to the way it should be.

Chapter Six

Lyndsey

I've never claimed to be smart. I didn't go to college. I wasn't top of any classes in high school. But I never thought I was stupid. So I can't understand why I thought being back in Seattle would make everything easier. I reasoned with myself that the old adage "What happens in Vegas, stays in Vegas" was really true. Deluded myself into thinking that, once I was home, I would be able to push Aiden and his stupidly toned body right out of my head.

Obviously, I was wrong. Instead I'm reminded of him even more. Every hockey fan I walk past on the street still wearing Spears gear, even though their season is over, reminds me of how elegant he is on the ice. Every time I close my eyes I'm hounded by memories of his tattooed skin and stormy eyes looking down at me filled with the lingering effects of sleep. Now today is my first day back at Bloom and Blossom since we got back and I'm dreading it.

When Ellis was put on bed rest towards the second half of her pregnancy last year Aiden stepped up for me. Well, I guess he stepped up for Liam but he helped me all the same. He would be in the quiet little flower shop every day after practice just to see if I had everything under control.

No matter how much I told him I didn't need a babysitter he would still bring me a coffee and sit with me while I closed up for the night. We would laugh and he would listen, really listen, as I told him about my day. Frankly he was one of the first people in my life outside of Ellis who I started to feel like myself around. My guard was still up, I kept him at bay with flirting jabs and a well-placed flick of my hair to hide my blush, but it was all for nothing.

Eventually he got bored, he still showed up until baby Charlotte was born but something had changed. About a few months before Ellis went into labour there was a shift in our dynamic. I couldn't explain it, he still bought me coffee and he still listened to me talk but there was a different aura around us. It was no longer charged with sexual tension, it was just tense. Like he wanted to be there but felt like he shouldn't be.

At first, I thought maybe Liam had told his captain to back off but Ellis and Liam seemed to be rooting for something to happen between us so that didn't feel right. I kept my questions to myself though, maybe I shouldn't have, maybe I should have confronted him and asked why it felt like being in my presence pained him. But I was scared, scared that I was pushing away one of the only people who seemed to care about me, even if it was only for a while.

So I resigned myself to friendship, we were going to be in each other's lives for a long time because of Ellis and Liam and I was not going to let my clearly unrequited crush make things uncomfortable for everyone else. So I kept it to myself, I sat in that uncomfortable feeling for months. I watched him when he wasn't looking, knowing it would be all I was allowed. Until I woke up in his arms.

Now it's harder, I can still feel his warm breath on my neck. I can't hide from the memories of him holding me tight against him and now I have to go to work. Another place plagued by images of him and I won't be able to avoid it for long. Ellis is going to have questions, she may have kept her cool during brunch but I doubt she was hungover enough to not notice the mounting tension between Aiden and me.

Taking a heaving breath – I must face the music – I push open the doors of Bloom and Blossom. Memories of Aiden aside, it is one of my favourite places in all of Seattle. With its walls of flowers coordinated by colour, somehow always warm but never stifling, this shop is a happy place. Many people hate their jobs but I feel privileged to have mine. Ellis doesn't like letting go of control and the fact she is willing to give it up for me is a blessing. Today is one of the first times I have walked in here grimacing as the little bell announces my entrance; at the sound, Ellis rounds from the back room, face split into a wide grin. Her eyes still seem heavy but between the amount she drank this weekend and the sleepless nights of a baby that isn't a surprise.

"Lynds! God, it's good to be back, right?" She beams. I wish it would put me at ease but it doesn't, I'm waiting for the probing questions that I know are coming. A part of me wants her to ask. That way I could get rid of some of the weight on my shoulders. Though I know that isn't fair, I want to keep everything with Aiden under wraps, and yet not telling Ellis feels wrong.

"Yeah, sure it's great. Let me just hang my stuff up and I'll get started on the online orders?" I want to be in the back, hoping that if she is in front of house and I'm in the back I can escape for a while.

"You're amazing, you know how much I hate them. I go cross-eyed if I look at that screen too long." I know that of course, she complains about it at least once a week since I started here. She likes real paperwork, warm pages straight off the printer, something tangible.

Once my jacket and bag are on a hook, I slide into the spinning computer chair that reminds me of the nook in my childhood home. That's where my dad's computer was – my brother Peter and I were allowed time on it each day, him more than me because he was older, I know it was because he was the golden child who did no wrong. My mom didn't want me searching too much and filling my head with "the word of Satan". I was to be a God-loving child and only use my internet access to learn more about the Lord. That's not what I used it for, but what she didn't know wouldn't hurt her.

Every time I sit in the little office in the back room of Bloom and Blossom for a moment, I'm right back there aged ten wanting to know everything about the world outside of my bubble. What an amazing world it is too.

Each time Ellis comes back for something when we aren't busy the hair on my neck stands on edge. I'm a skittish cat, all but hiding under the desk when she walks into the room, but it never comes. I lay awake last night mentally preparing how to shut down her barrage of questions and she is yet to ask me any. I would think she was trying to lull me into a false sense of security but that isn't like her. At least not with me, she is honest, never beating around the bush, which is why I thought I would walk into an interrogation this morning.

Paranoia is a difficult thing, I have driven myself crazy all for nothing. Ellis is her usual self, tired but determined, and I don't know how to handle it. My phone keeps buzzing on the desk in front of me but I ignore Aiden's texts the way I have every moment since we walked out of the meeting with Cassie about our impending divorce. He wanted to meet up to talk about what happens next but I ignored it. I don't want to talk, I want to leave it in Vegas even though I know I'll never be that lucky. My sins follow me, a looming shadow.

"Okay, I told Liam I would leave it but I can't, what's going on?" Well, shit. Ellis finally breaks the silence and I guess he told her to wait for me to be ready. She would be waiting a long time for that though.

"Nothing's wrong. I'm all good. Allll goodddd." *So smooth, Lyndsey, way to go.* That was nothing like what I practised. No, I was supposed to be sure and steady not a babbling moron.

"I call bull. Lyndsey, you have sat here growling at the computer for the past three hours and you want me to think nothing's wrong? I wasn't born yesterday. Is it something to do with your ex?" She's right. I'm not slick but I didn't plan for this, for her to draw it out for hours before asking me questions, the Ellis I know should have blurted them out as soon as she saw me.

"Speaking of born, how is my beautiful god-daughter?" It's a cheap shot, I know it is, and by the way she raises her brows at me Ellis knows it too.

"I know you're deflecting but it's going to work because you have to see the picture I took of her smiling, her teeth are cutting so she is covered in drool but it's so damn cute I don't care." That should give me at least another hour.

Ellis pulls her phone from the front pocket of her pink apron and starts scrolling through it. I can tell the moment she finds the picture she wants to show me because her eyes sparkle before she even turns it around. When she does mine must sparkle too. Charlotte is nine months old and I love her deeply.

I haven't been around many babies, my parents stopped after they had me. A lot of super-religious families aren't keen on birth control, but they were realistic in knowing they couldn't afford any more kids after Peter and me. They always said they had the perfect kids: the older-brother-younger-sister dynamic, with a pet cat to finish the family. They wanted to have that picture-perfect ending and, when they achieved it, they were as happy as they could be.

That meant that I never had any younger siblings to play with, just a brother who hated my guts from the minute our parents brought me home. Ellis never had that problem, her older son Jack adores his sister. She is the apple of his eye and it is clear to everyone that, when she grows up, he is going to be so overprotective that it will drive her crazy.

Charlotte's little face beams up at me from the phone and Ellis didn't understate it, her jaw is covered in drool that soaks her flowery onesie. My phone vibrates again and I decide I'm going to turn it off in the hope that it will make it easier to focus on keeping Ellis distracted. That plan is paused though when I see who has been texting me, because it sure as shit isn't Aiden.

Kayla.

It feels like centuries have passed since we split, but it definitely hasn't been centuries since she last texted. I wish there was a delicate way to put it, but there isn't. Kayla has a drinking problem. I too have had my fair share of binge-drinking episodes from my early twenties, but from being with Kayla… I saw how it rapidly became a disease. She hid it well in the beginning, her fancy clothes bought with her father's money, the fun stories that she conveniently forgot to mention happened while she was hammered.

I'm not completely unobservant. When we went out to dinner, I noticed her throwing back the gin and tonics but I thought it was just first-date nerves. She told me she had a similar story to my own: parents not accepting of her sexuality, but that wasn't the truth. The truth was her parents were trying to save her, they wanted her to be willingly admitted into a rehabilitation unit. I always pictured them as sterile places but when I looked up where they were suggesting, I was floored. Lush green gardens, plus a spa, it was complete with all the luxuries money can buy. Kayla, of course, refused. Rehab didn't have the one she wanted; I thought that one thing might have been me, perhaps she would miss me, miss us, too much. But I was naive.

Once I found out the truth, I wish I could say that I ended what we had. As hard as it was, I was not strong enough to be her saviour and it wouldn't be fair to either of us for me to try. For months I believed her promises that she would change. That she wanted to stop but she had just had a slip-up. I wanted to be the reason she would change but that wasn't fair to either of us. Eventually, I had to put myself first and told her that enough was enough, that it was hurting too much. Still, every few weeks the texts start to roll in. Begging for me to come back to her, then switching to saying I ruined her life. Then she sobers up and apologises. Every time I block her. I will not be her punching bag and yet she uses daddy's deep pockets to buy another phone to contact me again. This cycle has been happening for so long I'm becoming desensitised to it.

> Doubt it all u want we are gon be 2gether
> Lynds baby we r soulm8s

Her text is kind of legible so she must be in the early stages, drunk enough to click on my contact but sober enough to form almost sentences. I don't even realise Ellis has moved until her hand comes to my shoulder. My nosy boss and best friend has just read the text over my shoulder. Her hand tightens as she takes in the message but she must be in disbelief because she grabs for my phone, yanking it from me before I even register her coming for it.

"What the fuck is this? Is she still harassing you? Is this why you have been acting all skittish?" Finally she starts asking a bunch of questions, they just aren't the ones I thought I was going to get today. Maybe she and Liam were both drunk enough not to notice the shift between me and Aiden.

"It's just Kayla. Again." Ellis' eyes widen slightly, my dating life is not something I'm good at talking about seriously. I can tell a bunch of bad-date stories but when I fall for someone it feels wrong to divulge all of our relationship. "She isn't harassing me and I haven't been acting skittish. She gets drunk and texts me sometimes. No biggie." I don't know if I'm trying to soothe her or myself but I don't think it's working either way.

"Yes biggie. Lynds, it's eleven in the morning, if she's drunk now it's only going to get worse." I hate putting extra drama on to her. Ellis is a disabled mom of two, she doesn't need to be cleaning up my messes but I know she will. With the drop of a hat she would take my problems on as her own because she cares. Cares about me.

"I know, look I've been dealing with her but I can't exactly stop her, she just gets a new phone when I block her." Ellis tries to interrupt me but I ignore her. "I'll just let her wear herself out until she crashes and eventually apologises."

"You shouldn't have to deal with this. Do you want Liam to go talk to her maybe, get her to back off?" Now that's an image. If I thought it would do any good to send a huge ex-hockey star to her door, I would probably agree, but I know it will just anger her more.

"I'm flattered but it's fine, she's harmless, just gets text-happy when she drinks." If Liam tries to intervene Kayla will just harass me more, I know she will poke fun at me sending a man to fix my issues. The conversation of my bisexuality was a sore spot for her, she wanted me to admit I was a lesbian and never talk to her about any ex-boyfriends I had. Not that there was a lot to tell. She didn't like the idea of me being around men. Sending Liam to her would just open that old wound.

"If you're sure." Ellis doesn't want to drop it. That's not the type of person she is, but she will. She will tell Liam all about it, I'm sure, but I know they won't intervene unless I give the go-ahead.

"I am, thank you though, El, really it means a lot." And it does. My parents wouldn't be willing to help me fight this battle, hell, any battle – that's what makes this little family I have found myself falling into all the more special. "Can you do me one favour?"

"Sure, anything." She nods tentatively.

"I know you're going to tell Liam, I know you guys don't have secrets or whatever but ask him to keep his lips zipped around the guys, yeah?" I pierce her with a hard glare. One I saw my mom do a hundred times growing up, it is stern but not overtly intimidating.

"Sure... but why?" She speaks slowly, trying to wrap her head around my strange request.

"I love them, I do, but they will be overbearing and pushy and I just don't need that right now. Aiden can't find out, he will lose his mind and I just can't deal with him, okay?" Aiden will go into protector mode and I don't need a protector, I just need a new phone. No big deal.

"We'll keep it to ourselves, but you know they would just want to help, especially Aiden. You know he cares about you." She is trying to soothe me but her words rile me up more than Kayla's texts ever could.

"Well, I'm none of his business!"

"Damn!" She laughs, shocked at my outburst.

"Sorry, just please, promise me. Aiden won't find out about Kayla from you or Liam?" I hold out my pinkie to her and she instantly interlocks our fingers together.

"I promise, I still think you should tell him, he might be able to get Cassie to help." Ah, Cassie. She is a small but mighty force. She rules those giant men with an iron fist while wearing pretty dresses and heels high enough to make her curvy stature almost average height. She is a spitfire that might actually be good to have on my side. She, Ellis and I are the unofficial women of the Spears. I might have to start a group chat.

"Maybe, I'll keep it in mind." And I will, I also might ask Cassie if she has any tips on keeping my husband in line. Damn, *husband*. My life is a wreck, but at least the Spears are a family around me.

The Spears team is like a family, I always thought sports teams had to be close because they worked together but if the rest of them are anything like these men, then that isn't the case. The Spears men care about each other. Aiden cares about his team like they are his brothers. Edge is like a strong, silent protector ready to pounce if anyone disrespects his teammates, he is the only one allowed to antagonise them. Felix, the goalie, is a little more distant but if anyone needs him he is willing to drop anything to help as best he can. Rook is the comic relief: when they lose, he is there to show them the silver lining; when they win, he is leading the charge to the nearest bar.

I don't know if their dynamic will change now that Liam has retired but I'm sure about how they feel about Ellis. Every member of that team from the players to Coach Mitch have embraced Ellis, Jack and Charlotte and I guess inadvertently me too. She pulled me right along with her into this family unit unlike anything I ever saw growing up.

I can't speak for every family in the church, but my family wanted to be seen as a solid unit *so badly* that it was what caused the cracks the most. Mom's insistence of perfection in everything; our appearance, our schooling and our faith were always under scrutiny. Dad was like those classic dads in cheesy TV sitcoms that hate their wives and kids but need them to function. Without mom he would have starved to death years ago, that or rotted in his own filth. The man has never lifted a finger. His mom cared for him and now his wife cares for him, and I suspect he wants me to care for him in the future too. He is the master and we all his humble servants.

He would have a conniption if he saw the way the Spears men treat the women in their lives. With care and gratitude and love. Familial love or romantic love, it doesn't matter. If you are one of them you are in for life, and I'm going to count myself lucky that I have been allowed in.

There's just one, insignificant issue: I never intended to marry one of them.

Chapter Seven

Aiden

Doom is a palpable thing.

I love my house – when I found it, it felt like it had been built just for me. It may be a little big for just me, but I never imagined it just as mine. It was supposed to be a family home, even though I have taken zero steps to get there. A modern expanse on the outskirts of the city, I wanted land and big windows so I could look at that land. Growing up in Texas, people assume my views back home were vast deserts and rolling hills, but I grew up in the suburbs, my only view was of the house next door. I loved to sit on our porch as a kid and listen to all the wildlife, but I never got that big open-space feeling until I saw this house.

Right now, my house feels the opposite to the comforting armour keeping me from the world; today I need protecting from inside my house. Sat on my glass coffee table is a letter. Just a small, unassuming letter, but it's the handwriting that curves out the letters of my name that scare me. It's my grandfather's. I love my pops, dearly, but we don't see eye to eye about a lot of how I live my life.

He wanted me to leave hockey behind after Mom and Dad died. To move back home and become the man of the house. With both of our parents dead my sisters needed my strength, according to him, but when I broached the topic with my twin Alice, she smacked me upside the head and told me she would flay me open if I didn't go out there and show the world what I could do.

When he didn't get his way there, he told me I needed to settle down, that I couldn't run amok all over the US and that I needed a solid woman to keep my bed warm just like Nana Lulu did for him, but it wasn't that simple. I want to get married some day in the distant future, to have a family of my own, but I'm the captain of the Spears, I all but adopted a bunch of hockey players overnight, and finding a woman who would not only be okay with me travelling all the time but also with the fact our relationship would also include my team has proved difficult. Plus, once I come home from the rink, I don't want to have to be the perfect boyfriend, I want to slob out with a beer and watch game tapes. Not have arguments about how much I travel or how many hours I spend with everyone except her.

And now here I am, married to Lyndsey, and my wife is avoiding me. Not that I blame her, she made it clear she didn't want to be married to me, but I could do with the support of a loving partner when I open this damned letter. My pops is an old man, made even older by the fact he had to step up in a big way when my parents died, he had to step up in an even bigger way when I wouldn't stay home. At first he had help from Nana, but when she died three years later he was alone with us. Alice and I were adults but we were still under his care.

Instead of doing the mature thing and opening the letter on my table, I procrastinate by spinning my phone between my fingers. I text Lyndsey, asking to talk about our impending divorce, but I'm pretty sure I won't be getting a reply. She doesn't want to talk to me, she only wants to talk to the lawyer. I need something to distract me though, that's why when the phone does start to ring, I nearly drop it. But it's not Lyndsey's name lighting up my screen, it's Alice's. Great. I love talking to all three of my sisters, but my twin has a special knack for pissing me off. Everyone says it's because we are so similar, but I think it's because she takes pleasure in finding every way to get under my skin.

Still, I answer like a good dutiful brother.

"When are you coming home?" Her voice is short. *Well damn*, straight to the point like usual.

"Oh hi, Al, it's nice to hear from you. Yeah, I'm doing good, glad to be getting rest, how are you?" My voice drips with sarcasm, but if I can be prissy with anyone, it's Alice.

"Yeah, hi and whatever, look – can you answer my question, or have you taken too many pucks to the head?" She is the cause of a lot of the pucks I've taken, she was just as good on skates as me when we were kids. But she was smart enough to get into university on a full ride scholarship for her exceptional academic ability so she could study marketing at Texas Tech University, instead of needing a sports scholarship and staying on the ice like I had to do.

"Soon, probably." I'm noncommittal, as always.

"Jesus, Mary and Joseph, you drive me crazy, I swear." I hear the sound of her throwing something down on the other end of the line and the loud noise makes me cringe, bringing the phone away from my ear.

"Why do you want me home anyway, ya miss me?" I ask, hoping she will let me off, I want to avoid Texas like the plague.

"Like a hole in the head. Look, Pops is getting bad. You know I wouldn't say that unless it was true. I just know he ain't gonna make it to the end of the year, Aid, we need you to come home."

With her words, my heart sinks. She wouldn't tell me something like that unless she meant it. She knows what I'm like; she knows I'll want to fix it. But from all the way over here I can't.

I eye the letter again.

"What if I come home and piss him off so much that I kill him?" My voice throbs. It's a baseless fear but still, he and I love each other through our endless spats. What if I turn up and he croaks it because my life choices upset him that much? Hell, what if the letter tells me that he knows he's dying and that I better keep my ass away?

"You're on too many steroids because you sound five types of crazy, if you're not here you know you will regret it. I know you will." Her voice is sympathetic but stern, she reminds me of Mama when she talks like that. It's bittersweet.

"Shit, okay, I'll get a flight. I have something I need to do tomorrow but I'll be home before end of next week. Okay?" I reassure her. If the letter really does say to keep my ass away from Texas, then I'll just go and support my sisters, I don't have to go see him.

"Oh, you have something to do? What's her name?" she singsongs down the line.

"Fuck all the way off, Alice." That just makes her cackle at me before trying to catch her breath.

"Also, yeah, I do miss you, you know? You're my brother, I do like having you around," she says after she manages a full intake of air.

"Aw, that almost sounded sweet. I'll text you my flight info when I've booked something." *I just need to get tomorrow over with first*, I reassure myself. Go see little Jack's first official hockey game and talk to Lyndsey about the fact Mr Collins is going to take a few more days to finish up the papers, shouldn't be too hard.

"Bye, dickhead." Before I even get a chance to reply the line cuts, filling my living room with silence again.

The silence rises around me, a fog that I know how to wave away. I pick up the letter and whip the envelope open in a quick pull. The quicker this is over the better.

> *Aiden,*
> *Son, I know I'm no spring chicken. I've been in this damned home for three years and it's given me a hell of a lot of time to think.*
> *About you, about the girls. About your dad.*
> *Losing him cracked my heart in a way I tried to hide, but now I have to face the music and soon I will meet my maker the way he had to. We have all suffered an immense amount of loss in our lives, you and the girls suffered it earlier than anyone should have to. But I like to think I stepped up and was the best guardian I could be.*
> *All that to say, I have been thinking about wills. I don't have much to give apart from the house, I don't have a lot of money or things to pass down to you the way your father did. You might not believe me but I never agreed with his decision to put his belongings under conditions. I*

wanted you to find love the way both your father and I did but I wouldn't have put it in writing. Still I cannot argue with a dead man, he chose to make it a requirement for you to be married to get your part of the inheritance without consulting me. I would like to see my son's medals before I go.

You know I don't agree with your choice to not marry, and it brings me a lot of sadness to know you are missing out on becoming a real man by pushing the need to settle down aside. You have lived the high life as a professional athlete for a long time and it is high time you saw your life for what it is, a gift that you are throwing back in the faces of those who love you.

Your father was hard-headed, we both know that. But even I never imagined he would put a stipulation in his will that you would need to be married to gain your inheritance. Regrettably, but I understand it. Without a good woman by your side, you are missing out on the best parts of life. Your father knew that better than any of us.

I loved your father, and I love you too, but I agree with him. You will not be a real man until you know how to love someone other than yourself. Your father found it and I did too. I want you to find that before I go. Your running around the country instead of settling down has had an impact on everyone. I want to see my son's medals back at home – one last time.

Come home, Aiden. Find a woman and look after your sisters the way you always should have done. I do love you. I just want you to know what love really feels like.

Pops.

My hands shake around the paper before scrunching it into a ball. My fists squeeze and shake as I turn a ghostly shade of white.

Those things are mine. My dad wanted them to go to me. I don't think he knew how long it would take me to find a wife. I know Mom made him happy, but I don't understand why I'm being punished for not finding the same kind of love? I did everything I should. I worked hard. I played hard. I answered to every call.

What do they think would happen if I never married? Now Pops is trying to guilt me, putting pressure on me to marry before he dies? That wouldn't be real love. He implies I'm somehow selfish, but his words are completely self-serving. It has nothing to do with my happiness at all. If Alice is right and Pops will die soon, what does he want me to do? Marry someone just to give a certificate of proof to my dad's lawyer and get the medals for him?

Without conscious thought, I storm down a flight of stairs to my home gym. There are treadmills and weights littering the room, but I head straight for the punching bag. I don't take the time to wrap my hands, they are already clenched into fists. Then I swing. The hook above my head creaks with the force but I push ahead. Swinging in a constant meditative rhythm over and over. Right, left right right. Left, right, left left. Again and again.

Punching until it is all I can feel. Every thought pushed through my fists into the fabric of the bag. It swings as I hit it but I wish it would grunt like when I hit someone on the ice. I'm not a violent player, I only fight if it is necessary and, right now, it is necessary. Players around the States should take comfort in the fact that the Spears didn't make it to the playoffs because if I were to be on the ice this week, I'm not sure I would have the control to keep my temper from flaring.

My plan is to keep swinging until I pass out, but soon the bag starts to be speckled with blood from my knuckles. The cold air hitting the small wounds stings me back to the present. As I'm finding myself back in the room, the fog inside my mind begins to lift – if only for a moment.

I *am* married.

Well, I have a marriage certificate. If I can get Lyndsey to put off that divorce, I can get what is rightfully mine.

I can get my father's things, make my grandfather happy, and maybe, *just maybe*, life can go back to how it was before.

Chapter Eight

Aiden

I've never crashed a car before. Even as a teenager driving was never a challenge. But today... today, I feel like I could be sideswiped any minute. Not because I'm being chased or anything else quite as dramatic, but because for the first time I feel like my multitasking skills are eluding me. When I take to the ice as the captain of the Seattle Spears there are hundreds of things on my mind: my team, the opposing team, every play and every penalty flows through my head and I can organise them. It's what makes me so good at my job, being able to compartmentalise all of the background noise and focus on what I need to do, what my team needs to do. Today I'm tripping over my own damn feet and I can't find a way through the sludge of thoughts.

Music is a great distraction when your mind is spinning. When you're driving you are supposed to be completely focused, but no one has ever been solely focused on one thing. I'm thinking about four things this morning. Driving to a youth hockey game. Excitement for my favourite nine-year-old. Vegas. Lyndsey Stone.

I tried to distract my brain by playing my favourite songs. Some country songs that my mom used to sing when I was a kid mixed with a selection of 2000s pop songs that were on the radio while I was in college. I'm a man of habit. When I find something that I enjoy it becomes a part of the routine, including these songs. In the same way when I meet a person who I come to care about, they become a part of me too.

Jack is one of those people. Jack is the son of my NHL teammate Liam Ruinsky. Well, technically he is his stepson; but Ruin would beat me up for even thinking of Jack as anything other than his son. Which I suppose makes me Jack's unofficial uncle, in a way. Even if Liam did retire last year, so he isn't even technically my teammate any more, we've still remained like a family. Right now as I drive, I'm trying to focus on him. He is playing his first official youth hockey game and I couldn't be more proud. As a team we saw Ruin become Jack's dad, and as his captain I was proud to see the man being a father turned him into. Not only a father to Jack, but also to his and his fiancée Ellis' baby girl, Charlotte.

The only downfall to watching him become a dad is losing him from the Seattle Spears. When his life became family-centric there wasn't enough room for hockey in his life any more, and we all miss him on the ice.

I can ignore how much I miss him for now because of how excited I am for Jack. I saw that kid learn to skate – hell, I let him chase me around the ice and blast pucks at me for "target practice". At least that's what Liam called it. All of the team wanted to be here, but we aren't idiots. No matter what our PR manager would want the world to think, we knew that if we all turned up today the eyes would be on us, not on those kids. Edge called dibs as he is baby Charlotte's godfather, and I pulled the captain card so I could come too. We didn't play fair.

And, of course, I know I'm in for a storm from outside the rink today. Ellis has invited her best friend. Lyndsey Stone. *My wife*. Beautiful with long strawberry-blond hair and terrifying green eyes that see through bullshit. Mine more than most. Especially the day we woke up in Vegas.

Vegas is the thing I push to the recesses of my brain the hardest. We only got back a few days ago, and my life has taken so many turns since I boarded that damn plane. All I wanted was to celebrate the end of the season and Liam's retirement, and instead I'm a different man. I'm someone's husband, purely by accident. And now I need to find a way to make this work to my advantage.

By the time I get to the arena the parking lot is pretty busy. Minivans line the spots closest to the doors, apart from the black Range Rover that I know is Edge's. He took Lyndsey home after our meeting with Cassie and I have been dodging his questions about it since. If they are here together I'll have to pull her aside at some point. Hopefully it won't feel like I am accosting her.

Luckily for me, she is sat by Edge. I could find her in a crowd of a hundred but today she stands out more than normal. Her hair is twisted up in a complicated braid leaving her long feminine neck exposed. She is wearing one of Liam's jerseys and it takes more patience than it should to not get angry at the sight of his name across her back. As I come down the steps towards them I still haven't seen her face but I can imagine the excitement that I will find there. Jack is important to her, she sees him as her nephew and she has been there with us watching him find his love of the ice.

"She will love me more, I don't need to buy her affection," she taunts Edge. I still can't see her but his eyebrows raise at her words.

"Charlotte Ruinsky is my girl, Lyndsey. I'm sure she will love you too but I'm her best guy." Edge sounds completely sure in his conviction – if I didn't know Charlotte couldn't talk, I'd think she'd told him that herself.

Of course the two of them are having this conversation. Lyndsey is Charlotte's godmother and Edge is her godfather, not only do they both love her fiercely, they are also two very competitive people. Damn stubborn too.

"Does that help you sleep at night?" she taunts.

"That and the Egyptian-cotton sheets." He winks at her but when he sees me behind her he nods in acknowledgment of my arrival.

Lyndsey spins around on her seat, looking up at me. That's not strange, even when she is standing she has to look up at me. As soon as she sees it's me she spins back around just as fast, effectively ignoring my presence.

"I think I left something in my car… I'm going to go"— she coughs—"go check." Still not meeting my eyes, she edges past me like the wind.

My momma taught me manners but they go out the window when I jog right after her without saying a word to Edge. He will forgive me, he likes the quiet. I'm sure he will have questions eventually but he can wait. Lyndsey is like a rocket shooting down the corridors back towards the arena.

"You can't run forever, darlin', Jack's gonna want to see ya," I yell after her as she rounds a corner out of my view. When I round it behind her I find she has stopped. Lyndsey is stood with her forehead resting against a painted blue wall, breath heaving.

"That isn't fair," she whispers to me, and I know it went below the belt, it was the only way I knew I could get her to stop. The Ruinsky kids are her soft spot.

"You are gonna have to talk to me eventually, you know?" I lean against the wall next to her but when I try to put my hand on her shoulder she jerks away from me before finally looking me in the eye.

"You shouldn't touch me, last time you did our lives went to shit." Lyndsey is trying to joke but I hear the truth in it. Our lives did change in Vegas. When I woke up with her wrapped in my arms.

"Lyndsey…"

"Aiden, listen, it's probably a good thing we are talking actually because we need to get this shit over with ASAP. Where're the papers?" she asks me, slicing the air with her hand.

"Look, I know we need to eventually, but I can't do that right now." I wanted to go about this gently, but I don't think that is going to work out how I planned.

"What are you saying? We aren't staying married, Aiden. Have you lost your mind?" Her voice is stern through gritted teeth. She might be right, all things considered. But she just doesn't understand.

"Maybe, but I have some family stuff going on, okay? And I need your help with it." I *do* sound like I've lost my mind. I know I should tell her everything. I'm planning on telling her everything. About my sick grandfather and my sisters struggling to deal with him. Before I can get to this point, she cuts me off.

"I'll help you… When we divorce." Her voice kicks up at the end and I know she is getting mad. I don't blame her.

"Lyndsey, all I'm asking is for us to stay married for just a little bit." I try to reason, rationalising to myself how I can get all this squared away in a few months. I hope.

"You can't make a unilateral decision about my life! We. Are. Getting. *Divorced*," she growls out, baring her teeth at me. Practically ready to attack.

"Pot calling the kettle black much, Lyndsey? You're unilaterally deciding we are getting divorced," I push back, realising that I still hadn't got to tell her everything before I got on the defensive. I need to be smarter about this.

"I'm not talking about this here." Lyndsey looks angrier than I have ever seen her.

"Well, darlin', we're gonna have to talk about it soon." My hand comes out to hold her elbow but she pulls that free too, shaking her head up at me.

"Don't *darlin'* me! No one can know." I can feel myself starting to heat up, my chest feels tight with frustration so I let out a deep breath to expel it the way I do on the ice.

"Lyndsey. You are my wife, people are going to find out." I try to lift the atmosphere, but it doesn't work. Instead, my statement falls on the wrong ears.

"What?" Liam yells from my right. Every muscle in my body tenses at the sound.

"Nice going, cowboy." Lyndsey pushes past me quickly, sweeping out towards the exit of the arena. I'm left standing with one of my closest friends and his fiancée… Lyndsey's closest friend. Jesus.

"I'm sorry, I think we might miss the game. I'll call you later." I stop them before they get a chance to question me. Their questions will come – thick and fast, I'm sure – but I can avoid them for now.

I pace after Lyndsey, jogging out of the arena back into the late springtime sun.

If I was ever to get married, this isn't how I pictured the newlywed period.

Chapter Nine

Lyndsey

I burst through the doors of the rink, not bothering to look behind me. I don't know what I need but I know I can't be in there any more. I didn't want anyone to know. I kept this shit from my best friend even when it was weighing me down just for him to blab without a second's thought. Now not only does she know, I'm not the one who got to tell her.

The air is crisp but my lungs can't seem to take a deep breath. As I walk, I remember that Edge drove me here so I don't have the sanctuary of my car to hide in. I have no way to escape. Knowing Aiden will follow after me I dart around the corner, my bag slips off my shoulder but I don't stop to pick it up. My hair sticks to the sweaty skin of my neck. My clothes feel too tight.

I want it all off.

I can't even see past my own nose through the fog in my mind. I can feel everywhere my clothes are touching me. I'm blinded by the sunlight. I can feel the hair that rests on my neck and I want to cut it off. With every step I take I can feel my heart pounding in my chest. My knees buckle under me and I slide down the brick facade of the building to hide.

I can feel everything but there is nothing I can do about it. I just can't seem to move from my spot on the ground. It's as though my legs have locked into position. I can feel heat prickling over my chest but there is nothing I can do about it even if I wanted to. People think the fear responses are fight and flight but there are actually four.

Fight.

Flight.

Fawn.

Freeze.

I'm doing the latter. Every part of me wants to run, to take flight, but there is not even a twitch. The only part of my body that I seem to be able to move freely is my head. It rocks back and forth, lightly hitting the wall behind me. The feeling is grounding, reminding me that I won't float away.

The noise of children in the arena becomes a quiet hum in the background overpowered by the sound of my heart beating in my head. Yet I feel myself instantly start to calm now that I'm out of the line of fire. Now that my lungs feel like they can inflate again, my brain rushes with the reality of the panic I was consumed by.

My parents would be celebrating if they could see me now. Married to a man, the perfect straight daughter they always dreamed of. I know deep inside that just because I'm married to Aiden that doesn't make me any less bisexual. They wouldn't see it that way. They would say that I'm over my little tantrum and that I'm making the choice to be straight. I didn't make any choice here. I don't remember making the choice to marry. I didn't get to make the choice to get a divorce instead of an annulment. I have no choice but to deal with Kayla sending me message after message on a constant loop. Everything in my life has been decided for me over the past few weeks and I hate the way it feels.

Beside me the heavy metal fire door swings open and out the corner of my eye I see Aiden rush to my side but I make no move to meet his eye. His knees hit the pavement in front of me and his hand comes up to cradle my face. For a split second I see him hesitate as though he is worried I might pull away from him but he moves anyway. He pulls me into his lap and I feel his shoulders relax under my tears when I lean into his touch. His thumb rubs light circles on the side of my cheek and I can see his eyes scanning me to find some clues as to what he is supposed to do to help.

"Darlin', what's going on?" His voice is low, I suppose not to startle me, but when my eyes meet his, the tears fall even harder. He is looking at me like I'm broken and, in a way, I guess I am. The cracks I try so hard to cover are exposed to him.

"They already hate me. I just wanted to be enough. Why am I never enough?" My breath heaves between each word punching me in the gut. "They are going to think they were right. They are going to think I lied. They already hate me." It's true. I have never felt as much hatred as I did the day my father kicked me out. I'm so overwhelmed that everything is pouring out of me: every time a little part of me has wondered if they were right; every dirty look I have been given when people have found out about my sexuality; every little thing that has knocked me down over the years – all of it is laid bare. I'm talking about my parents, but I could also mean Kayla – she hated that I had dated men, and she might think she was right that my bisexuality was a phase now that I'm married to Aiden.

He tells me that I'm safe, mumbling against my hairline. I rock in his lap gently as he tells me that everything is going to be okay. He has no idea what I'm rambling about but he holds me steady, refusing to let me succumb to my spiralling thoughts. When he left the house today, I highly doubt he thought I would be crying into his shirt… again.

Back when Ellis collapsed at work and had to leave for the hospital, it was Aiden who came to comfort me then. He let me cry against him and held me together. That was a big shift in our relationship. It became less fun that day, we went from easy flirtation to him putting a solid wall between us. Now here I am again, crying into his solid chest as though he is some saviour.

"My parents hate me, Aiden." My words are spoken against the skin of his neck. He holds me tight enough to keep me together. I don't mention Kayla, it would lead to too many questions.

"Nobody can hate you, darlin'." He sounds so sure. As though the thought alone is crazy to him. It almost makes me laugh. The idea that this man who barely knows me would be so steadfast in his opinion of me. He has only really seen the good. The light, fun mask I wear. The one time he saw the cracks was when he pushed me away and, still, he is so sure of my goodness that he is angry at people he has never met.

"They hate me because I'm not straight." My admission renders him speechless for a change. I take the moment of silence to look at him. I'm rarely this close to him, here I can see the light stubble on his chin. The way his eyes crinkle at the sides from where he smiles.

"Then I hate them for hating you," he tells me, holding me tighter to him. The fierceness in his voice makes a small laugh bubble out of my chest.

"Stop trying to make me laugh." Even though my face is still pushed against his skin I know he can hear the smile in my words. He puts a hand behind my head, pulling me out of his chest to see my face.

"I'll never stop trying to see you smile, darlin', it's a sight too pretty to hide." He says it like it's a determined truth. The feelings I have for him are too confusing. I know he is attractive, I have eyes, but I also do not want to be married to him. I liked harmless flirting between friends but now? Now I feel this burning anger whenever I look at him. "At least this has taught me something," he says, rubbing his hand up and down my spine.

"What's that?" I hiccup out a reply, still struggling to get my breathing steady. Hating myself a little for being vulnerable with him. But he is here and he is soft so I'll accept the comfort for a little while longer.

"That I leave you breathless." He winks down at me and I can't contain the small laugh that bubbles out.

"You're not funny." I slap his hard chest, trying to ignore the feeling of his muscles beneath my hand. I want to be mad at him.

"I'm a little funny," he says, nudging me, and I do what I can to bite back the smile that is trying to burst through.

I know it isn't entirely his fault that we are in this place. I must have had some say in all this, but because I don't remember it, it feels easier to put my emotions onto him. He is a hockey captain, shouldn't he be responsible enough to know not to get blackout drunk and married in Vegas? Still, I know him better than that. He is a playboy, the one who is always flirting and putting a smile on everyone's face. He probably took it as his responsibility to make sure everyone was having a good time that night, it's just a shame we had too good of a time. I'm reminded of just why I'm mad at him and sitting on this floor after a panic attack when he opens his mouth again.

"Lyndsey, I know I'm asking a lot by asking to stay married but, please, for me, just hear me out."

The sigh that flows out of me is filled with lingering emotion, but I nod for him to continue anyway.

"My dad was in the army, did you know that?" he asks, but when my eyes widen a fraction, he knows this is news to me, "He un-enlisted when my youngest sister Cece was born, said he wanted to see us grow up. But him and Mom died in a car crash years later, the night of my first college game. He had a will made, when my mom nearly died giving birth to my baby sister, I think he thought more about his morality."

"Aiden, you don't have to tell me all this. If it's too painful you can stop." I use my sleeve to wipe a stray tear away, I don't think he even realised he was crying. I give him time to find his words and the chance to stop if that's what he wants but he shakes his head before continuing.

"No, I want you to understand. God, I loved that man but he was hard work. He had kept all of his army stuff, his medals and things, the stuff he kept in his bunk, he put a stipulation in his will because he decided I hadn't earned them." He sighs and for the first time I can hear how deeply tired he is. Usually he wouldn't let anyone see him sweat. Everything is like satin flying over him but this is something real. Something he has grappled with alone.

"That's fucked up," I interrupt. I have been thinking so hard about how many choices have been made for me recently and here he is being commanded by his father from beyond the grave.

"He had this old-school mentality, that I'm not a man until I have my own family. I tried to argue with my grandfather about it but that got me nowhere and now my grandfather is sick. Alice, that's my twin, she had to put him in a home because he was too much work for the three girls alone. Now I get a letter from him that he wants to see his son's army memorabilia before he dies, so he is demanding I marry to get my part of the inheritance." And now he is married. To me. Yes, it might not be a love connection but in the eyes of the law he is my husband, our marriage certificate would be enough to get his dad's stuff, but without me there to back it up everyone would question his intentions.

It might sound crazy but I'm considering helping him. I know it would be wrong lying to his family, but I hate that he feels like this is his only option. I want some control over my life and this feels like a good way to get it. If I stay married to him and we tell the public, well, that would mean Kayla would find out and it might be the final nail in the coffin of her leaving me alone. There is always the chance she would harden her efforts but if I have Aiden on my side, I could ask him to talk to her without it looking like I'm getting a man to save me. I'm getting *my husband* to save me.

Then there is the fact Aiden isn't the type to ask for help. He never lets anything get to him, every problem is like water off a duck's back, and yet he needs me now. As long as we are both benefitting from it then maybe it would be worth it.

"I'll do it." I don't even think about the words. My mind is filled with images of him having to bury his grandfather without getting to grant his dying wish. My family don't care about me but I know he doesn't have that same problem. He loves his sisters and I can hear how much he loved his parents. Now I have the power to make a family happy in a way I could never make mine.

"Lyndsey—" he starts, but I interrupt him again.

"No! He shouldn't have kept that stuff from you. We can stay married, they have to give you what's yours." I'm enraged on his behalf but more than that I'm determined. Some good might be able to come from our drunken marriage; I just have to make sure I don't get myself hurt in the process. "Can you make me one promise?" I ask, ignoring the way his lips press against my hair. "Once it's over, when we have your stuff back, you have to let me go. We will divorce and stay friends. I can help you, I'll help you, but I can't stay married to you."

"What's in this for you?" he asks, his voice filled with wonder as though he can't believe I would agree so easily. I know that I shouldn't but I know we can make this work. As long as we don't kill each other before we pull it off.

"Let's just say I could do with a partner of my own," I tell him. Hopefully I won't have to tell him about Kayla and, if I do, well, I'll wait until I'm out of other options. I think me actually moving on will show her that we aren't meant to be together. She might try to fight it but I know deep down she will see me being married to a man as a big enough betrayal that it could be the final push she needs to let me go.

"Okay, if that's what you need. That's what we will do," he tells me, silence settling between us both. I don't rush to leave his lap, I want some comfort and he is giving it so willingly that I can't help but soak it up. After today though, once our marriage is public knowledge I won't do this again. Take comfort in my reluctant husband. Even if we need to prove it to everyone else that doesn't mean we have to be any closer than we have to be. I inhale sharply, considering my next words, because they even manage to terrify me.

"We need to speak to Cassie… and the press."

Chapter Ten

Aiden

As the team pile into the locker room I question if this is a good idea. It's not for the first time, but Lyndsey thinks it's better if everyone is on the same page. It's my family we have to convince, not the team, and it's better that we lie to as few people as possible. I agree with the logic, I don't want to hide it from them, I just wish she were here with me.

Lyndsey is off telling Ellis the news while I tackle telling the whole team about our nuptials. I don't think it's fair that I have to deal with the reaction of these idiots all alone. They all file in and take a seat on the benches, looking at me expectantly, waiting for me to give them more game plays or yell at them for something or other, that's what it usually means when I call one of these meetings on an off day. Usually, I'm calm and collected when I command my team but this is different.

I stand proud in the centre of the room, my shoulders back and my feet planted apart. I exude confidence, the braver I look the easier it will be to convince them I know what I'm doing. I think I do. It's not like it will be hard to pretend to be attracted to Lyndsey because I am, the only lie is going to be about us being happily married. I know deep down that this is going to work and I just hope the team don't ask any questions I haven't thought about yet. I'm going to roll with the punches and figure this out as it goes, I can't predict how my sisters will react so there is no point stressing about it.

The plan is foolproof. Give the bank where my dad's lockbox is our marriage certificate to gain access to the inheritance. Spend a couple of nights in my childhood home and visit my grandpa once or twice to show him his son's stuff. Easy-peasy. Then we can come home, sign the divorce papers and move on with our lives.

"Okay y'all, I'm just gonna come out and say it." I clasp my hands in front of myself, trying not to rock on the balls of my feet.

They all look up at me waiting in near silence for me to continue and I can't help but let the anticipation build, a little bit of drama and panache might soften the blow.

"Lyndsey Stone and I are married." I bring my hand up to show them the gold band on my ring finger that I slipped on again for the first time since that morning in Vegas.

There is a moment of stunned silence and then the room erupts into rambunctious laughter. Rook doubles over, his face going bright red as he laughs. Edge doesn't laugh as loud as everyone but even he rolls his eyes at my apparent joke. Felix's eyes flick between me and the ring, his smile slowly slipping as I don't join their laughter.

"Wait, why aren't you laughing?" he asks, and everyone but Rook stops laughing, looking at me, waiting for me to crack a smile.

"We got married, she's my wife," I tell them again, and when they all look at me slack-jawed I try once more: "Sorry I didn't let ya'll plan a bachelor party."

My joke falls completely flat but it at least makes me smile. The guys lose it again but this time they aren't laughing, the room explodes in uproar. Yelling, asking if I'm serious. Asking how this happened. How long has it been going on? I don't answer their questions, instead I just stand in front of them, waiting for them to calm down instead of adding fuel to the fire. Once they realise I'm not talking they eye me suspiciously.

"Are you going to let me explain?" I ask, and they all fall silent watching me again.

"Oh, go right ahead. Please," Rook says, still smiling like this is still fun and games. He really does remind me of a young me. Things roll off of him the way they do me, there is so much levity even in the hard moments.

"So the actual wedding part is a little fuzzy. In Vegas we woke up in bed with each other the day we were flying back home with rings, a marriage certificate and no idea how we got there." I fill them in on everything. From our flight home to our meeting with Cassie that Edge interrupted and to Pops' letter. The more I explain the more confused they look until I get to the crux of the issue. "So Lyndsey is going to pretend to be my wife for a little while until I can get Dad's stuff," I finish to the silent room.

"What the fuck is wrong with you?" Edge's voice cuts through the silence, almost shaking the walls. He storms across the room until he is toe to toe with me, his face bright red with anger. His fists clench the fabric at the front of my shirt, pulling me up a few inches until he is right in my face. "You can't use her like this, I won't let you." His voice is like gravel as he speaks through his teeth, trying not to yell.

"That's not your choice," I tell him, ignoring how tight my shirt is around my throat. I won't let him think he can scare me out of this. It's between me and Lyndsey, not him.

"She likes you and you're using her for this bullshit." He lets out a humourless laugh. "It's not right." The rest of the team watch on silently. I can see Rook over Edge's shoulder with Felix holding him back by the elbow.

"It's none of your business, Jay, put me down." I'm done with this shit. I use his first name hoping he can hear how serious I am, but the rage behind his eyes doesn't waver.

"Edge, put him down. Now!" Rook yells from behind and I've never heard him sound so serious. Edge glances over the shoulder to see all of our team looking at him with worry and it must bring him back down to earth enough that he loosens his grip on me.

"Tell her it's off," he tells me, shoving me lightly, his voice still just as angry as before.

"Why? You want to fuck her or something?" I know I shouldn't say it, I should think more about my words before I say them as captain, but when my emotions are this heightened it's difficult. It's the only reason I can think about why he would care so much about this. He has only known Lyndsey for about a year and a half and he has never shown any signs of being into her but he is a quiet guy when it comes to relationships. I might have missed it.

"Not everything is about sex," he huffs, shaking his head before pinning me with a glare again. Rook must have shaken off Felix's hold because he comes up to stand by my side as Edge continues, "She is my friend, a good person, and she deserves better than this shit."

"She agreed to it, says she has her own reasons," I tell him. It's not like I'm blackmailing her or anything. She told me this will benefit her and I have to trust that she is telling the truth. "It's just a trip to Texas for a few days and then it's over."

"You're gonna let her go?" He raises a brow at me as though he is giving me one last chance to not make this mistake. But I don't believe it is a mistake. I think this is going to be good for Lyndsey. I don't see why she would do it otherwise. She isn't the type of woman to be pushed around so if she says she is in, then I have to think that she is right. All she has asked is for us to divorce when we get back and that is something I can offer.

"As soon as we land," I tell him earnestly. Nodding once, he turns on his heels and storms out of the room, pulling his phone out of his pocket as he does. Probably to call Lyndsey and find out her side of the story, though I know she will tell him the same as me.

Slowly and wordlessly, everyone leaves the room, leaving me with Rook. He slaps my shoulder once before following everyone else. I end up alone again, feeling equal parts relieved and in a state of dread. On one side I'm glad to have this over with, telling the boys was always going to be some kind of battle. I'm glad to have step one of this plan crossed off. But that is where the dread comes in. The next step is convincing my sisters that this is for real.

At least with the boys I could be truthful, but lying to Alice, Eden and Celia is going to be difficult. Those three girls know me better than anyone else. They have seen me grieve and rage, they have seen me at my highest of highs and there is not a lot I keep from them. I have always been an open book when I'm close to people and there is no closer than my damn blood.

Alice is going to be the hardest to convince. Not only is it strange for me not to tell her when I'm dating someone but the idea that I would get married without my twin there is almost inconceivable. She will be looking for every crack in our story, questioning everything to understand why she was kept out of the loop.

One battle down, a lot more to go.

Chapter Eleven

Lyndsey

It's not rare for me to be at Ellis and Liam's home. Usually to spend time with Ellis when she is feeling overwhelmed or if I'm here to spend time with the kids. Jack has been my little bestie since he was born. Back then Ellis had nobody by her side, her ex Michael kicked her out when she told him about her pregnancy. She hired me not long before that and I think having me around to help when she became a single mom bonded us. Still, I was surprised when she gave birth to Charlotte that she asked me to be her godmother.

Edge and I are in constant competition to be the favourite godparent and I'm winning. He would disagree but he is wrong. So when I told Ellis I wanted to see my favourite kids she didn't bat an eye. It wasn't until she opened the door and I found it impossible to look her in the eye that she probably started to suspect something is wrong. I'm sitting on the floor with Charlotte on my lap as Jack explains to me the difference between ice hockey positions.

"My dad says that Anders has the hardest job but I think Edge does," he tells me excitedly, and I try not to flinch at the mention of Aiden. Jack started calling Liam 'Dad' not long before Charlotte was born and Liam is a better dad than he would have ever guessed.

"All right, bud, get your shoes on, we're going to the park!" Liam calls as he and Ellis come out of the kitchen where they have been talking about me. They thought they were being slick but I know them well enough to know Ellis wants to find out what's wrong with me.

"No! My babies!" I snuggle Charlotte closer to my chest but she bursts out of my arms and crawls over to her dad, babbling as she goes.

"Stop using my kids as a buffer," Ellis admonishes, her English accent still as strong as the day I met her, flopping onto the sofa behind me. Liam just laughs while I mouth "traitor" at him as he rallies the kids towards the door. Pushing myself up from the floor I settle onto the soft brown leather cushion until I'm next to her. Still I don't look her in the eyes. "You want some tea?" she asks after a moment of silence. I think she is doing that mom thing where she is trying to trick me into getting comfortable before she starts badgering me.

I came here with the intention of telling her about the fact I'm a married woman but now that I'm here? I don't want to disappoint her. She is the closest thing I have to family any more and if she feels less of me, I would hate it. I doubt I'm going to have her full support in this stupid plan but I just need her to trust that I know what I'm doing.

Because I think I do. A few days in the Texas sun while Aiden collects his dad's stuff. A well-placed press release to show Kayla I have moved on and to strengthen the validity of our claims.

"Got anything stronger? Tequila?" I ask, finally looking at her.

"Okay, that's enough. What the hell is going on?" she demands, hitting me with a cushion, which makes me laugh.

"I'm just going to come out and say it, I'm married to Aiden." There is no grace to my words. I have thought about this conversation maybe a hundred times since Aiden and I decided to pretend to be married and every time I get too scared or I basically choke on the words. Now that it's out there I bite down on my lips to stop from over-explaining, I don't want to overwhelm her with this.

"I think I misheard, can you say that one again for me? Because when he called you his wife, I thought I must be going crazy." She shakes her head lightly, a smile on her face clearly thinking whatever she heard was a joke.

"I married Aiden in Vegas. Surprise!" I do a shitty jazz hands to soften the blow. It doesn't work.

Ellis stares at me and I stare right back. I can almost see her mind coming to terms with what I said. Her mouth opens and closes as she tries to find the right words to say but she comes up with nothing. That is when I start to worry, I'm so used to her having an answer for everything. She is only a few years older than my twenty-seven but she has always been more wise and put together. I think it is because she had to grow up so fast because of her shitty childhood.

"Please say something," I ask, pulling her hands into my lap, needing that physical connection, hoping it will ground her somehow.

"Like what? Congratulations? Are you two together now? I was rooting for you two to date but I thought maybe a nice meal or go to the museum not this," she rambles all at once. Her words meld into each other as though she can't order her thoughts.

I remember last year when she and Liam first started dating and Aiden and I had a lot of tension. She was a big supporter of us dating but it would never have worked. I mean, he is the type of man who could have any woman in the world and I'm just a normal woman from Seattle, I'm a dime a dozen.

"We aren't together... technically," I start but she yells out again.

"You're married!"

"Okay, listen." I squeeze her hands once to settle her before I try my best to explain how I got here. "We got drunkenly married and are planning on getting divorced but we have to stay married for a little while and go to Texas together."

"Why?" She is getting frustrated and I don't blame her. It's a lot to take in, I'm really married but also pretending to be married to fool my husband's family. Though I don't want to go into the details of the inheritance, I don't feel comfortable sharing all of Aiden's secrets without at least his go-ahead.

"That's Aiden's story, but this will be good for me too," I promise. It might seem like I decided to do this whole thing a little off the cuff but I know deep down that it makes sense. I know Aiden will help me if I need it, plus there are worse men to be married to for a couple of weeks. As long as that is all it is.

"How do you figure that?" She laughs as if I'm crazy. She might not be wrong.

"It's going to get Kayla off my back, she will see I've moved on and leave me alone." The words come out sure and steady. I have to believe this will work, I have tried everything else, what is one more attempt at trying to get her to leave me alone?

"You are not that naive!" She frowns but her words take me aback. She sounds completely outraged and I wasn't expecting that reaction.

"What?" My jaw drops open and she pulls me closer to her along the leather seat until our legs are touching. She throws one arm over my shoulder.

"It might just make her more mad, what then?" she asks, genuinely worried, but I have thought about that too. I'm not usually a planner but in this case all I can do is run through every eventuality.

"Well, I'll be in Texas so it's not like she can confront me. By the time I get back she will have cooled off and have moved on to the next thing." I'm sure of it. Kayla is a lot of things but she gets bored easily. Outside of her texts to me I never saw her care about anything for longer than a few days, a week at most. Whether it was her quitting a job because the boss asked her to clean up her mess, or when she wanted to take up tennis but stopped because she thought the coach was too overweight to be any good at sport, there was always something that made her give in before things got complicated.

"I hope so." Ellis sighs, pulling me even closer under her arm and I take comfort in how much she cares. For a long while I thought I would never have people that cared about me and about keeping me safe. I'm so lucky to have found her. And, I guess, the hockey team she brought with her.

"I've thought about this, El, I swear, it'll work," I assure her, pulling her into a full hug, wrapping her taller frame into my arms.

"Well… I guess good luck, Mrs Anders." She laughs and I pull back with a groan. She is going to love teasing me about this. She knows how big of a crush I had on

Aiden, I have done since the first day I met him – hell, before even then. Now I'm his wife, it would almost be serendipitous if it wasn't so ridiculous. "So how about that tea?" El slaps my leg before standing up and walking to the kitchen, leaving me alone with my thoughts.

I'm so glad she doesn't hate me. I didn't think she would but the Spears players are an important part of her life now. More important than me. It wouldn't have shocked me if she had chosen them over me, she is going to be married to a man who is always around those men. Her son loves them and her daughter already adores her uncles and, as much as I'm a part of their lives too, I'm used to being expendable.

If I was expendable enough for my parents to toss me aside then why should I expect anyone else I know to pick me when it comes down to it?

Chapter Twelve

Wedding Bells for Spears Captain... Updates from Hot Hockey News

Yes, if you listen closely, you can hear women weep around the world as it is announced that Captain Aiden Anders has officially tied the knot.

A year after the pair were introduced, Aiden Anders and close friend to the Spears team, Lyndsey Stone, have married in Vegas. The pair have supposedly had a whirlwind romance, and despite the team captain initially wanting to keep his privacy, have now decided to share their nuptials to the world.

Their elopement was attended by friends of the pair and fellow players. While inside sources claim they didn't plan to marry, once they touched down in Vegas they knew it was the right time.

Lyndsey Stone was apparently introduced to the Spears captain when ex defenceman Liam Ruinsky made his romance public with his fiancée, Ellis Ainsley. Lyndsey, previously spotted with Ellis on a number of outings, appears to be a close friend of Miss Ainsley, and is even reported to be the godmother of Liam and Ellis' young daughter. She grew up in Blue Ridge, Seattle and is no stranger to ice hockey – with a brother who played himself.

The Seattle Spears PR manager, Cassie Fitzgerald, released the following statement this morning to ESPN:

"Aiden and Lyndsey are a very happy couple. Everyone here at the Spears family are overjoyed about the news of their marriage. We wish them a long and happy life together and are excited to see what Aiden will bring to the ice as a happily married man. Congratulations to the newly-weds."

Chapter Thirteen

Lyndsey

I'm a professional airport goer. If I could profit from it I'd be up there in the hottest billionaire lists. I was prepared with my slip-on shoes for security, all of my electronics near the top of my bag for easy access, all for Aiden to swoop in and take us through premium security and straight to a VIP lounge. Who would I be if I squandered that opportunity?

VIP lounges aren't my usual scene, surprise to no one, but I could get used to this. Being fake married to a hockey star is starting to have its perks. Aiden is sat in some comfortable-looking recliner as I explore; he trusts me more than he probably should because I have already stuffed three cookies into my carry-on in case I get peckish on the plane.

Now I'm making myself a quinoa bowl and a cocktail while we wait for boarding to open. We must be compatible in some ways, because Aiden seemed just as eager as me to get to the airport early. I'm an *arrive three hours before the flight* type of person, who ignores anyone who tries to tell me it's pointless. Aiden, for once, didn't disagree. He picked me up in an Uber with enough time to kill that I can explore the lounge to the fullest extent.

It never occurred to me how people dress when they aren't flying in economy. These business- and first-class folks are in a different realm to me. I saw a woman in heels – *heels* – at the airport. It is some unwritten law that airplane shoes should be comfortable, have room for expansion in the air and be easy to run in, in case of emergency. Apparently, that isn't some universal law, just a personal one.

For my personal flying style, it is either a lounge co-ord or, like today, it's leggings with a vest and a beige button-up cardigan over the top. Aiden has joined me in the comfort-over-style approach by wearing sweatpants with a T-shirt, so I don't feel completely out of place. If he had shown up like the man snoring next to him, in a suit with a damn tie, I might have died of embarrassment and run back up to my apartment to change.

"Darlin', you know they serve food on the plane, right?" Aiden's voice startles me as I slip another cookie into my bag.

"Shit, cowboy, you trying to give me a heart attack?" I turn to slap his arm, but he is closer than I expected. Aiden looms over me, eyes scanning from head to toe, he is so close the scent that rings completely true to him permeates my personal bubble. My hand is still swinging though, hitting him in the ribs instead of his bicep. He wheezes out a breath.

"Lynds, how many cookies have you got there?" He tries to peek into my bag but I pull it tight to my side avoiding his grey-eyed gaze.

"Look, I have to make the most of being a WAG while I can, this is one of the only perks so far." I shoulder past him as I talk, shaking the food container in my hands to mix the quinoa and salad to distract myself while his eyes burn into the back of my head. Until his hand shoots out to grab my elbow to pull my back against his chest.

"I can think of a few more perks for you." His southern drawl whispered against the shell of my ear sends chills down to my toes. I'm glad for the cardigan as it hides the goosebumps that raise over my arms.

"You'll have to find someone else to join the mile-high club with, *husband*," I tease, falling into his chest further. His hand slips from my elbow to my wrist and up again, pulling the fabric with it. The contrast between his tanned and tatted skin and my pale freckled arms looks like something from an editorial magazine cover. The bright lights make my skin appear even brighter and paler and make his tattoos look almost alive. The snake wrapped around his forearm almost slithers as his muscles ripple as he massages my arms.

"This marriage might not have been completely intentional, but does that mean we're never going to consummate it?" In an instant his hands dart out and snatch the food from me before he pulls away and slinks back over to the recliner, digging into my lunch.

"In your dreams." I flop onto the chair facing him, trying to appear annoyed but, more than that, I'm trying to disguise the blush covering me as anger rather than the truth that he affects me more than I wish he did.

The little asshole just keeps eating, only sending a wink my way before moaning around a fork full of the food I made myself.

"What happened to the food on the plane you told me about, you thief?" I huff.

"What? I just wanted a meal made by my lovely wife, that's not a crime." His smile is sickly-sweet, his lashes bat against his cheeks too and if it wasn't for the piece of lettuce stuck to his teeth I would have melted.

"No, but murder is, and I'm getting hangry." I try to appear serious, but judging by his unaffected expression, I know he sees right through me. That is one of the things that is scaring me so much about this trip. With Aiden, I don't have anywhere to hide.

"Why don't you eat a cookie?" He points *my* fork at my bag and if I wasn't so hungry I'd have thrown one at him in spite. I pull one out and start to chew almost violently. He laughs in response. Smug. But for all his annoyances and marriage grief he has caused me, I don't hate his laugh. I wish I did. It would make my life so much simpler if he were a troll who snorts when he laughs and spits when he talks, but just my luck that I ended up married to a nearly perfect specimen, when I didn't want to be married at all.

"Dick," I mumble around a mouthful of white chocolate and strawberry crumble cookie.

"I'm not putting that in your mouth here, Lynds." He leans forward in his chair and stage-whispers as though the woman at the table behind him didn't stiffen at his words. I watch over his sandy hair as she reddens and untucks the hair from behind her ear to hide behind.

I shoot a glance around the room, wondering how many others must have heard every word. When I'm by his side, I forget that others exist until that illusion is broken. I know he's teasing me, he can't help himself apparently. Even when he needs me to be his fake wife, to do him a favour, he wants to get under my skin. To everyone around us, he is a husband teasing his wife as they get ready to go on their honeymoon, at least that is what I would think as an outsider looking in. I roll my eyes at him, reaching into my bag again, this time pulling out my trusty neck pillow.

"It's only a three-hour flight, that might be a bit unnecessary, darlin'." His words are laced with lingering humour and without even looking up I know his lips will be pulled up into a smirk.

"Well, when I found out you don't have a private jet I had to prepare for the worst." I smile over as I wrap the pillow around the back of my neck.

"You wound me." His hand flies to his chest, those southern dramatics are no joke. Then again that might just be Aiden, he never gets to be this laid-back on the ice so he must be overcompensating.

"Do you even fit in a plane seat?" I ask, flicking my hand in his general direction. His legs are out straight in front of him, crossed at the ankle: it is a reminder of how big he really is. When he is around other players, they all even each other out and make it seem normal, but each of them are over six foot tall – in the eyes of the rest of the world they barely fit.

"No, that's why we are flying business, extra legroom. Need room to move and to cuddle in case the need arises." He has the nerve to wiggle his eyebrows at me but before I can think of a barb to throw back my phone vibrates on my lap.

Kayla has been texting me on and off since I got back to Seattle, but even more so since articles went live about my and Aiden's nuptials. When I didn't pick up any of her calls she turned up at Bloom and Blossom. Luckily I was out that day doing a delivery for a wedding. As soon as she left, Ellis called me and filled me in. Apparently Kayla only wanted to give me her congratulations, she told Ellis how happy she was for me. I don't know if I believe it but her texts stopped after that. Well, I thought they had. This morning I woke up to a text from a number I didn't recognise.

> Your secret won't be a secret for long. Your husband will know.

It's the most literate text she has sent in a while, maybe ever. Hopefully if she can stay sober for a few days for a change, she will realise that sending baseless threats isn't worth it. I don't even know what secret she is talking about. We weren't together long enough for her to know about my childhood, never mind any deep-seated secrets I have. There are a few things I wouldn't want Aiden to know about me but that text makes it seem like she knows something big.

I decide to just delete the text and block the number. I have enough on my plate right now. Right as I slip my phone away our flight announcement comes over the speaker that it is time to board. Aiden walks over to my chair and offers me his hand to help me up, what a gentleman. Then to prove that even more he takes my bag from where it sits between us and swings it over his shoulder without a word. Just as I go to slip my phone into my pocket it vibrates again.

> You can hide for now, but not forever.

What the hell? What would Kayla care enough about to be texting me like this? Again the spelling is right and it makes sense so I think she must be sober but I can't imagine any sober person texting like that. All cryptic and angry for no reason. I don't hide, I hid enough as a child for a lifetime. I try to think if it could be anyone else but apart from my family I haven't had anyone truly hate me for who I am. Whatever she wants to hold over my head I won't let her, I just need to find out what she is talking about first. It can wait until we land though. Aiden's hand rests low on the bottom of my back, but not low enough to be inappropriate, as he guides me to our gate.

Still my eyes dart around as we walk. The chances that Kayla is here are slim to none but the weight on my chest doesn't take that as a comfort. She wants to date me again and holding something over me to get it isn't her usual MO – no, that is usually begging and then a drunken swing to yelling that I ruined her when I broke up with her. Aiden senses the tension in me but doesn't comment on it. I let him take the lead as we walk to the boarding desk. My eyes seem to snap from person to person trying to find her pixie cut but it has been so long since I've seen her that she might have grown it out by now. She could be hiding in plain sight and I wouldn't know until she wanted me to.

I have been able to take her texts with a grain of salt because I know she is struggling but that is not my cross to bear. I block the number from the second text as I slip into the seat beside Aiden, I think this might be what she wants. Maybe she is sober enough to be feeling her rage at my marriage, she doesn't know how fake it is. Maybe she is seeing it as a betrayal and is trying to scare me back into her arms. Little does she know it is having the opposite effect, if anything she is pushing me closer to Aiden. Who better to hide from a crazy ex behind than a six-foot-three hockey player who put a rock on my finger?

"Are you scared of flying?" For the second time today Aiden's voice brings me out of my stupor.

"What?" I ask, shaking my head to clear it of all thoughts of Kayla and her drunken nonsense.

"You just got super tense when it was time to board, if you don't like flying you should have told me." He is being too sweet for his own good. I'm not afraid of flying but he knows that, if I were, I'd probably keep it to myself so I wouldn't be any trouble.

"No." I fumble for an excuse, not wanting to worry him with my nonsense. "I'm scared about meeting your family is all. They might not like me."

"Trust me, darlin', everyone who meets you falls under your spell, they are going to love you." His hand wraps around mine, I have never met a man as open with physical affection as Aiden. He never shies away from touching me, a hand on my back or folding my hand in his. If he thinks it will bring me comfort, he will not blink before giving me that reassurance.

"You have to say that, you're my husband." I nudge him gently in the ribs, I want him to know that even though meeting his family does make me nervous (even if that's not why I'm tense right now), I won't go back on our plan. I'm in this by his side for as long as he needs me. Until I have done my part as the doting wife.

"Lyndsey, trust me when I say I never say something I don't mean, my family will like you because they think you love me and I love you, they wouldn't try to get in the middle of that." His family is worlds apart from mine. My family love to get in the middle, that's why it was so hard to hide my sexuality from them. There was no privacy, every little thing I did was under a microscope to make sure I didn't stray from the path they wanted me to walk, and if anything tried to interfere they would be in the middle of it before I could blink.

I do wonder what my life would have been like with different parents but it is too painful to consider because I didn't get different ones. I got parents who care more about making God happy than making sure their children are happy. Aiden's family seems nice: despite the adversity and trauma they have suffered, they are bonded together stronger because of it.

"I want to go over the plan again." I shake those thoughts away too. A small metal tube in the sky isn't the right time to be dissecting my childhood and my parents' minds. He rolls his eyes but humours me anyway, not commenting on my almost obsessive need to change the subject.

"When did we get married?" He turns in his chair so he is facing me fully, pulling me along with him until I'm cross-legged in the chair with both of our hands joined together between us.

"May twenty-sixth." I remember the entire plan, but what better way to distract myself from my phone than to go over the lies I'm about to live for at least a few weeks?

"Good, why didn't we invite everyone?"

"It was last minute, we couldn't go another day without wearing a ring." I make an overdramatic gagging sound that makes Aiden roll his eyes.

"When did we start dating?" I don't think he notices but with every question his thumb traces the ring on my left hand.

"That's a tricky question, we didn't go on our first date until July last year but we had been seeing each other casually since last April." We had to make it sound believable. Aiden isn't the type to jump into a relationship – sleep with someone, yes; but introduce them to his family, not so much. His sisters would be suspicious if we met and started dating right away, like he may have lost his mind because of a pair of pretty green eyes. His words, not mine.

"See, we have it down, don't stress your pretty little head, darlin'. You're going to be perfect." He must think I'm still tense because he lets go of my hand to lift his to cradle my cheek as he speaks. He wants me to take the words to heart and I can see the sincerity reflected in his eyes.

"Show me pictures of your sisters so I know which is which. I don't want to embarrass myself." I should pull my head away from his touch but I don't. I don't melt into him either, I stay stock-still, unwilling to disconnect from the warmth of his hand.

"Okay, but I swear it's unnecessary." He waits a beat himself before he pulls his hand away to slip his phone out of his jacket pocket.

We sit shoulder to shoulder the rest of the flight. We thumb through pictures from childhood all the way up until today. He regales me with stories of his sisters bossing him around good and well their entire lives. The reverence he talks about them with puts an ache in my heart. I wouldn't be surprised if my brother Peter never said my name in his life, never mind talked about me with love and affection. Aiden tells me about his parents and what his grandfather was like before the people he loved started to die.

The entire flight I sit with my phone wedged under my thigh. I don't know why. I put the thing on airplane mode so no texts would come through anyway but a part of me is scared that the minute my phone reconnects it will be flooded with more thinly veiled threats. So I tuck it away. I tuck my phone away but I also tuck the thoughts away. Push them to the back of my mind and try my hardest to focus on the now, on Aiden's stormy eyes and his fuller bottom lip. I wish I could be one of those people who live solely in the moment so for now I pretend to be.

I'm pretending to be a wife, what is one more thing to hide from the light?

Chapter Fourteen

Lyndsey

Turns out Aiden really didn't grow up on a ranch. I have always been teasing him, calling him "cowboy". But *this*, this is so ordinary, the least Texas suburb I could imagine. The street is lined with quaint detached houses, all fronted with a picturesque porch each; real American dream stuff. Kids play in their gardens as their parents sit together sipping iced tea, their conversations pausing as we drive by.

I'm not sure if they are noticing that their home-grown celebrity Aiden Anders is back or if they are just shocked by the car. When we made it to the rental desk I wasn't expecting the near monster truck Aiden picked. The SUV is huge, an imposing figure tearing down sweet suburbia. I guess I won't be living my rodeo fantasy in any way. No cattle or ranch hands to watch, no classic truck and no cowboy hats. Frankly, I think I should just go back home.

"So, did you *ever* drive a truck?" I ask, trying to connect the man in the car with me to the one I imagined as a kid.

"The idea you have of teenage me is so wrong, darlin'." He laughs at me as I pout.

"Why?"

"I wasn't the hotshot quarterback, I wasn't getting lucky in the bed of a truck with the popular girls." He turns his eyes on me then. "I played hockey, drove a beater to and from the rink and that was my life. Looking after the girls and trying not to flunk out."

"So, you want me to believe the girls weren't falling at your skates? Yeah, right." My eyes roll, struggling to believe him. Aiden is attractive. Unless he blossomed overnight, I can't imagine him not having a gaggle of girls fawning over his deep eyes and swoopy hair. And probably enjoying every second of it.

"Okay, maybe a few, but still: no truck." He winks.

When Aiden pulls to the end of the quaint little street, we come to a house that looks older than the rest. The porch has a bench swing that is swaying slowly in the light breeze. There are trees along the edges of the garden, giving it a more secluded edge, considering where it is. There is a two-car garage off to the side and if I'm not getting cowboys this is a good close second. The panels outside are painted a pale sea-foam colour with white trim, it looks like something from a postcard.

It's hard to picture Aiden living here, his house now is all cold lines and untreated wood, this feels so opposite to the man I know now. He showed me hundreds of pictures on the plane, all of his sisters playing in this very garden so I can see them here, but Aiden wasn't in a lot of the pictures. He was the one behind the camera. The one making the memories for the girls he loves so wholly.

The car is barely in park before the door at the top of the porch steps swings open and a flurry of green fabric comes flying down the stairs. Aiden jumps out at lightning speed just in time to catch who I think is his youngest sister Celia. Alice and Eden come down the stairs next as they seem just as pleased to see their brother, though they keep their feet on the floor as they take turns hugging him. I have to fight the urge to stay hidden in the car because Celia makes her way around to the passenger door, swinging it open and pulling me out.

I was told they were huggers, but I guess I assumed that wouldn't apply to the woman who married their brother without inviting them. Apparently not. Celia's arms wrap over my shoulders, pulling me to her.

"Hey!" she exclaims, her green sundress tangling between our legs. I'm not opposed to hugs, I just didn't think to expect them so intensely. Once she has had her fill, Celia passes me over to Eden, her hug just as tight.

"Nice to meet ya," she whispers in my ear before pulling away.

Alice doesn't pull me in like her sisters. Her eyes flow over my travel attire, clearly appraising me. Once she is satisfied, she nods slightly before wiggling her eyebrows at Aiden. Only then does she pull me into a hug after all, relieving the tension. Her hug is not as tight, but it feels like acceptance. Not only is she Aiden's twin, she is the oldest girl. Something about her approval feels most important. If she hated me, I think this whole thing would fall apart before it even began.

I try not to read into the affectionate squeezes as signs of full acceptance. This could just be that southern hospitality I have always heard about. Catch more flies with honey than vinegar, so the saying goes. If they lure me in with kindness and sweetness it will be easier for them to break down my walls when I need to keep them up.

But my walls won't be broken down here. That isn't why we came. That isn't why we agreed to stay married for a while longer.

For a moment, I wish there was a world where I could get to know these three women fully. Without the performance of my fake marriage. Without the pressure to be a pretend wife. But this is not that time.

This trip is a visit full of lies and deception. I can't let them in, even as they grin and welcome me with open arms. It will only hurt them, and me, in the long run when Aiden and I inevitably end our charade. It will be less painful for everyone if I can remember that this trip is a farce. We are basically here for a job: to help Aiden get his father's things, to keep Kayla at bay until she moves on, and to run before things become too serious.

Celia slips her hand through mine and tugs me up to the front door, only yelling at Aiden to grab the bags over her shoulder. The three Anders sisters corral me into the sitting room where they have a pitcher of iced tea, and a plate of what I think might be home-baked cookies is sat on the low wooden table. It looks pretty as a picture but I know an inquisition when I see one. There are two mismatched couches either side of the coffee table and I'm herded to one while they huddle on the opposite facing me. Eden busies herself by pouring out four glasses of tea, the ice clinking against the glasses is loud around us.

Aiden finally makes his way in, leaving our bags in the entryway and joining me on the sage-coloured sofa.

"Oh darn, I forgot to get bread for dinner." Alice slaps her knee, trying to sell the obvious lie. "Aiden, be a doll an' drive into town for me." Her smile is almost genuine. If I didn't know her twin so well I think it would have even fooled me.

"Alice." Aiden's voice is full of warning, but she doesn't flinch. Masking her face with a look of confused indifference, she shrugs.

"Come on now, we can't exactly break bread with your bride without bread now, can we?" Beside her Eden tucks her lips into her mouth, trying to contain her laughter. She isn't quite as practised as Alice seems to be.

"Lynds…" My husband is clearly torn. We all know why they want me alone: an interrogation. But if he doesn't go now, they will just manufacture another way to isolate me. Getting it over with might be the best way to do it.

"Don't worry so much, Aid, we don't bite." Celia tries to wave him off, but his eyes are still on me. Waiting for me to protest, I assume.

"Yes, you do." Alice laughs under her breath, causing Celia to smack her arm – which causes all four siblings to burst into laughter. I'm obviously not in on the joke, but at least the tension in the room is broken.

"Well, I don't bite *any more*." Celia smiles at me as though that would be comforting, but that one look is the thing that breaks my composure. I have been on edge since the airport lounge and this twenty-year-old girl telling me she won't bite me is what makes me crack. Giggles burst out of me in a trickle like gas out of a helium balloon until we are all laughing together.

"Hey, it's fine. If they kill me and bury me under the porch at least I go out with cookies." I give my assurance to Aiden.

"Fine, I'm leaving." He lifts his hands in surrender, yet he doesn't walk out. He edges towards the door, keeping his eyes locked on mine until I nod again, giving him a small smile. "Be nice!" he yells as the door finally closes behind him. The sound echoes around the otherwise silent room.

"So…" I break the heavy silence. "Who wants to go first?" Luckily all three laugh at my bluntness and Alice nods before doing just what I assumed. Interrogating me.

"What do you do?" she asks, crossing her legs. For the first time I realise how tall they all are. It looks like they are all genetically blessed. Alice is the slenderest of the three, whereas Eden and Celia have curvier frames. Eden actually reminds me a little of Cassie, but with a cheerier disposition. All three sisters share their brother's eyes and dirty-blond hair, but beside that they are all starkly different.

Alice is poised and clearly the leader of the family. Eden is all smiles, even with her curvier figure she has the aura of a Miss America contestant: perfect posture and an open soul. Celia is clearly more naive than her sisters. She is openly welcoming and comforting. She is the only one not staring me down as they wait for my answer.

"I work as a florist, the one Ellis Ainsley owns. That's how we met, through Ellis and Liam." I tell them the truth. Aiden and I decided that was the best approach. The more lies you tell the easier it is to get caught up in it. As long as we err on the side of truth, it should be more believable.

"Are you a gold digger?" Eden is blunt. I think she even shocks herself. Her eyes widen slightly, as do her sisters' in her direction. She was obviously desperate to ask, but had probably planned to go about it in a gentler way.

"Damn," I reply, stunned myself. "No, I'm not after Aiden for his money. Though I don't think he has as much as he claims. He made me fly commercial." I laugh, settling the dust a little. Judging by their approving nods, they see I'm not being serious. Celia sips her tea, letting the other two continue to ask their questions as she observes from beside them.

"Are you close with your family?" Alice fires.

"No, not any more." I try to sip from my glass but my shaky hands clinking the ice around highlight the nerves I'm trying to disguise.

"Has Aiden met them?" Eden asks.

"No, he probably won't." God, please stop asking about my parents. I should have lied and said they live abroad or something, but that doesn't follow the rules Aiden set out of being truthful wherever possible. So I go for evasive instead, hoping they will take a hint and drop it. I'm not that lucky.

"Why are you getting all clammed up talking about your family? Are you ashamed of my brother or something?" Alice's voice is sharp and direct. I've inadvertently hit a nerve.

"God no! I'm ashamed of *them*. My parents suck and my golden-child older brother is a dick. They don't like how I live my life, but Aiden tells me that's their loss." I think it best not to disclose the reasons behind my and my family's feud. My sexuality doesn't feel like a first-meeting conversation. I know Aiden has never blinked twice, but the south isn't always the most inclusive. I can't imagine Aiden would allow me to meet his sisters if they were huge homophobes. But still, I decide it's best to wait and ask him about that, if we need to take that step. I don't yet know if I'm in enemy territory.

He told me himself that his grandfather is old-school, which is sometimes code for something else entirely. I doubt it means he's a strong defender of the LGBTQ. I guess now wouldn't be the first time I've had to shove myself back into the closet. I thought if I pushed through enough awkward interaction with my family after coming out that they would realise I'm still their little girl, the same Lyndsey they raised. But I think instead I showed them time and time again that I would never be who they wished I was. I will never be the good, straight little Catholic they used to love.

"Well, damn," Celia whispers.

"Okay then." Eden nods.

Alice sits between them and they all share a silent moment before their heads all turn back to me while smiles paint their faces.

"I think we're good?" It's phrased as a question, but I think it's Alice's way of telling me I've passed whatever test they set out for me.

"Before he comes back, do you have anything I can use as leverage? A wife's got to get what she can while she can." I laugh and Celia nods enthusiastically. It feels strangely normal to refer to him as my husband. Aiden has called me his wife a hundred times since Vegas but using the words myself, referring to us as a married couple, still feels odd on my tongue. Like they will be able to hear the lie threaded in the letters, I worry that I'll choke on the words each time I say them, but the girls seem none the wiser.

"Oh, do we have stories, she asks? Of course we do." Alice laughs, pulling a book from the cushion behind her. The words "photo album" are painted in gold lustre. Alice flips the book open before laying it on the table between us, spinning it around to a picture of Aiden wearing the prettiest princess dress next to Alice in a knight-in-shining-armour costume with broad matching smiles.

I think by the time Aiden makes it home I'm going to be stocked with leverage over my fake husband. It's strange seeing Aiden this way – young, innocent and sweet. To know Aiden Anders as more than just the captain of the Spears. As more than just my fake husband.

A sense of betrayal lingers in my gut as I peek behind the curtain of Aiden's life. When we are ready to go back to our real lives, I need to leave behind all the things I learn while I'm here. It was never mine to keep.

Knowing Aiden inside and out isn't part of the plan.

Chapter Fifteen

Lyndsey

It's a few hours later when the five of us sit around the old wooden dining room table. Once Aiden got back from the store, he found us girls laughing and he tried his best to hide his shock. I think a part of him thought I would sit silently and wait for him to save me but I'm not the type of woman who likes waiting for a knight in a shining hockey jersey.

Alice serves up the food and the rich aroma causes my stomach to rumble, this is the first thing I have eaten since the plane and until right now I didn't realise how hungry I am. Still, I do the polite thing and wait for everyone else to be served before digging in. I'm so focused on shovelling food in my mouth that I don't realise until too late that Aiden is reaching for me. His hand comes to rest on my right thigh and the touch shocks me so violently I jump in my chair, my knees hitting the underside of the table.

All three girls fall silent, watching us from across the table, their forks forgotten in their hands. They are all looking at me differently: Alice has a small smirk pulling up one side of her mouth; Eden looks like she is trying to hold back laughter; but Celia looks completely and utterly confused. Why wouldn't she? It isn't exactly normal for a wife to flinch at her husband's touch.

"Babe! Not in front of your sisters!" I say with a giggle, trying to brush my reaction under the rug, and it seems good enough because they start to eat again.

"Oh, don't mind us." Alice laughs and, instead of talking, Aiden hooks his hand under my chair, pulling me closer to his side until our seats are connected.

Leaning into my space, he kisses my cheek lightly before sliding his lips across my skin until he is at the shell of my ear, his warm breath puffing against my blushing skin. I have to fight the need to push him away, I want to scoot my chair back to where it was, but I know how bad that would look.

"If you were my wife, I wouldn't be able to take my hands off you. You need to relax." My face heats at his whispers but I think that is even better for our ruse, like I'm so worked up by him. Before he pulls away, he nips at the soft skin of my earlobe, laughing as I gasp in shock.

"Okay, that might be a touch much for the dinner table." Eden laughs, throwing a napkin at her brother. He catches it with a wink before hitting me with a blinding smile that causes my blood to heat.

It is wildly unfair how attractive he is. Especially because the last time his lips where on me, it nearly broke my heart.

I'm primped and preened ready for Aiden's New Year's Eve party. As much as I want to throw on my sweatpants and hide under the covers, I won't miss Ellis' engagement for the world. When Liam told me his plan to propose at midnight I melted. He loves her in a way I thought only existed in Hollywood movies. I hid my bitterness behind a blinding smile because as excited as I am for my best friend to get everything she deserves, I'm wishing and hoping for a man to love me like Liam loves her.

My hair is pulled back into a slick ponytail, the rosy strands curled to perfection; my make-up is just as precise. I wanted to feel my best which is why I find myself wearing heels instead of the fluffy socks that are calling my name. My black sequin trousers make me feel super festive but I keep my top simple with a black turtleneck sweater. I look like I'm ready for a party, it's the inside that is causing problems.

When my taxi pulls up, I do everything I can to push Aiden from my mind. I have a job to do tonight and I won't let my stupid unrequited crush ruin this night for Ellis and Liam. It's a known fact that Liam doesn't have a good poker face, I need to keep Ellis from grilling him about why he is suspicious. I also need to make sure she doesn't get too drunk. She isn't breastfeeding because of her chronic illness so she doesn't have to pump and dump. I can't let her get drunk in case she falls asleep before midnight or, God forbid, she vomits on him when he is on one knee before her. I'm taking my job very seriously. It's the only distraction I can think of to keep me from following Aiden around like a lost puppy begging for scraps of his attention.

By the time midnight rolls around I'm disgustingly sober. But so is Ellis. I did my job to perfection and now as it is minutes away from the ball dropping, we all congregate outside to watch the fireworks. I have felt Aiden's eyes on me all night but whenever I look his way his attention snaps away from me. When I got dressed up, I wanted to catch his attention but I regret it now. He looks incredibly attractive in a pair of grey suit trousers and a crisp black shirt. Dressy but effortlessly casual, that annoying way men can. Over the night he has rolled up his shirtsleeves and I wish I had bought a spare pair of panties because every time I get a glimpse at his tattooed forearm my thighs clench together to release the tension there.

I watch as Liam drops down onto one knee. He speaks in low tones, his words only for Ellis, but I have to wipe a tear from my eye when she throws herself into his arms. Of course she said yes. It was never a possibility that she wouldn't in my opinion, even if Liam was nervous that she wouldn't be ready. They kiss as everyone around us starts to count down from ten. I look to my right to see Aiden walking towards me.

Nine.

He pushes through the crowd of his teammates.

Seven.

The crowd of hockey players get rowdier by the second.

Five.

He stops a foot away from me. He holds my eye as his hands clench at his sides.

Two.

I hold my breath, staring up at him.

One.

He kisses me. One hand slips around the back of my neck, pulling me against his chest as his lips drop to mine. I kiss him back readily. His tongue swipes against mine as fireworks light up the sky around us. Fireworks go off in my chest as he tightens his hold on me.

Just as quickly as he started, he stops.

"Shit, that... that shouldn't have happened. I'm sorry." Then he is storming away. Leaving me alone with the taste of him on my lips and his aftershave still in the air around me.

Pain lances through my chest as his retreating figure disappears from sight. I struggle to catch my breath as everyone cheers and celebrates around me. I'm frozen to the spot. There was so much disgust in his eyes when he pulled away from me. It's something I'll never forget, the anger on his face while my lipstick stained his lips.

I don't pause to say goodbye. I run back through his house as I book a car to take me home. I'm suddenly freezing cold as my hands shake around my phone. I need to be away from here.

As far away from Aiden Anders as possible. For one second, I thought my dream was coming true, that he truly wanted me. That he was bringing me out of the friend zone, but I'm an idiot. A man like Aiden, a man who can have any woman in the world, doesn't want a poor lonely queer florist like me.

It isn't until I'm sat in the back of the car that the tears start to fall. I cry silently as I watch Seattle pass by. Fireworks light the sky. People celebrate in the streets and I just want it to stop. How dare they get to be happy but I just tasted sweetness for a second? How dare they celebrate when my heart has just been stepped on like it is meaningless?

Aiden has brought me so much pain. He led me on thinking he might want me just to pull away the second I showed an ounce of vulnerability. Then he plies me with friendship just to kiss me at midnight and rip that kiss away a minute later. I brought in the new year watching him walk away from me.

That might be as much as I can handle. Pulling my phone out again, I bring up his contact. Aiden has hurt me for the last time. He might be Liam and Ellis' friend but that is all he is going to be. I take a deep breath and block his number.

After that I only spoke to him when it was necessary to keep the peace between me and the rest of the team. All the way from New Year's until Vegas I maybe said twenty words to him. I refused to be another notch on his bedpost.

I need to remember that now. How many women's ears has he whispered into? How many earlobes has he nipped at? He is a ladies' man through and through and the reminder of that is a bucket of cold water over me. Still, I know I can't pull away, it would ruin everything and we have only been here for a matter of hours.

The girls try to pull me into conversation, ask about Bloom and Blossom and how long I have known Ellis, but when Aiden's fingers weave into mine, holding my hand in between our dinner plates, I find it hard to concentrate. I fight against my instincts to elbow him in the ribs and focus on making the girls like me.

My phone vibrating on the solid wood table draws all of our eyes, I want to ignore it in case it is another stupid threat but with all of their eyes on me I know it would look strange if I ignore it. Clenching my hand once before I reach out, I ready myself for what it has to say next.

> Run and hide, the truth will find you.

My heart starts to thunder in my chest and I drop my phone with a loud clang as I stare at it like it is going to grow legs and attack me. It feels like it has. How does whoever the hell this is know I'm not in Seattle? How closely have they been watching me? The press release said nothing about our little getaway, so nobody apart from our friends should know.

"You okay?" Aiden asks quietly turning my face towards his with a gentle finger hooked under my chin. His eyes bore into mine before flicking to my phone.

"Just Ellis, nothing to worry about," I reassure him, but even I can hear my voice waver around the words. I plead with my eyes for him to stop it. It's a cheap shot but I flick my eyes over to the girls before coming back to his, hoping he understands that now isn't the time to discuss this. It might never be because I don't know what whoever this is wants and I won't pull him into my drama. If this is Kayla, it's surprising that she has managed to stay sober all day. I mean between the text before the plane and now there's a lot of time for her to spiral down the bottle and yet here she is still sounding coherent. I should probably tell Aiden when we are alone but what am I supposed to say, "Hi, fake husband, I think my alcoholic ex might be sending me threatening texts but maybe not because she is usually drunk and these texts don't really sound like her usual nonsense." Yeah, I'll pass. I'm here to help him with his family and get out.

Besides, in a few days' time we will be getting ready to go back home and getting a divorce, by that time I won't be his problem any more. He nods lightly before pulling his hand away from my face and picking my hand up again, going back to his food with his free hand. Suddenly my appetite has disappeared but I won't be a bad house guest and not finish my meal. I shove forkful after forkful into my mouth, even though I'm no longer tasting it. I laugh when I'm supposed to and say perfectly placed flirty comments to keep the girls none the wiser, even when my heart feels like it's going to beat out of my chest.

Just a few more days, Lyndsey, you can keep everything under wraps for a little while. Or at least I hope I can.

Chapter Sixteen

Aiden

I try to hide it from my sisters, but I'm a coward. I'm not scared of spiders or hard work, but lying to my sisters scares me. The fact they might pick up on my lies scares me. I might never know what made my sisters accept Lyndsey but she did it. By the time I got back from the store the four of them were laughing and sharing stories like they were childhood friends. Seeing her sat in my childhood home, with the women I love, stopped me short. That might be why I pawned Lyndsey on to Eden when it was time to settle down for the night. Told them I would lock up and Eden could show Lyndsey to the room.

Key words there being *the room*, I may have conveniently forgotten to tell my wife that we will be sharing my bedroom. I don't know why I bothered hiding it from her, it should be a given that a married couple would be sharing a bed, and yet I didn't confirm or deny it for her. I know when I walk in there I'll be walking into a verbal lashing, that's why I make sure to check the doors and windows twice before dawdling in the kitchen for a while. I busy myself pouring us both a glass of water while listening to the floorboards above me creak as someone walks along the hallway.

"You're so full of shit." Alice's voice cuts through the darkened room.

"What have I done now?" I can pretend to be mad but I'm not going to pretend it's not nice to have an excuse to avoid upstairs a little longer.

"You're not in love with her. She's great but I know you, Aid, you're not in love." Shit. Her voice is sure and steady, there isn't even a speck of hesitation in her conviction.

"Alice," I try, but she just raises her hand to shut me up. She always has to have it her way. But she is right. Alice was always going to be the hardest sell, having a wedding without her by my side would just be wrong, plus if I even thought I was getting serious with someone she would find out. If anything was going to be our downfall, it would be my twin refusing to accept that she wasn't there when I tied the knot.

"No, just wait. I'll keep it from the girls but you have to promise me something." She takes one of the glasses of water from my hand, sipping it down as I glare at her.

"What?" I growl out, snatching the glass right back from her.

"Don't let her go. I don't know what you need to do, but I like her." Alice smirks. "And I know you like her even if it might not be love so, at least give it a chance to grow. You deserve to be happy." With that she slaps my cheek lightly.

"I'll sure as shit try." My resolve is strong.

Lyndsey and I are never just going to fall into each other's arms, she is far too stubborn to admit it even if she did want me, and I keep putting her at a distance. I know she is single now, I know she finds me attractive and I know we would be good together. She needs someone who will give her a soft place to land, she has to be so strong every day, no family support and outside of Ellis not many friends so she needs a shoulder. It will be hard to keep her at arm's length when she is sleeping right by my side.

"Good, try not to fuck this all up," are Alice's parting words before she takes her leave up the old wooden stairs.

"Love you too, Al," I shout at her departing figure.

Finally putting on my big boy pants, I start walking towards the stairs myself, only to stop again. Lyndsey Stone is in my bedroom right now. For all I know she might be getting changed into her pyjamas, she is up there right now in my bed waiting for me. Sure, not in the way I wish she was, but all the same my wife, my bed, that's a pretty picture.

It has been longer than I'd admit since I shared my bed – really shared it, I mean. I have sex, but no sleepovers. And sure as shit no sleepovers in my childhood bed. The idea of Lyndsey with her pale skin and rosy hair against my white sheets makes my heart shudder in my chest. How am I supposed to breathe easy and rest while she is beside me? When all I want to do is look at her. All I can think about is touching her. She might not want to be married to me but that doesn't mean I can't admit how drop-dead gorgeous she is.

The delicate curve of her neck, the freckles that splatter her chest that flushes red when she is angry. She might be angry now, angry that I didn't tell her about the sleeping arrangements, but I couldn't risk her getting cold feet. Hell, that usually comes before the marriage, but then again so does sharing a bed. I have spent so many years putting my all into hockey. Into making sure my life still had purpose after my parents died that I have neglected my heart and its wants. My pops has me pinned there, I did want a wife and kids one day in the future, I just don't like the ultimatum laid out for me. I'll play this game how I need to. It's my life, my family and *my* decisions.

My drunken marriage was a wild coincidence, but I'm not one to look a gift horse in the mouth. I'm going to sleep in my marriage bed beside my beautiful wife and tomorrow I'll introduce her to my grandfather. We will pretend I never got his letter. That it must have arrived while we were travelling, so I'm clueless to what it says. Then Lyndsey will woo him, the same way she seems to with everyone, including my sisters. That's the plan, and nothing more.

Once I will my strength to walk up the stairs and down the hallway to my bedroom, I wonder what waits for me behind the door. Will Lyndsey be ready for war or will she be pliant and welcoming?

Ready for war it is.

The door swings open into the pale blue room I grew up in. It's been decorated over the years. My old posters are no longer on the walls, it's less my bedroom now and more of a guest room. Not that they ever have any guests that aren't me. The queen bed is the same though, large in the corner of the room covered in white sheets and a soft blue comforter. A comforter that is covering Lyndsey's legs as she sits stock-still with her back against the headboard, arms crossed over her pert chest.

"You got a sleeping bag around here, cowboy?" she asks, head cocking to one side.

"No, darlin', but that bed does look cosy." I try to flirt, to make her smile. It's unsuccessful, as it usually is.

"One bed, Aiden? Really?" She rolls her eyes, clearly exasperated by me.

"In my defence you shouldn't be surprised, we are married after all." That's a bullshit excuse.

"Bullshit."

"Fine, but we are adults and it's not some small kids' bed. There is more than enough room," I tell her, walking into the en suite. If she had been in a lighter mood I might have tried to change in the room with her. See if I have an effect on her the same way she does on me.

"Don't be surprised if I kick you," she hollers through the door.

"Don't be surprised if I cuddle you," I laugh back.

"Don't you dare." Her voice is low.

"Oh come on, Lynds, what's wrong with a bit of cuddling between husband and wife?" Once I'm out of my jeans and into some sweatpants I saunter back into the room and can't help but notice the way her eyes sweep over my bare chest, her eyes snagging on each of my tattoos.

"Get in the bed, Aiden, before I send you down to the sofa." I don't need to be told twice, sliding in beside her, making sure I'm on the side closest to the door. Just in case.

"Yes, ma'am." I laugh low as she rolls her eyes at me. "Last time we were in a bed together things were a bit different."

"Aiden, if you don't shut it." Her elbow lodges itself into my rib but that just makes me laugh. She can fight all night long but I saw the attraction in her eyes when she looked at my body. I think the truth is she thinks about me the same way I think about her. Which involves a lot of nakedness and a hell of a lot of time to explore.

"I'm just saying, darlin', there were far less clothes involved." I wrap my hand around her arm to stop her from trying to puncture my lung through my ribs.

"Yuck, don't remind me." She gags to drive home her point, but as she turns onto her side away from me, I see the smile she is trying to hide.

"You lie like a dog but you're beautiful so I'll let it go." I lie down beside her then pull the blanket up to my chin and push my chest to her back. Well, it would be if she hadn't shuffled all the way towards the wall.

I'll give her that space. If she needs it tonight she can have it but I doubt it will last long. This house is old, I love it but it does have its flaws, one of which being it gets damn cold. In a few hours' time I won't be surprised if she burrows towards a heat source. Me.

I didn't lie to her. I'm a cuddler. I'm a big physical affection kind of guy but, especially at night, I love wrapping my arms around things. Pillows, people – hell, even Edge once but he gave me a swift kick in the knee to remind me of my place. Planes are cramped, I can't be held responsible for that. I'm going to have to fight my natural responses, how am I going to stop my unconscious body from pulling her back against my chest and wrapping myself around her? I don't have control of my sleeping actions, but if Lyndsey wakes up tomorrow wrapped up in my arms I think she will be madder than Edge.

Her anger won't be for the same reasons but, all the same, Lyndsey will be angry because she will have to admit to herself that being in my arms, in my bed, isn't all that bad.

I will myself to sleep. I can feel the bed dipping with every one of her even breaths as she sleeps soundly beside me. Sleep eludes me though. I'm plagued with fear that we'll wake up tangled together. Fear that anything we do behind closed doors might affect how we act in front of others.

I inch myself away, resisting the urge to inhale the smell of Lyndsey's shampooed hair as it fills the room. It's what we must do. Because knowing Lyndsey inside and out isn't part of the plan.

Chapter Seventeen

Lyndsey

When I wake up every morning, the first thing I feel is a chill. I love my apartment but it is old, the windows are thin and no amount of blankets seem to keep the early morning chill away. It is something I've grown to appreciate though, at least if I wake up cold there is no chance of me rolling over and falling back asleep. My apartment gave me my independence from my family so it will always be my pride and joy, even with the windows and the fact it takes the water a long time to heat up for scalding temperatures for my shower.

My mom always said once I was over throwing my tantrum and realised my life was better the way it was that she would welcome me with open arms. My tantrum has been going on nine years now and I'm no closer to running home with my tail between my legs. Granted, if I was thrown out on to the street by my landlord my childhood home wouldn't be in the first ten places I would try and crash at. My childhood bedroom was warm and light for the darkness that was hidden inside its walls, the door that locked from the outside, the closet with rows of frilly knee-length dresses and cardigans that I hated wearing.

My youth wasn't traumatic for an outsider looking in. I had food and a roof over my head, clothes on my back, two parents and a brother. A perfect nuclear family. But if you peeked through the cracks, you would see a little girl who just wanted to feel loved, even if it meant losing that safety and security. It was never safe for me anyway, not really. There was always a threat, either my brother was mad and I was his outlet or my parents were putting me over their knee to teach me how to be a good sin-free little girl. Then when I needed their safety the most, I got nothing but disgust and hatred from the people who were supposed to love me unconditionally.

I thank every star in the sky I was able to save money from my weekend job over my teenage years so when they told me I could no longer stay in their house I had a bit to fall back on. It wasn't enough for a deposit but it was close. My old boss, Mr Jenkins, let me sleep on a cot in the back room for a few months until he got me in touch with a friend of his who was letting out an apartment. Apparently the woman who lived there before me found a millionaire to marry and was breaking her lease. Good for her and even better for me. Since that day I have had my own space. A space that I could find my own safety in; it would never be the same as my childhood home and that is a blessing in itself. My cold bedroom is my sanctuary.

Which is why I'm confused as hell to wake up feeling warm. I'm hot. Surrounded by the comfort and warmth that I've only heard about in movies. The need to bury myself further into the heat is staggering, it's a compulsion pulling me further into the sheets.

Then just as sleep is about to overtake me again, I'm jolted by memories of where I actually am. Texas. Aiden's bedroom. Aiden's bed. Snuggled into Aiden's side. He is the warmth. I'm not in my solace. I'm laid up in bed next to my husband for the foreseeable future. Perfect.

Remember the plan, Lyndsey.

I huff to myself, knowing this is what I signed up for, but still feeling unprepared. I've heard of bedbugs but Aiden is a cuddle bug. This giant hockey player of a man is wrapped around me like my own personal weighted blanket. His chest is tight to my back with one arm thrown over my waist splaying his hand over my abdomen. My natural instinct is to suck in my gut, or elbow him in his, but I refrain. Plus, who cares if Aiden feels my stomach? He isn't like my ex-girlfriends, I don't need to impress him because he isn't mine to keep.

Still, I think it would be best for me to slip out of his grasp before he's up. He will probably be like the cat who got the cream to see me wrapped in his arms. He would give me that annoyingly handsome smirk and make some joke about being his wife. That's the last thing I need – that and I don't think I'm ready to hear his morning voice again.

I try to glide out of the bed. *Try* being the key word. The minute I attempt to lift his tree-trunk arm, he tightens his grip. Aiden presses his hand harder against my stomach, pulling me tighter than I thought was possible. Then he tucks his legs in behind mine. That's when I feel it. Hard and unmistakable against the curve of my ass. Aiden's hips grind ever so slightly against mine, the friction of the clothes between us must bring him some kind of relief because he grunts softly against the back of my neck. That sound sends lightning through my body. Shit. I can't wake him now. If he wakes up there will be awkward apologies and conversations I'm not ready to have without coffee.

But I sure as shit can't stay here while he rubs himself against me. I wish I could say it's because I'm grossed out, that the idea of him fucking me makes me feel nauseous. But that would be a lie. Despite what I think of Aiden – a notorious flirt, unchained by responsibility, and overall an overgrown himbo – I can't hate it. I hate that I like it. I should hate it, I should roll over and slap him awake because how dare he force me to share a bed with him just to grind on me like a teenager? Instead I feel like a teenager myself, I'm hungry for it. I must not have control of my body, I'll blame the fact I have only just woken up as an excuse as to why I find myself pushing my ass harder against him. Why I have to bite my lip to keep from moaning when his head moves into the space where my neck meets my shoulder.

The size of him is so different, this is the first time I've ever woken up with a man clinging to me. I'm not used to waking up next to anyone, truth be told. I slink out before the sun rises, or I kick them out before dawn is even a mirage. Feeling every inch, and I mean every inch, pressed tight to my body is overwhelming. The heat of him alone is seeping into my bones but with every breath he takes I feel the muscles under his skin flex against the satin of my pyjamas. I knew he was big. Aiden is over six foot, no idea the exact measurements, but taller than Liam and shorter than Edge. It is easier to compare the team to each other rather than the riff-raff one might find on a night out in Seattle.

The Spears players are a league of their own and, somehow, I ended up married to their leader with his dick rubbing against me in his childhood bed. What has my life become?

When you date women, there are always expectations from straight people that there has to be some kind of gender role in the relationship. There is always someone who thinks they are well meaning asking, "Who is the man in the relationship?" They have this fascination with wanting to know how two women can have sex, as if porn isn't available to them to figure that out. It's never that straightforward. I have never been a cuddler, so I haven't ever figured out if I like to be the big spoon or the little spoon. Right now though, small spoon feels pretty damn good. I like feeling protected, it's a new feeling, but it's nice all the same. Having Aiden wrapped around me is exhilarating.

I remember it was my plan to slip out of his arms but I can't bring myself to do it. I like feeling him. My husband hard against me. It's a thrill. One I never imagined to have. Then he moans against me. A bone-deep moan, gutturally washing over my heated skin. If I thought I was hot before it had nothing on this. Aiden's hand tightens against the fabric of my top, fisting the material as he rolls against me. I know I need to get out. If I don't, I think I might go too far. How far would I let it go? I don't know but I seem to be weak when it comes to him.

He makes me weak and needy and oh-so hot. Hot and wet. Damn it, I don't want to admit it to myself but it's true. I'm wet at the feeling of my husband's hand on me, holding me, the idea of his long fingers tangled in my hair instead of my clothes. The thought of his body thrusting over me with nothing between us except heat and sweat, my hands linked behind his neck as he fucks me hard. I need to get out of this bed before I do something I can't come back from. Like roll over and hitch my leg over his hip.

Get out of the bed, Lyndsey. Now.

No longer worried about if he wakes up, I bolt from the sheets, scrambling for the door of the en suite, not bothering to look back. Just in case I meet his eyes. My clothes are already half off before I have even locked the door behind me, I need a cold shower so I can think. I don't wait for a second before I duck under the water, the cold like bullets against my overheated skin.

Damn you, Aiden Anders, and your stupidly sexy moans. I can hear them echoing through my head. The cold water is useless against the onslaught of images my mind is painting. I have always had an active imagination and now it will be my downfall. I can see everything so intensely clear. His tanned skin flushed with desire. His grey eyes piercing through my green ones, until he sees my soul. I can almost feel his fingers drifting over my skin as I think about how much of my breasts his big hands could hold, the way the snake tattoo around his forearm would ripple under his skin as he plays with me. I have average breasts but I know he would dwarf them, his trim nails leaving scratch marks where he digs his fingers into my hips. I can see it all so vividly that he may as well be under the water with me. My skin becomes flushed, a heat that even the water can't cool.

I yearn to hear his sounds again. His moans against my thighs before he consumes me. Against my shoulder as he takes me from behind. From above me as I get on my knees for him. I need to hear every sound he can make, I deserve them. I want to make them mine, keep them for myself so I'll always have a piece of him. I want to make him growl and gasp in ways he never has before, in a way he never will again. I want to ruin my sweet little husband so when he discards me in a few months' time I'll take a vital part of him with me and I'll leave him something in return.

That thought alone is what crosses my mind as my hand slips down my body. Following the same path as the water trickles over me, my fingertips trace every part of my stomach, feeling where he held me. I can almost imagine how his stubble would redden my skin as he kissed down my body. When my hand reaches my pelvis, where I can only imagine Aiden touching, I picture his hands. I keep my fingers feather-light even though I know he would be more desperate, I want this to build. I want to take my time so I can paint an everlasting picture. When my fingers slip through my soaked pussy it's his hand that is touching me. It's his long, callused fingers that strum against my clit, bringing me higher and higher.

The roughness of his fingertips is heaven against my sensitive skin. I want to fist my fingers in his dirty-blond locks, tug until he moans against me. I imagine it all as I push one finger inside.

It kills me to keep my sounds to myself. I want to scream and call for him, drag him in here with me and make him fix what he caused, but I'm stronger than that. I'm stronger than anyone gives me credit for so I don't. Instead I slip my finger inside myself again, knowing Aiden's would reach places I can only dream of hitting with my own hands. Still, it is enough for now. The steady rhythm of the water beating down onto my sensitive breasts combined with my frantic fingers pushes me closer to the edge.

My other hand comes to play with my nipples, twisting and tugging with the strength I know Aiden would have. If I ever gave in to what is happening between us I know he would snap. I doubt he would be able to be gentle, he wouldn't be able to fight the fire that could burn us alive. That is why I touch myself without him. I keep my movements tight and strong as I picture his tattooed arms instead of my bare ones until I feel myself reach the peak I need.

Hopefully the loud water hides the sounds of my gasp as I orgasm with my husband's name on my tongue. I don't believe in God but if there is one they will have kept him asleep. Aiden can't know how he affects me, it would just cause problems neither of us needs. For now though, I bask in the afterglow of my orgasm, turning up the heat of the water to wash away the chill that still paints my skin. No longer is it a cold chill though – no, now it is the chill of regret. Knowing that the image of Aiden might never be enough.

I can come one hundred times at my own hands but I know the truth is, if I let Aiden touch me, the feeling would be unmatched. The things he would do to me would shatter me apart and I can't afford that, I need to keep my wits about me. Even if that means fucking my own fingers every morning until we divorce.

Chapter Eighteen

Aiden

There is something bittersweet about knowing I'm going to finally get my dad's stuff. I'm excited but more than that I wish he was here.

Lyndsey is with me now while the bank manager takes us to the lockbox room. Before we got this far, there were a bunch of forms that needed signing, and they took a copy of our marriage certificate as proof of meeting the requirements of the will. I know what is going to be in the box in general. There will be a few medals, but my main motive is wanting to see what stuff my dad had with him when he was overseas. I have wondered for years what were the things he kept, we sent hundreds of letters and pictures over the years and I know there is no way he could have kept every drawing, I have no idea which stuff was precious to him. After pulling out the large box, the bank manager leaves us to it. My hands shake as I bring the key to the lock but I'm trembling so badly that it slips from between my clammy fingertips.

"Can you?" My question is open-ended but Lyndsey knows what I need. A lot of the time she knows before I do.

She slides in front of me and unlocks the box with ease, but she keeps it closed. Turning to face me, standing between me and the box I have obsessed over for so long, Lyndsey cradles my jaw with her hands, looking me right in the eye.

"Whatever is in there is yours, Aiden. You deserve these things but if you want to leave right now, we can turn around and try again tomorrow." God, I really care about what she thinks about me. It's a stark realisation, I'm quickly going from reluctant husband to really enjoying having her support, even if that makes me selfish.

"I can do this." I want to drop my head and kiss her but I don't, she wouldn't be receptive anyway. I wouldn't be surprised if she slapped me.

"Not going anywhere." I never plan on letting her go.

Then I open the box.

Just like I thought, his medals are on the top and as much as I'm happy to finally have them it is the rest of the stuff I'm here for. There are letters tucked neatly back in their envelopes but I can tell from the worn edges that they have been read over and over. I recognise my own handwriting on some of the letters as well as the girls'.

Under those, though, is a different one, a letter written in my mom's loopy handwriting. I remember her writing every Friday, she would talk about what happened each week, from family news to stupid small-town gossip that he probably didn't care about but she told him anyway. When I asked her why, she said she wanted him to feel some normalcy, she didn't want to lament about how much she missed him, said that much was a given, she wanted him to know what he had waiting for him when he came back home.

I pull her letter out first, stroking over her black penmanship and basking in the memories of her. When I see the date written in small writing on the back, I'm shocked to see this must be the last letter she sent to him before Cece was born, before he finally came home. I find myself not wanting to leave Lyndsey out of this and I start to read it aloud.

Hi my love,

I'm going to get all the news out of the way because I want time to complain.

1. Aiden got a concussion yesterday, I love how much passion he has for hockey but the mom in me wanted to ban the whole sport. Then I heard you in my head reminding me that risk is a constant, if he is going to be at risk at least he is doing something he loves.

2. Alice is a dream, I never asked her to and yet each night after I have tucked everybody into bed, I hear her sneaking into Eden's bedroom to read her a story. I don't know who loves it more but our daughters are something special.

3. Eden is finally having no bed-wetting accidents. If you asked Alice she would take responsibility but to me it's just telling me they are all grown. Scary stuff.

Before you beat yourself up for missing it, know it is worth it when you come home. When you get to hold them again they will tell you all of this stuff themselves and you will be just as proud. You might miss it in the moment but they get to see your face when they tell you all of their stories and it brings them so much joy. Eden has even started journaling so she remembers all the things she wants to tell you.

Now, my love, I'm going to complain. If you get me pregnant one more time I'll kill you. My poor ribs never get a break from this little monster, her foot is basically wedged in there all of the time. She is so strong that the others like to sit and watch her move around like a little alien. An alien I'll love when she comes out but right now I get to be mad.

Outside of the Anders home there isn't much happening, I wish I had more gossip but I have been staying in more than usual. I'm so ready to pop that I get scared I'm going to go into labour in public, I would never live down the embarrassment. I hope you are hanging in there.

We miss you and love you and when you do get home, I might have forgotten how much pregnancy sucks so bring this letter home with you to remind me. It is your duty as my husband.

All my love
Your Darlin'.

I don't realise I'm crying until Lyndsey swipes her thumb under my eyes. I pull her to me. Tighter than I should. I had forgotten my dad called Mom darlin'. It just felt so right when I met Lyndsey that she was my darlin' and finding this letter, this reminder, makes me feel like my parents approve.

The paper falls to the table next to the box as we stand together in each other's arms.

"They really loved each other, didn't they?" Her voice is a quiet mumble against my chest and I finally let her go, pulling myself together.

"I've never seen anything like it, they were two halves of the same soul, I swear." I shake my head lightly, putting everything back into the box, lingering on each piece of memory. "Dad, he called Mom his darlin'. I'd forgotten." I don't know if it makes me sad or happy.

I'm sad that I have started to forget things about them already. And yet I'm happy to have a connection from my parents to Lyndsey. The fact Dad kept this letter with him breaks my heart. Every time he read it, it must have come with the instant reminder of what he was missing. What made him want to come home and reclaim what was always his – in the same way I have come to reclaim these things.

—

Silence isn't always a bad thing. Sometime silence can be how people connect, this is not that silence. Lyndsey has been quiet, too quiet. Not that I'm any better. I'm not sure if it's her anxiety or something else keeping her lips locked but for me I just don't know what words would be worth breaking the silence for. I love my pops. He has been the man in my life for so long. Even before my dad died he was away a lot when I was a kid, Pops stepped up to teach me how to shave and to open a car door for my woman while my dad was deployed. As I grew the lessons changed. Instead of making me into my best self he wanted me to be my dad, he wanted his son back and I was as close as he was going to get, but that isn't me.

My dad was brave beyond measure and I don't think you could pay me enough money to join the army, I'm just not built for that life. I'm good in a team. I'm a good leader. I have a strong mental capacity. All things the military look for. But there is something I lack, the willingness to leave the people I love behind.

"My dad would hate this." I break the silence, my hands gripping the steering wheel until it creaks.

"Hate what?" she asks, uncapping a bottle of water and taking a sip as I find the right words.

"That I'm lying to make Pops happy." I sigh. "He would rip me a new one if he found out."

"Was he a hard-ass?" she asks, I realise that she is doing so much for me and she barely knows the man she is helping. I don't talk about my parents a lot, it hurts too much. Now seems like a good a time as any to reminisce.

"Yes and no. He had strong morals but as soon as we looked at him with puppy-dog eyes, he would give us anything." I think that's why I'm always so sure things will work out for me, my dad instilled the idea that as long as I wanted something bad enough, I could get it.

"I think if this makes your grandfather happy then it would be worth whatever your parents would say, it's a small evil for a big reward," she reasons, and I try to release the tension in my shoulders. I just need to believe that as much as she does.

Pops has been in Sunnyvale Care Home for three years, since his most recent stroke. Not because the girls didn't want to look after him but because he didn't want them to. Always so stubborn he wouldn't hear them when they told him they would just be paying him back for looking after them. No, he said that they should be living their lives not holding his hand at the end of his. It was a noble decision and I understand why he did it but there was a big change in him when we moved his belongings into his room. He became so sure he was going to die any day. Three years later and I think he has some life in him yet – well, I did last time I saw him. If Alice is right, there might be less time than I want to believe.

I just can't imagine it: Pops dying. It feels blasphemous to even think about. This man is the face of strength for me, he is invincible. Alice has told me he is coming to the end and even though I know it isn't something she would lie about I don't want to believe it. I want to believe it was just a ploy to get me home and if it was Cece who told me I might still think that. But not Alice.

"So how often do you talk to him?" The silence is broken by Lyndsey this time and I'm not sure if I'm glad for it.

"Not as often as I should, I make way too many excuses but none of them seem worth it now." Lyndsey has this way of making me tell the truth, even if I don't know it's the truth until I say it.

"So I'm about to walk into a cold war between two Anders men?"

I try to laugh but its barely even audible. "I love him, I just don't like to be around him. It hurts us both. I can never be what he wants and he will always see me as a lesser version than his son." I look over in the car to see Lyndsey as she processes that.

"So you are both just stubborn men?" she asks, her head shaking with a deep sigh.

"What?" I find a space to park the SUV near the back of the visitor lot.

"Trying so hard to hide how you feel you have let it split you apart from someone you love. Classic men." Then she opens the damn door and jumps out before I can reply.

"Well shit, darlin', you don't take it easy on me." I follow her towards the big glass door that leads to the reception. The building is bright and open, unlike the prison-type buildings I imagined care homes were when I was a kid.

Lyndsey smiles reassuringly but it doesn't really help. She isn't wrong though. There is a gorge between me and Pops and as much as I want to put all the blame on the old man the truth is I'm just as much to blame. I ran away instead of holding my ground. Shit, I'm here pretending to be married instead of just admitting to him that I'm not really holding up my end of the bargain when it comes to Dad's will. I take down grown men on skates for a living but the man who raised me is a step too far.

I don't recognise the woman who takes us to Pops' room. I barely even see her. She's a short woman in clinical blue scrubs. My mind can't focus on anything except Lyndsey's hand linked in mine – it somehow found its way to mine, but I'm not willing to question why too much. She must be able to feel my anxious energy. Or perhaps she's anxious herself. I don't blame her. Or, like I suspect, she's playing her wife role. Going with the plan. I use the feeling of her skin as distraction from the impending sense of doom I feel with each step closer.

Alice warned me of what I would see. I don't know why I'm surprised to see him, and yet I am. His skin looks almost grey where he sits in an armchair looking out of the window. The room he lives in is nice. The whole place is nice. I wouldn't have put him somewhere dated to spend his days, that's one thing we can agree on. The window is big and looks out over a garden dotted with trees and flowers; outside I can see another elderly resident, a woman, shuffling around aided only by a walker.

When he hears the door open, Pops looks up to see who has disturbed his day, only to light up when he sees me. His posture is hunched and folded and he looks so much older. When I picture him in my mind he is still the man in his late fifties that he was when I was a kid, the man who ran after me and taught me how to change a tyre. That man is a distant memory compared to the image in front of me now.

"Aiden, my boy, about time you showed your face." His voice is a lot quieter, everything about him is quiet.

Fuck, I'm a terrible grandson. I might just be a terrible person because I'm trying to swindle this man. It might not be for money, but into believing the love-marriage display I'm about to put on. All the same, it feels wrong to lie to a man who can't fight back. I swallow hard. I'm doing this for him, so he can see his son's stuff one last time. So that I can see it too. It has to be worth it.

Instead of answering him, I lead Lyndsey over to his side before hugging him lightly, scared that if I hold him any tighter, I'll break a bone. His eyes slide from me to Lyndsey as he pulls out of my arms. He smirks at me then.

"Well, hello there, ma'am, I'm William, who might you be?" He is definitely turning on his southern charm as he lifts her hand up to his lips.

"Nice to meet you, William, I'm Lyndsey." I can see the humour in her eyes, I think she might have been expecting something different: a sinister, evil old man, not this.

"She's pretty, Aiden, too pretty for you. If I were a few years younger, and all that." He waves his hand in the air, floating his joke. They both laugh at that before he gestures us over to sit on the end of the bed nearest to him.

"I'm sorry I haven't visited much, time slips by so quick." It's a weak excuse but it's the only one I have.

"You can blame me, it takes a lot of time to put up with me. Aiden is pretty much a saint for loving me." I can hear how tight Lyndsey's voice is but that's just because I know her, to him it probably sounds sweet and apologetic. Exactly what she was hoping for.

"Well, I can't begrudge that, I'd spend all my time with you too." He smiles at her. She has him wrapped around her little finger so quick. Must be an Anders-men gene.

"I'm sure anyone would be lucky to spend so much time with you." She winks and I feel some tension flow out of her as her fingers loosen in my hand but I don't let go. I can't.

"I like her a lot, you should get her down the aisle before someone nabs her from you." Pops moves his gaze to me and my pulse hammers in my neck at the open door he has given me.

"That's actually why we're here. Pops, Lyndsey is my wife."

Stunned silence fills the room. Lyndsey's grip tightens again, her ring finger now the focal point of the room. Then he starts to laugh. It's quiet at first, just an air-filled sound wheezing out of him, until he coughs out a louder one. His cardigan-covered shoulders shake as he looks at us. For a split second I think he has us to rights, he knows we are full of shit. Then he reaches out for Lyndsey's hands, pulling her into a hug like the one he gave me.

"Congratulations, my boy! You've just made my damn day. Hell, my year." He shakes my hand, his grip weak but his smile strong.

"Thanks, Pops, I'm sorry I didn't tell you sooner, I didn't want to get everyone's hopes up if things didn't work out." My heart doesn't feel like it is going to slow down any time soon. Seeing how all I have done is lie the last few days, you would think I would feel calmer than this by now.

"In case I got sick of him, he means." Lyndsey and Pops laugh and, when she sits down beside me again instead of taking my hand, she places her hand on my thigh squeezing to try and calm me. It just works me up more. The heat of her hand through my jeans is strong and distracting.

"She reminds me of my Lulu, gonna keep you in line, that's for sure," Pops chuckles.

"I'm sure she will... Lulu was my grandmother, the love of his life. Her and her baked goods were some of the best parts of my childhood," I explain to Lyndsey, before facing my grandfather again. "Pops. I, erm, I have something for you." I change the subject, pulling the box from Lyndsey's bag. Based on the sharp inhale I think he knows what it is.

"Aid?" His voice is weak but stiff with emotion as I place the box on his lap. He doesn't open it straight away. No, he rubs a shaking hand over the wood. I consider giving him a minute alone but I also don't want to miss this. So I don't. Lyndsey and I sit as he opens the box filled with memories of his son. There are hundreds of emotions: sadness and grief, of course, but I can see how happy he is to see this stuff again. After all this time he has a piece of his son back again. He is gentle as he riffles through it, looking at the drawings and letters, lifting the medals into the light to see how they gleam. The sadness is lifted the more he explores. We sit in silence for a while before his eyes jump from the box to my eyes. "Say, did you get my letter?" he asks, effectively stopping my heart. It's no longer just beating fast, it's hammering.

"What letter?" I cough. Lyndsey squeezes my thigh again, keenly noticing my fear.

"I sent a letter a few days ago, I never know how long these things take nowadays," he grumbles, like a clichéd old man from a film.

"Nope, I didn't see anything before we left, is everything okay?" I don't think I have ever said nope to him before, this is not the time to expand my vocabulary. I catch Lyndsey out of the corner of my eye biting her lip at my terrible lying skills.

"Everything is just right, Aiden, you can throw it right away when you get back, there's no need for it now that y'all are here." He shakes his head, gratitude and relief washing over him. *Well, that sounds like a plan to me.* Sensing my need to move on, Lyndsey distracts him with questions about me as a kid. As if she didn't get enough ammunition from my sisters.

The three of us talk for a while, but I can see the energy that our news gave him starting to wane. Being the strong, stubborn man he is, Pops doesn't ask us to leave nor does he drop the mask of strength he is trying to hide behind. If Lyndsey can see how tired he is, she doesn't comment on it. Instead she takes the lead in the conversation, asking fewer questions and telling him all about my current achievements, even if he doesn't seem as interested.

Pops spends time asking us questions. About her. About us. About everything. I was ready to fight and stand my ground if he pushed back on the validity of our marriage but, instead, he seems content to tell stories and listen to Lyndsey talk. It puts me on edge, I was so ready to be on the defence that now I don't know where I stand.

Lyndsey pulls another laugh from him but this one seems to hurt, the laughter shifts to a coughing fit so quickly it startles me. Pops pulls a tissue from one of his pockets, clearly used to coughing this way. The force of the coughing racks his small, frail frame until he is hunched in his chair. Lyndsey jumps up to pour him a glass of water but I just freeze. I can't look away as he coughs and wheezes in front of me. It's a reminder of how ill he really is.

Behind all his stories and smiles there is something darker going on that he is hiding from, but we can't hide from this. A nurse shuffles in, quickly shooing us from the bed before helping Pops to stand. That's when I start to move. I go to his other side, helping his nurse to guide him to his bed, and Lyndsey stands at the other side of the room unsure of how to help. I understand how she feels, I haven't felt this useless since my parents died.

We barely have a chance to say a proper goodbye before the nurse is all but shoving Lyndsey and I out of his room. When the door clicks shut Lyndsey wraps her hand around mine while the nurse guides us into a small office pointing at the sofa. Instead of moving behind the desk the nurse sits down on the other side of the sofa – it's less intimidating this way, but it also makes me think there is something big coming.

"I'm a direct woman. The doctor would probably be more sensitive but I don't think we have the time to wait for her," she starts.

"What's happening?" I want as much information as she will give.

"He is sicker than he lets on, the medication isn't helping him any more. His lungs are weak, and his heart is having to work harder than we would like." Lyndsey's hand tightens with each word out of the nurse's lips. I hold her just as tight.

"So, what does it mean? Different medication? Do I need to get him transferred somewhere else?" My voice strains.

"Mr Anders…" The nurse softens her tone. "It could be weeks, it could be days," she says delicately. Her directness is a harsh reality.

"Months?" Lyndsey asks, a tremble in her own voice.

"It's not likely. William is a stubborn ox but he can't run from time. I'm sorry." Lyndsey and the nurse continue to talk in low voices but I tune them out. All I can think about is how my family is about to lose another person. The final person we had to raise us is going to die and there is nothing I can throw money at to fix it.

I couldn't save my parents from the drunk driver. I couldn't help my grandma when age took her from us. Now I can't save Pops, the last guardian in my life is dying and I'm as useless as ever. All I could do was lie to him.

I couldn't be there when everyone else died, but I can be here now. It's all I have left to give: my presence. Even if it isn't as valuable as it once was. I can be here for my sisters as we face this together.

My eyes trace over my wife next to me. I hope Lyndsey is willing to be here for longer than was planned, because I can't leave yet. She hasn't been in my life for long, but I've brought her into my world. My family. My home. What would they think if my wife went back to Seattle when we need support most? Would they see through our fabrication?

It isn't an option. I need Lyndsey to stay. I might just crumble under the pressure without her.

Lyndsey's hand is on my lower back, guiding me out of the care home and towards the car. My mind is running through every option but her hands on me bring comfort.

"You're a terrible liar, you should have warned me because, damn, you have no poker face." I know she is trying to cheer me up or at least keep my mind busy but I can barely force a smile. "Seriously, Aiden, we will be found out if you say nope again, are you a teenager?" She tries again and that one does make me chuckle. Not a laugh but close enough, I guess.

"It just came out." She just hums at that as we make it closer to the car.

"You're going to be okay, you know?" She pulls me back to face her, not letting me get in the car.

"I'm not strong enough to go through this again," I tell her after a moment. The admission is quiet but the words feel like knives against my throat.

"What do you mean?" Lyndsey slips both of her hands into mine, standing only a foot away, trying to catch my eye while I do my best to look away.

"When my parents died, I came home from college, I had to be here but everyone was crumbling." I still refuse to meet her eye but I can feel her gaze against my skin. "No one should have to bury their child, but Pops fell so far into his grief that he couldn't help us with ours. Celia cried for days barely understanding what was happening and Eden all but stopped talking. Alice helped where she could but softness doesn't come easy to her, she wanted to rage, to break things and yell at the universe so I had to be the raft. I had to hold everyone together while hiding the cracks in my own heart. I don't think I can be the rock again, Lyndsey. It nearly killed me."

"Then I'll be the rock."

Then my eyes meet hers. We lock intensely. *There is no way she means what I think she does.* "What?"

"Your sisters will need you but when the load gets heavy, give it to me. I'll be right here, Aiden." One of her hands comes up to cradle my jaw, her soft skin rubs against my stubble. "This marriage has done me a favour too, Aiden. We're going to be free to go about our lives as we were meant to soon enough. And no matter how stubborn I might seem, I'm not stubborn or evil enough to turn my back just because I have what I want. I can joke all day long, but if you need a soft place to land, I can be that. You're my husband after all."

"I can't ask that of you." My voice is a whisper in the summer breeze.

"Well, I'm not giving you a choice," she tells me, stepping even closer still, until we are nearly chest to chest.

I know I shouldn't but I can't help but drop my forehead against hers. Up close her green eyes have specks of brown that I can't see from further away and it's hypnotising. I wish I could look at her this closely every minute of every day. Lyndsey's gaze holds mine as I silently take in the details of her face, the soft slope of her nose, the small scar above her right eyebrow that I wish I knew how she got. I look at her fuller bottom lip wishing I could taste it, I wonder if she wears a tinted lip balm or if they have a naturally rosy sheen to them. Every second I watch her I find something I haven't noticed before. I have watched her over the past eighteen months I have known her but I think forever would be too short to find out everything about Lyndsey Stone.

Before I know what I'm doing I feel myself drifting even closer to her, desperate to feel her lips against mine. I need to feel the way she would melt under my hands or whether she would fight me. My lips are a hair from hers when a phone starts to blare between us. Lyndsey leaps back a few feet and jumps into the car while I pull my phone out to see Rook calling me. Irritation rattles me to my core.

Though it might have been better that he disturbed us. She might have kissed me back. We don't need to complicate things further by kissing – falling into the unknown at a time when everything is already falling apart around me.

"Hey, Rook, what's up?" I hope he can't hear the tightness in my voice.

I try to pay attention as he asks about our trip and about Pops. He continues to ramble into my ear as we get into the car. I watch Lyndsey shifting uncomfortably in her seat, glaring at her own phone like it has personally offended her. I link the call to the car's Bluetooth to fill what I know will be a tense silence, letting Rook distract us from what almost happened.

What *can't* happen.

Chapter Nineteen

Aiden

Turns out Alice wanted to wait until I saw Pops for myself before we told the girls that he is close to the end. They didn't take it well. Celia went straight into denial, the same way I did, she asked about new medications or admitting him to a hospital somewhere to make him better. It made me sick to watch her break down. Eden went straight for rage. She yelled, mainly at Alice, about us keeping it from them. She was mad that Alice has known for weeks and I have known for a few days and kept them out of the loop. She hates that we still treat them like kids but it's hard to see them as grown-ups when, every time I look at them, I see those crying girls at our parents' funeral.

Alice let her yell, we both knew she needed to get it out before she could engage in a rational conversation. Eventually Eden got tired from yelling and flopped onto the couch where Cece sat quietly sobbing. She took our youngest sister into her arms as they cried together. I had no joke or comment that could make this better. I felt so useless and with Lyndsey waiting upstairs because she said we needed to do this as a family, I wanted nothing more than to hide with her. Instead I had to take charge, I moved over to the sofa and wrapped my arms around them as their sobs turned to sniffles. As much as they hate it, they know we wouldn't lie to them and that we would have done everything in our power to help Pops if we could. Since then we have all clung to each other and spent most nights together talking or watching TV as we all work through our thoughts.

Lyndsey has been here for all of that. Cece has clutched on to her a lot. Eden is still a little mad at Alice so she has been mainly by my side as Alice has spent all of her free time snapping photographs of the sunsets around our childhood home. That's why finding a minute alone in a house with four women, three of which are my sisters, is a difficult task. Basically impossible. Unless I'm in the bathroom there is always someone around. When it's Lyndsey I don't mind the company, but Alice wants to talk about what happens when Pops dies and that's too much for me right now. Eden wants to talk about the kids she teaches in her first-grade class, I think she is trying to do the opposite to Alice but there are only so many kid stories I can listen to, especially when it makes me a little homesick for Jack and Charlotte – those kids have a place in my heart that Eden's students don't. Celia is quieter than normal but that's because she is researching for an interview, every second she is typing away and the click-clack of her laptop keys is driving me slowly crazy.

Earlier today the three girls went to visit Pops themselves. Now that we know he really is close to the end every minute with him is precious. Cece is still in denial, thinking some miracle drug is going to come out at the last minute and save him. Alice and Eden are more resigned to the truth now. We are about to lose the final parental figure in our lives. The only thing I was looking forward to was getting time alone with Lyndsey, but she keeps managing to escape me. If she is alone watching TV and I walk in suddenly her phone will chime and she'll excuse herself. When she was sitting on the porch swing alone and I brought her some iced tea she swung her legs up to take up the whole bench, leaving me nowhere to sit. I left her alone only because I was confused.

I thought things were shifting between us somehow. Between meeting Pops and our almost kiss in the parking lot I convinced myself we might be able to pull this off. She must be an amazing actress because, when the girls are around, Lyndsey reminds me of how she was when things were more familiar between us. Back when Ellis was on bed rest and I did my best to convince Lyndsey to go on a date with me. That was until I was told to back off. I did and yet we still ended up here anyway.

Each morning as we eat breakfast, I make Lynds her coffee – no sugars because she is sweet enough – and she plates up my food from whatever selection Alice has made. Every time, Alice smirks at me knowingly but I pay her no mind. I'm too happy with the domestic flow between me and my temporary wife. Whenever the girls are around, I take the opportunity to have my hands on her. Whether it's a hand on her back or a light kiss to her forehead, I love giving her physical affection. I tell her it's just because I'm a physical guy and it's true but still I have never been around a woman long enough to have an excuse to touch them. Now I'm taking what I can while I can. Because as soon as we are alone, she demands space between us. Time where she doesn't have to pretend to enjoy being my wife. I have to remember that, even if there is growing tension between us, we are not going to be husband and wife forever.

I never pictured marrying the girl. Hell, I don't think I ever seriously considered marriage in the distant future.

But being married hasn't been quite as terrible as I imagined it. I pictured arguing and a very dry sex life and I only have half of those things. I haven't slept with my wife but I don't think it would be a bad thing if we did. We could both scratch that itch and release the tension that has been between us for over a year. Though it will be hard to convince her to give in with my sisters right down the hall.

Right now, though, I have found a slight reprieve from the tension. I had to offer to make dinner for it to happen, but small wins. There are a few dishes I have mastered: my beef roast is one of my best, and I know it is Celia's favourite too. When I offered to cook, the girls basically dragged Lyndsey outside to drink some wine while they gave her all the small-town gossip about people she will probably never meet. She looks like she is having fun, when she isn't staring at her phone with a frown. I can see them all through the big picture window in the kitchen. The setting sun bounces off Lyndsey's hair, making her glow as she throws her head back in laughter.

Despite the fake romance we're putting on, my chest feels settled seeing her fitting in like this. I knew they would approve of her, there is nothing they wouldn't approve of. I know she was worried about her sexuality, but that was just her old southern prejudice that was causing her anxiety. There is nothing to worry about, of course. But no matter how much I told her she would be fine, she had to see it to believe it.

More than that, she just fits in. Fake wife or not. Her jabs and teasing smiles, the way she can calm me with one touch is unlike anything I have experienced before.

On top of it all, I can see how free she seems here. Whenever she puts her phone down, that is. Her phone fills her with tension and I'm not sure why but if I try to bring it up she changes the subject. I thought at first it might have been because of the online backlash that came when our marriage was announced, there were a few overzealous female fans who were picking her apart. She said it wasn't that though, and I believe her, she actually laughed at some of those comments – apparently, if these women knew me in real life they wouldn't like me as much. At least that's what Lyndsey thinks, that knowing that I'm not the growly man I am on the ice in real life would burst their bubble. She is probably right, those fans don't know me. They see the way I act on the ice, protective of my team. They see what I want them to see off the ice, the funny, happy guy releasing the tension even after a loss. But Lyndsey sees more, and she is with me basically twenty-four-seven, so I'll let her keep her secrets for now but only because, when she does put her phone down, she is so fully indulging in life. She is wearing her hair down more and wearing the sexiest little sundresses – don't get me wrong, she would look beautiful in a potato sack, but seeing her wearing dresses instead of skintight jeans is a change I'm enjoying.

I'm so distracted by the thought of my wife's creamy-white skin fanned by flowing fabric that I don't hear her walk in. It's not until she is right beside me rubbing a hand up my spine that I notice her.

"Smells yummy, you need any help?" Her hair smells like coconut and that alone makes her more delicious than whatever food I'm making.

"No, I'm good, darlin'. You enjoying yourself?" I ask, dropping the knife and turning my attention to her.

"Your sisters are a hoot, are you sure they are related to you?" She nudges my ribs. I can see redness on her cheeks – caused by either the wine or the sun, I'm not sure.

"You found my secret." I roll my eyes, making her laugh brightly.

"I knew it, you're lucky Alice looks so much like you." She goes to walk away but I'm not ready to lose her yet so I move to stand in front of her, forcing her back against the edge of the countertop.

"Aiden, what are you doing?" I see her throat work as she swallows.

"I'm thanking you." I pick up a piece of her rose-gold hair, curling it around my finger. The strands are soft and shiny, perfectly her.

"For what?" Our voices have dropped low and I love it. There is tension in her voice but I see the way her pupils blow wide as she looks up at me.

"I haven't decided yet, I just wanted to look at you." I bring my face closer to her, almost whispering against her ear.

"Aiden..." Her voice is weak. I know the feeling.

"Fuck, darlin', you smell like heaven and hell combined." I bury my face into her shoulder. Smelling the mix of coconut in her hair and sunshine on her skin makes me weak in the knees.

"Maybe we should..." Her protest falls away as my lips find her pulse; it hammers against my lips, causing me to smile.

"I need more of it, Lynds." My hand comes up to grip the hair at the back of her head, tipping her head back so there is more skin available to me.

"Aiden, we are blurring the lines, it's not smart." Yet she doesn't tell me to stop. She can't, she wants this too.

Lyndsey wants my hands on her, wants my lips on her skin, and it drives me crazy.

"I think we should erase the lines altogether, wife," I tease.

"That would be complicated." Her throat works under my lips and she gulps down air.

"Maybe, but it would be good too. We don't have to make it complicated, we do what we want now and then leave it in Texas when the time comes to leave." My nose slides up and down her neck from the join of her shoulder right to the soft skin behind her ear.

"This is fake. We need boundaries." Her hands come up to my chest and, if she pushes me away, I'll go. But that's not what she does. She grips the plaid fabric, tightly holding me right there against her.

"Fuck boundaries.'" I kiss her skin again, smirking at the low moan that escapes her. "Is our marriage legal? Yes. Is my ring on your finger? Yes. We just need to give in."

"Fuck! I can't, Aiden." Her voice is a high whine but she doesn't let me go.

"Admit it. There is tension here, darlin'." I pull away then, to look in her eye. I want to see her lie to me, want her to know I'm seeing through whatever bullshit she is going to try to spin.

"Yes, okay, there is tension." She never fails to shock me. "But we are getting divorced in a few months, tension or not. Then we will be going home and we will be around our friends again and it will just be too hard."

"I'm pretty hard already. Who cares about when we get back, we should enjoy it now." I grind my hips into her then, my jeans are tented as I rub against the softness of her stomach. Lyndsey blinks up at me, biting her lip as a beautiful flush paints over her chest and neck. "Imagine what it would be like, you and me. It would be fireworks." Letting go of the hair at the back of her head, my hand moves around to hold her jaw, the callousness of my hands are a polar opposite to her supple skin.

"I have imagined it, okay! It would be explosive and explosive is dangerous." Well, well, well, my beautiful wife is not as indifferent as she might want me to believe.

Before I have a chance to reply her phone pings loudly from her bra. Using the distraction to push space between us she pulls it out even though we both know it won't be important. If it was important, whoever it is would have called not texted. She can run but now I know. My wife wants me and she is going to get me, soon.

When she reads the text, I see the colour that was just there drain before my eyes. Whoever is texting her has fully pulled her away from the moment we had. I'm pissed at them not just for that but because there is fear in her eyes. It isn't fear of the feelings between us but I don't know what type of fear it is.

"Lyndsey? What's wrong?"

"Nothing. Excuse me, I, erm, I need to use the restroom." Then she is off. All but running away towards the stairs. I would like to think she needs to cool down because of the heat between us but I'm not delusional. She is running because of her phone. And she is going to put a wall up between us now. I had one moment where I thought she would fall with me, but she is holding me at arm's length.

I may have pushed her too far. I know I was coming on strong but that, mixed with whatever is happening on that damn phone, is going to cause a rift between us. That ping gave Lyndsey an excuse to get out of my arms but there is no way that will work forever. Eventually she is going to have to decide if she is ready to try and see what could happen if we slipped beneath the sheets or if she wants to keep those damn lines clear. At least now she knows which one I want, there is no hiding it now. I want my wife in my bed and she knows it. The ball is in her court.

I'm a stupid, stupid man.

Chapter Twenty

Lyndsey

The house around me feels so much smaller than it has the past few days we have been here. The blue walls are closing in every second. I ran away. Aiden had me in a corner and I ran. I knew I needed to leave, especially when I got another damn text. One thing is for sure, it's not Kayla. That idea has long passed. She is never this persistent. This vile. Plus, whoever this is has not asked me to date them once, which is a big clue. Then there is the fact that every text has made sense, not a single spelling error, no short-hand. Unless Kayla has completely sobered up then there is no way she would have been able to text me so clearly for weeks. But that now brings up the new question of who the fuck is threatening me and why? The white blanket in the bedroom that has kept me warm is starkly cold against my heated skin. Why did I think I had it all together? I thought I could come here, lie to everyone and go back home while being fucking threatened.

When the texts didn't stop, I should have told Aiden. But no, I kept it to myself and now I'm going to have to pull him into drama he doesn't need. So I'm hiding, not well, but I'm hiding all the same.

As soon as dinner was done, I excused myself to bed claiming a headache. Aiden didn't buy it. I could see it in his eyes that he wanted to come after me but the girls kept him distracted. I wish there was a lock on the door; keeping him out wouldn't be fair, but I'm not looking for fair, I'm looking for an escape.

Aiden wouldn't let that happen, eventually he followed me up, but when I gave him nothing he hopped in the shower. I wish I could wash away all of my worries. For the hundredth time since this afternoon, my shaking hands open up the one-sided text thread:

> You can't run forever.

> Secrets will eat you alive, stupid dyke.

> You can't ignore me forever, I will find you.

> Hiding in Texas won't keep me away.

> Does your rich little husband know you're using him for his wallet?

> Poor Aiden falling for your gold digger act.

> You have one chance to break his heart or I tell the world what a sick whore you are. Liar.

> Lyndsey, Lyndsey, Lyndsey don't say I didn't warn you.

> I will go away, let you keep up your straight girl act... for $10,000 that is.

That last one came through when Aiden had his damn hands tangled in my hair. So I ran. With each text my anxiety has grown but I don't understand who would care so much about my relationship with Aiden to go to all this trouble to scare me. Kayla doesn't need the money – hell, she has more than one woman could ever spend, her daddy keeps her bank filled enough for three people. Ten thousand dollars would be nothing to her, definitely not worth all this trouble, but there is nobody else.

I thought maybe Aiden had a point when he asked me about overzealous fans but their comments were more about my looks and their apparent disdain for redheads. There were no threats, nothing that would make me worry about them. Anyway, the first text came through before the hate comments, someone knew before everyone else. Someone was keeping a close eye on me apparently, because they know more than they are saying. I can feel it in their hatred.

My new priority is telling Aiden. I thought if I let them wear themselves out, they would get bored, but that isn't the case. They are escalating.

Asking for his money, wanting to tarnish his reputation through me. Whoever it is thinks Aiden doesn't know I'm bi, at least that's what I think. But then why would they think the rest of the world would care about some hockey player's wife's sexuality? It doesn't make sense to me. There seems to be some crossed wires but I haven't wanted to text them back, I think that would only encourage their behaviour.

Aiden is going through enough. I promised I would be his soft place when William dies, but now he is going to think he needs to fix this for me. That damn captain attitude making him think he needs to be everyone's lord and saviour and now I'm going to have to add more weight onto his heavy shoulders. However, I no longer have a choice.

When the en suite bathroom door creaks open I decide now is the best time to get this over with. That is until I see Aiden. Naked and dripping with nothing but a towel covering himself.

"I forgot to grab my clothes," he has the nerve to say. His words are dripping with deceit as I watch drops of water flowing down his broad chest. Blond hair trails down from his navel to where he is holding the towel up. His tattoos sprinkled over his skin look like something to explore. Every time I glance, I feel like I notice one I haven't seen before.

"You lie like a rug, Aiden Anders." My voice is distant, my mind is blank as my eyes slide over all of his exposed skin. I can see each muscle ripple as he laughs at me. I don't need to look at his face to know he is giving me that killer smile. He laid a trap and I'm falling right into it. Willingly.

"I don't know what you mean?"

"You forgot your clothes on purpose, you didn't even get any out to leave out here."

He just hums, no denial or argument. He wanted me weak. God, I must be weak because even though I shouldn't, I want nothing more than to fall to my knees and throw that towel away. I want to see every inch of his skin exposed to me even though I know it will only be sex. I won't be married to him forever, I should get to enjoy it while he is offering. Especially after I tell him what has been happening, he is going to drop me like a hot potato when he sees how much drama I'm bringing to his door. I push away those thoughts for now. He is here and, for now, he is mine.

"My eyes are up here, darlin'." He laughs, walking closer to where I'm sat at the end of our queen bed. Shit, it's not *our* anything. It is his.

I need to remember that but my brain has apparently turned off because I tell him, "I'm not looking at your eyes, cowboy."

His laughter is boisterous in the otherwise quiet room. I stay stock-still watching droplets of water cascade down his chest and down to the trail of hair where his pelvis is hidden from me.

"I wish it wasn't working but fuck you're sexy." I continue to soak in the almost pornographic view of the man I somehow ended up married to.

"Well, wife, it's all yours if you admit you want it." He wraps his hand around the hair at the back of my head and tugs so my eyes finally meet his. "Tell me, do you want to blur the lines? Or do you want me to grab my clothes and go?"

"Fuck the lines."

Then I pounce.

I all but leap from the bed into Aiden's arms. My legs loop around his trim waist as I kiss him. I have imagined kissing him a million times but this is more than my deepest fantasies could live up to. His lips are soft but demanding against mine as our tongues tangle together in a harmonic flow. He was right, it is explosive. I can feel his damp skin through my thin sleepwear but it just turns me on more. The fact I'm going to dirty him up. I feel safe in his arms, like nothing can hurt me. Not even those texts affect me when Aiden has his lips on mine.

His hands squeeze my ass cheeks, causing me to moan around his lips. Fuck, I can feel him on every inch of my skin, I tingle with hundreds of electric shocks bursting in my blood. My heart pounds against my chest and I wouldn't be surprised if Aiden can feel it against his naked skin.

I'm not easily dominated though, Aiden might want to run this show but I'm giving him a run for his money. My fingers tangle in his blond locks, tugging his head back for a change. He growls out a moan and I feel it vibrate against my lips as I kiss over the skin of his neck, the same way he did for me this afternoon. His skin is still wet from the shower and I can smell the soap he used, I want to drown in it. I would drown in him happily.

Then I'm airborne. Aiden tosses me onto the bed with such force I bounce twice before I can right myself. Just when I find a comfortable position his long fingers wrap around my ankles, completely pulling me down the bed so he can lean over me. With his weight steeled on one hand next to my head, his other hand tugs at the hem of my summer dress, pulling it up and over my head in one swoop. I try to sit up to help him but his body is so close to mine that there is hardly any room to breathe.

Even in my white lace underwear I'm not naked enough for Aiden because a snarl pulls from his lips until I move my hands to unhook my bra. When the fabric falls away I see his jaw work as he takes me in. From the freckles that cover my chest to the soft pink colour of my nipples, he enjoys his view. And, hell, I enjoy mine. I could look at him all day and its seems like he would be happy to do the same but I'm sick of waiting: I tug at the towel still around his hips to free his cock.

My mouth near waters at the sight. He is long and thick but not in a way that makes me think it would hurt, I would hate to not be able to take him all. It's a task I'm looking forward to and clearly so is he because just then Aiden drops to his knees at the foot of the bed.

Reaching up he pulls my white lace panties down my legs, they are more tanned than usual and it makes me feel sexier somehow. Like it isn't me doing this but some bronzed, more confident me lying naked in front of this muscle man with him looking at me like I'm a feast.

Pulling me even further down the bed, Aiden throws both of my thighs over his shoulders so his face is inches away from where I'm wet for him. I can feel his breath puffing against my wet skin.

"Perfect. All for me, isn't it, darlin'?" Chills skitter over my skin at the bass trembling in his voice, deeper than I have ever heard it, and I know that it's me driving him into this feral beast.

"Yours." My voice doesn't sound like mine but then neither does his so I guess that's fair. I want to pretend at least for tonight that I truly am his. That the affection he is giving me is genuine.

"Attagirl." Not wasting another second, his tongue plunges into me like a man starved. The stubble on his chin rubs against my sensitive skin, driving me even more crazy for him.

Aiden is messy, it's the most unbridled I think he has ever been. The wet sounds we are making drive me crazy and I don't care if his sisters hear as I moan out his name. We are married after all, they shouldn't be shocked at the idea we're fucking. Because that is what is happening, Aiden is fucking me with his tongue. Just as the thought that I need more forms, two of Aiden's long, callused fingers slide into me with ease like he can read my mind. I'm so soaked for him I think he could fuck me right now and his dick would slide right in with no resistance. Still, if he wants to eat me out I'm not going to stop him.

It has been my mind resisting him but my body is not on the same page. My body is a whore for him and now I'm just going to let her enjoy it. My back bows when his fingers bump against my G-spot, I feel the edge of my orgasm swimming in my blood. Lights flash in the sides of my vision and it is suddenly hard to breathe. Wetness gushes out of me, Aiden laps it all up like he has been stranded in a desert for a hundred years and I'm the elixir of life.

Sliding a third finger in is what pushes me over the cliff. Somehow I'm soaring and yet I feel so safe with Aiden between my legs, I knew he would make me feel good but this is beyond. My moans are a continued stream at this point, I don't think I could form any words except his name and pleas for more.

"Fuck, Aiden!" My head is thrashing against the comforter and my fingers are so tight in his hair I wouldn't be surprised if I pulled it out, but it would be his own damn fault. For being so fucking good with his tongue that it should come with a warning.

"Keep coming for me, Lynds, soak me." Even as my orgasm starts to fade and my body starts to sag, he never stops his ministration. His fingers pump and pump inside of me until I can feel the overstimulation creeping in. Only then do I untangle my hands from his strands and push him away, though my arms are so weak I'm surprised he even feels it. "I'm not done yet, wife, you're not tapping out already, are ya?"

My eyes flutter open to see him smirking that panty-dropping smile from between my legs. Too late for that, Aiden, my panties are long gone.

"Get up here." My voice is hoarse from moaning but that just turns his smirk from flirty to self-satisfied.

"Shit, I don't have a condom. There might be some in the bathroom, give me a second." He goes to get up but I just wrap my legs around his hips, pulling him back to me.

"I have an IUD and I'm clean. Fuck your wife bare, cowboy." It's my turn to smirk.

"Fuck, Lyndsey, you're going to kill me, aren't you?" His hips grind down, his dick rubbing at where I'm still dripping wet from the magic he caused with his tongue. The way his eyes bore into mine connects us even more than the feeling of him inside of me.

"I'll wait until after you make me come again." I try to do what I usually do, flirt and deflect, but it's hard when I want to bask in the feelings forming between us.

He doesn't bother with words, Aiden just grips at the base of his dick before sliding it into me in one thrust. My walls stretch to accommodate him and even with how wet I am there is still a touch of pain. I knew he would make me feel good but I had no idea what I was missing out on by pushing him away. I could have been feeling this euphoria for weeks if I had been less stubborn. My eyes flutter closed at the feeling of being satisfyingly full.

"Eyes on me, darlin', or I stop." Aiden grabs my chin, staying stock-still inside of me until I snap my eyes open again. He must find what he was looking for in my green eyes because as soon as they meet his grey ones he starts to thrust. There are so many emotions on his face but the biggest is reverence. He is looking down at me like I'm something delicate to him. Like I'm precious.

He doesn't go fast, no, Aiden slides in and out as though he has all of the time in the world. His thrusts hit deep, a slow, steady, breathtaking rhythm that is made to make me crumble below him. I manage to keep my eyes on his even when each of his thrusts feel like they are in my chest, he is pushing that deep inside of me. My moans turn to whimpers, pleading for more, but Aiden keeps his pace, building me up slowly until it is too much to handle.

"I need faster, Aiden, please." My words are a whine in the hot air between us.

"So pretty when you give in to me, wife, you need faster?" He nudges his nose against mine, teasing me with the closeness of his lips.

When I nod, he finally picks up the pace and I almost scream. He pounds into me then, quick but still as deep, like he wants to get deeper than anyone else ever has. He is imprinting himself into my soul. He grunts next to my ear and the sound of him enjoying the feeling of my body against his adds to the building pressure. That and the feeling of his bare chest rubbing against mine as he lowers to my elbows beside my head. The friction against my nipples is other-worldly and with each thrust my moans come out more ragged until they are almost silent from pleasure.

"I can feel you squeezing me, Lynds, come for me. I know you need it," Aiden whispers against the shell of my ear, but every one of my senses are on overdrive as I climb higher and higher.

The feelings are different than I'm used to. My orgasms usually come quick and short, not this one. I can feel the first pulses in the walls wrapped around him until my legs are shaking so hard I worry I'm going to give Aiden bruises on his hips from how tight my legs are bound around him. I feel each one of my muscles freezing up, wanting to expand the experience. My lungs struggle to take a full gulp of air. Then it hits. Full force. I can feel every cell of my skin vibrate under his touch, I can see colours no human ever has.

Damn, I think I might astral project, I come so hard.

Aiden grinds his hips as far forward as he can, holding his dick as deep inside me as it will go. The pulses of my orgasm spur on his own. When he grunts out my name, I feel the warmth of his come spreading through me and it's the strangest and most erotic experience I have felt. The warmth of his skin and the heat of his come combine to heat me completely. We are both panting when he collapses next to me, so close we are almost still connected, but I still grimace when his sperm starts to leak out of me.

As soon as he notices my discomfort Aiden slips off the bed and into the bathroom, coming back a few seconds later with a wet cloth and a smirk.

We don't speak as he spreads my legs again, this time carefully cleaning up every drop until he is satisfied. He mumbles something about grabbing some water but by the time he has slipped on some underwear and left the bedroom I'm already half asleep. Sated, satisfied and tired as hell. We can talk tomorrow, I can't do anything but cuddle further into the blankets as I let the darkness of the night overtake me.

Chapter Twenty-One

Aiden

Blistering warmth. That's the first thing I feel when I blink my eyes open. Last night would feel like a dream if it wasn't for the hair tickling my nostril. Lyndsey's body is cloaked over mine. I smile to myself, burying my nose into the hair at the crown of her head.

When I came out of the shower last night, I just wanted to push her, to take a hammer to the wall she was building between us, but I never thought it would be the straw that broke the camel's back. I just thought it would lead to some teasing jabs and get the image of me barely clothed into Lyndsey's head.

I wanted to chip at the wall but somehow that one simple act of "forgetting" my clothes was a bulldozer. Now I get to deal with the aftermath, with Lyndsey using me like her own personal mattress, lying naked on top of me. God, it is a breathtaking sight. Her alabaster skin, painted with a myriad of freckles, glows in the early morning light.

Both of us were too worn out last night to bother drawing the blinds and I'm so thankful to my lazy self. Her strawberry-blond hair is wild, spread over my chest with some flyaways tickling at my nose and neck, fluttering with each one of my breaths. The only thing that would make this better would be seeing her green eyes looking up at me with hunger or satisfaction, anything except regret.

If when Lyndsey wakes up she regrets what happened between us I think my heart would stop. She can feel anxious, she can feel vulnerable, I don't care, as long as she lets me feel it with her. I can't fathom her shutting me out again.

For a second when I opened the bathroom door in nothing but a towel there was something on her face that almost made me stop the plan altogether. Until it melted away, leaving nothing but longing. That is how I want her to look at me forever. Like she doesn't just want me. Like she needs me.

I would stay in the bed forever, even with how hot I am under her. The steady thumping of her heart against my chest is one of my tethers to reality. If it wasn't for that, I feel like I might float away.

When people talked about being on cloud nine I never really understood what that meant. I just thought it was a way to say that they felt happy, but no, now I get it. Cloud nine is where you go when the woman you have been falling for, for over a year, starts to hold your hand on the descent. Lyndsey might not admit it but I know she is falling too, I could see it in her eyes last night. In the way she held my face in her hands like I'm precious.

Men don't get to feel that very often. Like we are allowed to be loved back unconditionally. We are told to be distant and strong but Lyndsey doesn't need my strength, she needs my honesty. My vulnerability. It is not something I'm used to giving people but for her I will, if it means I get to wake up with her in my arms for the rest of my life.

I hate that it took us almost a year to get to this place.

To my sisters it probably seems like Lyndsey and I happened in the blink of an eye, but for me, it came just when it needed to. I have wanted this woman in my bed for the best part of a year. I have wanted her in my heart for nearly as long. The girls have seen the way Lyndsey and I interact. Sharing looks over breakfast. But even the way she interacts with them has shown them the relationship we have. Lyndsey has supported us all.

There is nothing wrong with waiting and building a relationship, so that is what I tried to do. I showed up to help her lock up Bloom and Blossom when Ellis was on bed rest. I brought her coffee and asked her about her family. If I never got to have her the way I wanted then I would have been happy to be her friend.

Even though it was slowly killing me that she wouldn't let me show her how I felt, I took a back seat because of other people's opinions and the fear that I might not be what she wants. But now I know the truth. She wants this too, she just needed to see I would be there to catch her.

My early morning musings are interrupted by a shattering sound from downstairs followed by sudden commotion. And in that second, I'm hit with painful clarity.

He's gone.

Pops is gone.

I know it in my soul.

It is not just Lyndsey's head on my chest, now there is a weight there too. I need to get down there and hear the news from my sister's mouth but I don't want to leave this bed. I want to pause this moment forever. A happy memory of a morning cuddle with my wife, not what is going to be waiting for us. It has been just over a week since we got here and went to visit Pops. Alice was right, he had less time than I wanted to believe, but there are no regrets in my mind. I got to see him smile before he passed. He looked at me with pride, and even if that pride was because of my fake marriage it was still enough for me.

"Lynds, darlin', wake up." My words are muffled in her hair but I know she hears me when her body unfurls like a cat stretching in the sunlight.

"What's wrong?" she mumbles against the skin of my chest, and even with what I know is coming I take comfort in the fact she hasn't jumped out of my arms. I think if she had, my heart would have broken for the second time today.

"I think Pops has died." Straight to the point, that's the only way I know how to do it. It takes a second for the words to process for her but when they do she jolts up in the bed, letting the cover fall around us.

"What?" Her voice is still a whisper but there is no more sleep in it, now it is just quiet shock. Her hands fly to mine, holding them tightly, as though she is holding me together.

"Don't worry, we knew it was going to happen." I don't know for sure, but my heart knows he has gone. I can hear the girls' voices downstairs, I can't hear what they are saying but there is urgency in their tone. I do what I do best: I hold strong.

Lyndsey hadn't known my grandfather long but in the time we have been here she has developed a soft spot for everyone in my family. I know behind her solid exterior that she is soft and loving, I know she will feel the pain for all of us.

"Listen to me, Aiden." She pulls me up so we are both standing toe to toe. "No matter what happened last night or whatever happens between us, I'm here. Right now I'm here with you, by your side, okay? Lean on me."

"Lyndsey..." I want to but I can't. It isn't her job to look after me, that's what I'm good for. All I know how to do is support the people who are important to me, it's what makes me a good captain.

"Promise me, before we leave this room you have to promise me you won't hide away from this, at least not to me." She makes it sound so easy. So easy that I want to do it. She isn't asking for something impossible, she isn't asking me to put my emotions above everyone, she is just asking me to feel my emotions with her. My grief, my anger. She wants it all. I think I'll be able to give it to her.

"I promise."

"I've got you, cowboy." With that she rushes to throw some clothes on and I follow suit. We move around the bedroom in what looks like a practised dance. There is silence around us and I can feel the tension forming in my shoulders, but just when I ready myself to put on my mask, the one I wear every time I step on the ice, Lyndsey's hand slips into mine. "Let's go."

I nod and we leave the room together. Hand in hand.

Walking downstairs feels like my legs are tangled in treacle, with each step I can feel time slowing down. In theory I know what is going to meet me, even from here I can hear Celia crying, even if it was just an idea before I know I'm right but still I don't know what state I'm going to find my sisters in.

More than anything I'm grateful that I'm here at all. There is a real possibility that, if Pops hadn't sent me that letter, I might have put off coming home again like I did last year. When I worry about being seen as weak, I run and hide. But thanks to Pops and Lyndsey I'm going to be able to be there for my sisters, as long as I can make it down the stairs.

My eyes scan the open-plan living room as my bare feet hit the hardwood floor. The first thing my eyes settle on is my Cece sobbing on the floor in Alice's arms. My twin has our baby sister held tightly, stroking her hair as she silently cries herself. Beside them is a glass with spilled orange juice and Alice's mobile cracked on the floor.

At first, I don't see Eden. But when I walk completely into the room I find her pacing alone by the sofa. Her skin is almost grey with shock, I'm surprised she can even stand with how violently her body is shaking.

I can feel Lyndsey's hand on the bottom of my back guiding me further in even when an alarm goes off in my mind that there is nothing I can do to fix this. I can't bring him back, I can't defeat their grief. Before I can spiral down that road, Eden looks up and meets my gaze.

Without a moment's hesitation, she takes off in a run and jumps in my arms. Instantly she begins to sob against my shoulder. I hold her tight to me, absorbing her cries and screams.

There is a knot the size of Texas in my throat but I swallow my own tears down.

"Don't hold it." Lyndsey reaches up on her tiptoes to kiss my cheek, slowly stroking Eden's back as she meets my eyes.

Giving me some space, she moves to the kitchen to grab a broom to sweep up the fallen glass. Something about that small act of helpfulness in a tornado of emotion is what cracks me.

With Eden sheltered in my arms I let myself break. Tears fall, tears of grief for Pops. Tears of pain for my sisters. Tears of relief that he is no longer in pain even if it means we have to take that pain on for ourselves.

Alice lifts Cece to her feet and guides her over away from the shattered glass Lyndsey is cleaning and into my arms. One benefit of being an athlete is my arms are big enough to hold the three of my sisters. We cry together, held tight in each other's arms.

Alice's tears are silent but fierce when she meets my eye. We have never really had that twin telepathy but right now we do, I see in her eyes that she needs to know I'm going to be here. With a nod I tell her I'm going nowhere. I'll be here to be their rock while Lyndsey is mine, my rock, holding me steady in the storm of what is to come.

Chapter Twenty-Two

Lyndsey

Losing a loved one is never easy. Whether that loss comes from death, or people just growing apart. When the people who you love, the people who loved you, are no longer in your life it shows you who is truly there for you. When my parents kicked me out, I had no other family to rally behind me. Even in their grief the Anders siblings are incredibly lucky to have each other.

I would like to think they are grateful for me too. Since William died last week I have taken a background role in their lives. I'm like the technical team for a musical, I'm not centre stage but the work I have been doing has been endlessly important for them.

Cece is so young, she is only twenty, if I had suffered the amount of loss she has in such a short amount of time I don't know if I would have been able to keep it together. But she is. They all are. First their mom and dad died in one fell swoop. Then they lost their grandmother, though at least then they knew it was coming. Apparently, she had been sick for a while, it's part of why William wanted to go into a home when he did. He saw his wife deteriorate and didn't want his grandkids to have to watch that happen to him.

That would be enough grief to take any person under, becoming an orphan and only having one adult left to raise you just for him to die now too. The only bright side is that at least they are all together, they all know how they grieve and find a way to work around each other.

Alice has been taking walks with her camera every day, needing to see the beauty in the world. Eden and Cece have both done a whole lot of therapy over the years, their words not mine, so they know how to manage their grief. Aiden needs to feel needed. He is making every call and meeting with the funeral director, promising the girls they don't have to worry about anything. Then when our bedroom door closes each night I'm there to hold him together as he tries to release the pressure on his shoulders. We haven't had sex since *that* night. I haven't known how to act about it. Did it mean something? Were we both just struggling, desperately reaching out, and it was each other that we found on either end? We've exchanged a few touches, but I can't help but flinch. I would feel terrible if he felt like he needed to have sex with me to keep me around. He could never touch me again and I would happily lie here.

He doesn't cry or fight, he just lies there in my arms taking comfort in my presence until he is tired enough to rest and he can grieve no more for the night. When we do talk, it's about the funeral, whereas the girls want to tell me about their memories of William. Want to share the joy he brought them over the years.

I feel a deep soul connection to the four remaining Anders family members. That is why I have made the decision that, even when Aiden and I decide it is time for our divorce, I'm not going to run from the girls. Even if they hate me for leaving their brother, I swear to myself that I'm going to be a good person for them. I refuse to be another person they lose. Aiden included.

Aiden has had Cassie release a statement for him to the Spears fans, he wanted them not to worry about the fact he wasn't being seen around Seattle. I think he had got some questions online about if he was leaving the team and needed the guys he plays with to know he will be with them when the season starts. They've released a statement briefly saying that he is needed at home right now, and will be back in Seattle and on the ice as soon as he can.

That brought some good for me too. Whoever has been texting me has only sent one text since William's death. The day the statement was released I received one final text.

> I am not a monster. Give your 'husband' my condolences, you have one month to get me my money, say thank you for my generosity.

Good and bad news there. They are giving me a reprieve that I'm taking with both hands. One month to support Aiden and his sisters. However, I'm not free, they will be back. I have tried to convince myself that over the time they are giving me they will become bored but I haven't been successful. At least for the past week and a half since William passed, I haven't jumped every time a message comes through.

Aiden was shocked when I told him that the Spears guys have booked a flight to attend the funeral. I assumed he would know but when I told him Ellis was sorry she couldn't join them because of the kids, he was dumbstruck.

"The guys are coming?" He sounded like a kid, scared and hopeful all at once.

"And Coach Mitch and Cassie, they care about you, Aiden," I told him as we clamoured into bed one evening. The picture of any normal married couple.

"But they didn't know him," he said, looking up at me, eyes full of confusion. It tore me up inside that he doesn't know how much everyone loves him, when it's so clear to me. It riddles me with guilt once again. Shouldn't I want to stay married to a man like Aiden?

Sure, *like* Aiden. But it can't be Aiden.

We're from two different worlds, and he agrees on that much.

"They know you. You have always been there for them so just this once let them be there for you," I reassure him.

"I can do that." Not long after that he fell asleep.

Every night has been the same. During the day I do what I can to be useful. The first few days, my main job was cooking. Not that anybody was especially hungry but I made enough to keep them from starving. I batch cooked some pasta sauce and some chilli so there was extra to freeze. I thought that even when it's time to go back to Seattle there will be food for the girls if they still don't have the energy to cook.

I'd rather them have that and know there is food for them so Aiden can know they aren't starving or only eating junk food when we leave. Hopefully that will give him some comfort.

"Lyndsey, tell my idiot twin that we can't play 'My Way' by Frank Sinatra." Alice comes storming into the kitchen with Aiden hot on her heels. I get a flash at what they must have been like as kids, both so headstrong and unrelenting.

"I just don't get why not?" He flops into the chair next to me, throwing a notepad filled with scribbles onto the table in front of him.

"Because it's cliché and unoriginal! He deserves something better than that." Alice might have a point, but there's no way I'm going to take sides. Especially where my opinion doesn't really matter. They just need to find a way to a middle ground.

"Do you know what William and Lulu's wedding song was? That might be sweet." I keep my back to them, cutting vegetables and letting them mull it over between themselves.

"That... that sounds beautiful. Thank you, darlin'." Aiden tugs at my wrist, pulling me from the counter to sit on his lap. Kissing my temple. I try not to blush but I don't think I'm successful. It's hard to tell for a moment if it's a fake display of affection for our audience, or if it's genuine. For a moment, I almost slide into believing it's reality. I feel comfortable with him. *Almost*. Until I remember what we're here for.

"How about I take something off your plate?" I hedge. I want to do more. Aiden might be the Spears team captain, but he's always been the rogue. He's rough and ready on the ice, but off the ice... he tends to just be rough. Full of energised chaos and spontaneity. I suppose that's how we got into this mess. But as he grieves a hard loss, it seems a slither of Aiden isn't here. He's lost a spark.

And I must admit, I miss him.

"You are doing so much already, Lynds, we can do this. As long as he just lets me do what I want." Alice laughs from the other side of the table, laughing even harder when Aiden kicks her shin.

"Jesus, Alice." He rolls his eyes. Holding me tight to him, my side against his chest. My pulse raises. *It means nothing.* It has to.

"Look, let me do the flowers, I know my way around the stems and it means you can focus on helping with the programmes with Celia. Or the eulogy with Eden," I blurt out as a way of distraction from Aiden's touch.

When Aiden finally agreed to let the girls help, they picked something that was important to them – except Alice, who wanted to do the same as Aiden. Take over. Being the eldest but also a twin has its disadvantages.

"If you weren't married to my brother and I wasn't straight I'd try and steal you for myself." Alice reaches over the table, grabbing for my hand, pretending to pull my wedding ring off.

"He doesn't need to know," I whisper-yell, making her laugh again. Hearing her laugh makes me smile, it shows me that me being here must be helping at least a little.

"I heard that!" Aiden's fingers dig into my sides, tickling me until I jump from his lap before escaping back to the vegetables I was preparing.

—

Sitting on the porch swing drowned by a soft blanket, sleep eludes me tonight, but out here on the porch swing under the night sky with only the cicadas for company it feels more like a dream than any other real thing I have experienced. It has been nearly two weeks since William's death and each day brings its highs and lows.

There is fleeting laughter and I have never seen love like that which these siblings share. It gives me hope that if I have kids some day they will love each other; not every sibling relationship is doomed the way mine and Peter's was. There have been lows, of course. Silent tears and short tempers from time to time. Four people all grieving under one roof is bound to bring some disagreements. Aiden wants to plan everything for the funeral but the girls are starting to push back, they want to be a part of it but he is having a hard time letting go of the reins.

Aiden is scared that if he lets them take some of the weight it would be his fault if they can't handle it. They can though. One day I hope I'm half as strong as any one of those women.

Creaking coming from the front door opening startles me out of the quiet reprieve of the night, but as I turn to see who has caused the disturbance I find there's no way to be disappointed at the scene that meets my eye. Aiden, stood in the doorway, clearly shocked that he woke up in bed alone. Pyjamas and mismatched socks bring a smile to my face that makes Aiden smile too. His bright eyes light up the darkness and I can tell by the glint in his eye that he is no longer worried that he has interrupted me. If it means I can see him smile like that I will be happy to let him disturb my peace any time he wants.

"Having trouble sleeping?" I ask lightly, as though if I speak any louder it would break the spell that we are enjoying together.

"Seems I'm not the only one." He nods, slowly walking towards the porch swing. Silently I lift one side of the spare blanket I found in the sitting room as an invitation to him to join me inside my cocoon. Cicadas fade into the background as he takes his rightful place next to me, it is as though we are the only people left in the world, which I admit would not be the worst thing I could imagine.

Alone time with Aiden could never be a waste. Plus if we were the only people in the world that would mean there would be no people for us to lose, or people there to try and blackmail me.

For a while we sit there in comfortable silence enjoying the darkness and the company of someone whose affection we can feel without feeling like we have to utter a word. Even if I knew what I wanted to say, I'm not ready to admit the pain that comes with being his *fake* wife. I hate that, once the funeral passes next week, he might be ready to write me out of his life.

It could be five minutes or five hours before I break the silence.

"I thought fresh air was supposed to make you sleepy but somehow I've never felt so awake." The truth is that I had lain in bed beside him tossing and turning but I could not find rest as thoughts of my growing feelings for the man next to me raced through my mind.

"All this fresh air is giving me a headache," Aiden chuckles. "I guess I'm too used to the pollution and noises that the quiet freshness feels odd after all this time."

Speaking in hushed tones which, if I was asked about later, I would say was because I didn't want to wake the girls inside the house, though really it's because this moment of privacy, just the two of us, feels special and undisturbed and neither of us wants to be the one who ruins it, I tell him, "Here, lay your head down on my lap so I can help get rid of that headache." Eyebrows raise at that. Sensing the turmoil in his eyes I nod to him and drop my eyes to my lap in an invitation that he can't turn down, even if he tries.

Shifting his weight so as to not rock the porch swing, Aiden lightly places his head on my thighs, clearly confused as to how I'm planning to help him. Basking in the way his stormy eyes look at me, as though I'm the only person who can bring him comfort, I forget for a moment that I have a task at hand, until he smiles up at me as though he is being blessed by the angels. After another beat I delicately place my hands in Aiden's blond hair, starting at the front and pushing his hair back as I go. A light smile settles on his lips and his eyes drift close at my continued contact. Applying slight pressure onto his skull, I hope it will make some difference to his headache. I hate seeing Aiden in pain and honestly I would do anything I could to ease him no matter where we stand with each other.

Bringing my hands back towards the front of his head I use my nails to scratch at his hair, making him shiver and hum in appreciation. Knowing that I'm helping him spurs me on and gives me a confidence I was not sure I would ever have with this man. In a split second, before I can even comprehend my own decision, I'm leaving a feather-light kiss on his lips. Immediately I expect an adverse reaction: for Aiden to sit up and storm back inside or for him to tell me off for making advances on him when he is struggling.

Aiden doesn't even open his eyes.

Heart thumping in my chest, I consider maybe I didn't actually even kiss him, maybe I just imagined the whole thing. But that can't be the case, which I'm clued in to by the red tint that is currently rising up from Aiden's neck, making his ears burn. Still he doesn't move, maybe hoping I might believe that he is really asleep and I'm praying to a God that I do not believe in that if he stays as still as he can that maybe he will let me do it again, maybe he will let me do it forever.

"I know you're awake," I say into the night air.

"Are you sure? Because I'm pretty sure I must be dreaming of you again, darlin'," he replies without pause as his arms wrap around my waist and his face nudges slightly against my stomach. Head falling back in a light laughter, I resume the ministrations on his head. The moment has been addressed and yet I really don't know where that leaves us as I drift off into a contented sleep surrounded by the smell of Aiden and the Texas air.

Chapter Twenty-Three

Aiden

Nobody would ever describe a funeral as a fun time. At least not a classic Catholic funeral ceremony anyway. We cut a lot of the religious text because Pops was never really a churchgoer, the only reason we are having it in a church to begin with is because he wanted to be buried next to his Lulu.

I've been to my share of funerals but until today I haven't had people there just for me. Funerals are for closure for the living more than for the dead so having people there to support me while I grasp for that closure means more than I'd ever have thought.

The last funeral I attended was my grandma's and I didn't have any friends there; the people I had at college were too busy with their new graduated lives and everyone else from my hockey team had moved on to bigger and better things. I didn't blame them for not coming, but that doesn't mean it didn't suck. I rely on my teammates and friends more than they know.

When Lyndsey told me the Spears were coming to Texas, I thought some of them would back out before the day, that they would make some excuse and only Liam and Coach Mitch would make it. I was very wrong.

They all stream in wearing their best suits. They look like a shitty impersonation of the Mafia, and the image has got my first smile of the day. One by one they come to give me their condolences, some even pulling me into hugs. Next to me Lyndsey is hugged and checked on and at that moment I don't know why I doubted them. Each one of these men have some of the biggest hearts, I have just been too scared to admit that it would matter to me that they were here.

"Anders, I'm sorry. Edge said that's all I'm allowed to say so I don't fuck up." Rook hugs me without hesitation, whispering that last bit just to me. Make that the second smile of the day. Edge is behind Rook and glares at him, knowing that the kid would never just do what he is told.

"You good?" Jay 'Edge' Brink is a man of few words but I can see in his eyes if I told him I needed something he would make it happen, even if it meant helping me run away from my grief.

"I will be," I say as Lyndsey slides under my arm, smiling up at him.

"How's our god-daughter?" she asks him.

"I've turned her against you," he deadpans.

"I'm sure you've tried. I'm also sure you failed." She winks. Ignoring that, he pulls her to him and kisses the crown of her head lightly. If it were anyone else jealousy would strike through me. Fake or not, she is my wife after all. But with him, it doesn't. We all know he doesn't have eyes for Lyndsey. His eyes are busy elsewhere – it's hard to not notice. Speak of the devil, Cassie comes up behind him, hugging Lyndsey first before coming for me.

"Need anything from me?" she asks, straight to the point. She and Edge are the straightest shooters I know. It's probably a good thing they have never dated, they might kill each other.

"I'm good, Cas. Thanks for coming."

"I wouldn't miss it." She moves along the line hugging my sisters too. She and Alice talk for a little while which is strange, they seem to know each other, but then I'm sure Cassie could pull anyone to reveal their secrets with only a few minutes.

The Seattle Spears have been there for a lot of highs. Our wins, relationships, weddings – but from memory this is our first funeral. God, I'm thankful for them. I didn't realise until I watched each person I work with step up to support me and my sisters. Pops might have been the last member of my family except my sisters, but even with the loss, my family is so much bigger than I realised.

Chapter Twenty-Four

Aiden

I never appreciated this porch when I was young. Kids never notice the beauty around them until it is too late. By the time I realised how beautiful my childhood home was I had already moved to Seattle, I traded open fields and glowing sunsets for a built-up city covered in rain and smog. I make sure to take time to look at this beauty whenever I'm home, though I wish now that I came home more often.

We have all been sharing stories about Pops and, sure, there are ones we all remember but the girls have so many more that I have missed out on because I ran away. I was so desperate to make being a professional athlete worth the sacrifices that I stopped showing up. I missed Celia's high school graduation, for God's sake. She is my baby sister and I was too busy. They don't hold it against me, but I do. I wish I could clone myself, have one of me here all the time, sat here on this porch swing so I never miss something important again. While other me goes back to Seattle and brings home the Stanley Cup.

If I did that though, I would have to clone Lyndsey too, because there is no way I could not have her around. She can be here, be my soft landing when everything feels out of my control, and then she can be in Seattle with me because I can't imagine going back without her. It feels like she fills all of the cracks I didn't know I had. She is the string pulling the broken parts of me back together. When I feel lacking she is there telling me all the good I have done. When I think about how much I missed she reminds me that I was here when they needed me most.

My job is to be a raft. I hold my team up so they can win. I hold my sisters when they cry. I fight against choppy waters so nobody else has to face the danger. I know the words the public associates with me. *Womaniser. Loose cannon.* Those days need to be behind me. If I can't do that, if I crumble, I'll pull everyone under with me. That is my biggest fear. I admitted it to Lyndsey last night as she lay with her head on my chest. Spoke the words for the first time.

"If I break, I can't keep them safe." The words drifted away in the late-night air.

At first Lyndsey didn't say a word. She shifted so her chin rested on my chest, looking up at me with so much warmth my heart spluttered inside. "Who keeps you safe?" she asked.

"What?"

"You can't expect to be the rock for everyone you know, all that weight will drown you." Her words were soft but the impact was a force against all of the walls around my heart.

"I don't know how to do anything else." I spoke around a lump in my throat, threatening to break me.

"Share the weight, I can take it."

She has proven that time and again since Pops' death. I'm just so worried that if I give her the weight, it will be what pushes her away. What pushes her to a divorce lawyer when we touch down next week.

Supporting me would be one thing, but she hasn't just done that, she has stepped up for my sisters. Even though I told her they would love her, there was a small part of me that thought they would ice her out, especially Alice. Then when Alice saw through my lies before the end of day one, I was sure she would tell Eden and Cece, but she didn't. She accepted Lyndsey – hell, she told me to make her my wife for real. I can't begin to explain how much it means that they want her around.

At every turn Lyndsey has stepped in to help. Whether it was the funeral flowers or silently cleaning so we didn't have to. She was the raft, she was the person keeping us on the path to grieving. She didn't give us anywhere to hide. It would have been easy to push the grieving aside, to busy myself with housework with the excuse I didn't want the girls to have to do it but she didn't let me. By being here Lyndsey forced me to grieve, forced me to face the fears that I'm not enough, and I'll be forever grateful.

A million thank yous will never be enough. There will never be enough kisses or bouquets of flowers that could articulate how important Lyndsey has been to me. I'm going to find a way. That is why I'm sat on the porch swing while the girls watch some cheese-filled romcom in the TV room. They have popcorn and the works, for a perfect movie night. I was kicked out, no boys allowed apparently. I could have gone into town, maybe gone to the rink to get some practice in, but I just couldn't. The thought of being half an hour away from Lyndsey was too far.

I feel pathetic, we aren't even a real married couple. Not the way Pops and Lulu were. For Lyndsey, she only has to be married to me for a few more weeks, but the thought of letting this all go feels wrong. As the time draws nearer to go back home, the dread sinks in deeper.

She was right when she said it was going to be complicated. If she demands the divorce, then I'll agree. It was always the understanding we had. But the idea of having to be around her afterwards is hard. I'll have to see her laugh with Ellis, spar with Edge and play with Charlotte without being able to act how I truly want with her. How am I supposed to heal my heart when she is going to be right there every step of the way? Shit, if she really wants the divorce it has crossed my mind that I might have to trade to a different team.

I would rather leave Seattle altogether, leave the team I love and the guys I respect than have my heart shatter watching her move on from me. Maybe if I find a way to thank her enough I can show her how important she is to me, how much I care about her. I just don't know how. Words aren't my forte, sport is my forte, sweat and pushing men against the boards is my forte. I wish I had my mom at times like this. She would know what to do, parents always do.

As a kid I would watch her with awe, the way she could raise us basically alone with a smile on her face. Lyndsey reminds me of my mom sometimes, not the way they look but the way their hearts are plastered on their sleeves. Even though it must have killed Mom, raising three kids, pregnant with a fourth while my dad was across the world, she never complained. She didn't yell at him or beg him to come home, she was a lighthouse, strong and steady on the edge of a choppy sea, bright and safe to welcome him home when his tours ended.

That's when it hits me.

Letters.

If they were good enough for Mom and Dad maybe they will be good enough for Lyndsey. I might take a few drafts, thank the lucky stars that the film is only just starting. Darting back into the house, I jog up the stairs like lightning, pulling sheets of paper from Cece's notebooks – I'll buy her a new one if I run through this one. It needs to be perfect, just like the woman I'm writing it for.

—

I was right, I needed nearly the whole notepad. Who knew spelling was so hard when you don't have autocorrect? It has been a long time since I wrote more than a few words down on paper – technology will be our downfall and all that nonsense. But it was worth it, as I look down at my chicken-scratch handwriting I'm proud and anxious in equal measure. Proud that I found the words, that I know I got out everything I wanted to. Anxious at the thought of giving it to her. It could be too much. I'm giving her physical proof of how much she owns me. If she doesn't feel the same, if she isn't ready to let me in, this might all have been for nothing.

> *Hey Darlin'*
>
> *Mom's letter has been on my mind all day. I remember her writing them, the joy on her face. The release it would give her to get her feeling onto the page. I need that release. You have shown me that I deserve relief and peace. So I want to thank you.*
>
> *Lyndsey Stone (Anders), I'm endlessly grateful for you. You have done more than I ever deserve*

and I don't think you have any idea how much you have stepped up.

You stayed married to me. This could have been over a long time ago for you. I know you had your own reasons for staying in this with me, but I know deep down you could have tucked and run at any time. Told me to shove my problems up my ass. But you are too kind for that. I saw in your eyes, when I told you about the will that first time, I could see the outrage you felt on my behalf. You were ready to burn the world to help me get Dad's belongings. You didn't have to do it. Yet you did. For me.

When you met my sisters, you could have kept them out. It probably would have been easy to keep a wall between you and them, claimed you were shy. Instead you got to know them. Each of them. You made room in your heart for them and I can see how much you care about them. They might not be your blood but you have made them your sisters.

When Pops died you could have left. He was not your family, you hardly knew the man and funerals suck for everyone. But you not only stayed, you helped. You gave me perspective when tensions got high, you ran around for us so we could focus on supporting each other. The flowers are something we would have let fall to the wayside but because of you they were a beautiful tribute to him.

Then there's me. When I could so easily have shut down and used planning the funeral or helping the girls to hide from myself you made me face it. You have given me room to feel my emotions without judgement. You can tease me but I know you want me to be happy. And you make me happy. Each night when I hold you in my arms, I feel invincible, like as long as you are by my side I'll be able to overcome whatever life might throw at us.

Because that's the truth, Lyndsey, you have been here for me and I will do the same for you. Even when you are no longer my wife I want to be the person you can lean on. It would be my honour to hold your hand when you need someone by your side. I cannot think of a better way to thank you than to prove to you that I'm going to be there.

I see you, Lyndsey, see the mask you hide behind because you fear no one will stay if they see you, but it's not true. I'll stay. Ellis will stay. The Spears showed up for me last week but they were here for you too because I might be their captain but they would follow you to war. I know you aren't comfortable talking in detail about everything that happened with your family. One day I hope you trust me enough to lean on me completely because I'm your family now. I'll see you and stay because every person who meets you is pulled into your orbit.

There is nowhere else I would rather be.

Thank you, my darlin', the words will never be enough but for now it is all I have.

Always, Your Cowboy.

By the time the letter is finished, the film has ended and Lyndsey has jumped in the shower. I was lucky that she was so tired that she didn't ask questions about what I was doing. As much as I have revealed myself in that letter I'm still a coward. I don't think I have the strength to sit in the same room as her while she reads it. Plus I think it will take the pressure off of her to be able to read it in her own time without worrying about giving me a reaction.

I leave the letter folded with her name written on the side against her pillow before I escape back out to the porch swing. Celia is reading on the sofa when I walk past and seeing her so relaxed is a balm to my soul. She has taken Pops' death hard, losing the only parental figure in her life threw her. She is the baby, I think it is a reminder of everything she has lost. Taking a quick detour, I lean over the back of the couch, placing a light kiss on the crown of her head, making her smile at me.

"If Lynds is looking for me, I'm just gettin' some air."

"Sure thing, you good?" She drops the book to her chest, tipping her head over the cushion to meet my eyes.

"I'm good, Cece. I love you, you know that, right?" I'll make sure the people I care about know it. I need to tell them more often. Especially before Lyndsey and I go back home.

"Love you right back," she says, shooing me away so she can get back to her book.

I pace outside joined only by the sound of cicadas and the hum of birds overhead. I love this porch so I shouldn't pace a hole in the wood but I can't imagine staying still. My blood feels electric pumping through my heart, it beats so fiercely that I can hear my blood in my ears. Every single creak I hear I think might be Lyndsey coming to find me and every time it is the sound of the old house settling.

I probably stand out here for five minutes and not the five hours it feels like until eventually the front door opens.

Chapter Twenty-Five

Lyndsey

I feel really at peace here. Settled on the old sofa next to Celia with a big bowl of popcorn between us. On the other sofa Alice and Eden match us with their own overflowing bowl of snacks. We took so long to pick what we were going to watch for our girls' night that by the time we pressed play on the Nineties romcom the popcorn was already half eaten.

Aiden has been sent up to his room on a no-boys-allowed basis, he acted offended but I know he has been desperate for some time to himself. Going from living alone to being in a house with four women, most of whom are grieving, is a lot. I have no idea what he is doing up there but I'm enjoying my time enough not to care. We will still get time together when we slip under the covers. That is our time to be uninterrupted and I spend most hours thinking about when I get to feel his warm skin against mine, the way his arms wrap around me.

"This is so unrealistic!" Alice exclaims after a while. Her sisters groan and Eden goes as far as to throw a handful of popcorn at her.

"Here we go again…" Eden rolls her eyes and Cece laughs but when Eden sees the confusion on my face she explains, "She thinks every romance is unrealistic, she can never just enjoy something."

"Well, it is! Fake dating to make your ex jealous just to end up falling in love with the fake boyfriend, I mean, come on! In what world?" She throws her head against the cushion in exasperation, making us all laugh. Though my laughter is a little more forced. She just hit the nail on the head with my and Aiden's relationship and she doesn't even know.

I'm falling for Aiden. Before I knew him, I had a crush on him. When I met him, I was falling for him, just to be put back on the shelf when he got bored, and now I'm married to him, living in his childhood home, laughing with his sisters, and I know my feelings for him are growing deeper day by day. Still, I can't drown out the sound of the voice in my head reminding me that he is a sweet-talker. He knows the right things to say but I can't believe him because who knows how many women he has said them to in the past?

We are supposed to be getting divorced and I have to remember that when we are back in Seattle, he will drop the whole falling-in-love act and go back to the way things were.

As the credits start to roll on the film, I realise I have been in my own head for so long that I missed the ending. What brings me back to the present is my phone vibrating on my lap. Instantly I'm on edge. My heart thunders in my chest, dreading what is coming next. I thought whoever sent the damn texts was giving me time. They said two weeks and it has only been one, I shouldn't have expected them to play fair.

That's my fault, getting comfortable here. With these people. Thinking I would get to enjoy some time as

Aiden's wife in the Texas sunshine without the threats looming over me. My hands start to shake and sweat so badly that I can barely pick the phone up. I don't want to look at this in front of the girls, I haven't even thought about how I'm going to get the money. I thought I had time.

Jumping up from the couch I stumble over to the stairs, leaving the girls calling after me asking if I'm okay. I yell back that I'm fine before running to the bedroom. Aiden went out on to the porch earlier on so luckily the room is empty for my impending breakdown. Trying to control my breathing, I click open my phone, preparing for the worst.

> Hey Lynds how are the Anders doing? Any ETA on your homecoming. Thinking about you, Cas.

My knees nearly buckle in relief. It was Cassie, just Cassie. Asking after us all. I'm still so keyed up that my hands still shake as I type out a reply letting her know our flight is next week. My knees still knocking, I stumble into the bathroom, resting my weight on the sink. The woman looking back at me in the mirror looks tired. My red hair looks dull and even with the tan I'm developing here I still seem white as a sheet.

Between the sweat still damp on my back and the sick feeling lingering around the edges of my mind I feel dirty all over. Turning away from my reflection I switch on the shower and strip off my clothes. Once the water has warmed, I slip under the stream trying to calm my mind.

Even though I know the text was from a friend and not a foe I still can't shake off the feelings of guilt.

The guilt from not telling Aiden what is happening, guilt from running from the girls. Running from my problems. I just can't put more on their plates, especially not now. They are still grieving their loss and I won't make this all about me. I just need to wait out the clock and then I can get a loan to pay off whoever this is. Or maybe once news of our divorce hits the papers they will leave me alone. They are only doing this because of my marriage and that will be over soon.

Plus there isn't exactly anything Aiden can do. He can't fight some troll on the other end of my phone. Aiden would probably offer to pay them off but even when I think about getting a loan something feels wrong about it. I don't want them to get away with this, never mind get away with a bunch of money on top.

Eventually, I turn off the water and wrap a big fluffy towel around my body. I peek through the crack in the bathroom door to see that the room is still empty, Aiden nowhere in sight. I throw on a pair of leggings and an oversized T-shirt, squeezing the water out of my hair. Only then do I notice the note on my pillow. Aiden's handwriting stares back at me.

Snatching the letter up I unfurl it to find the most beautiful letter I could ever imagine. The words wrap around my heart, warming me from the inside out. The vulnerability in his words, the way he is using his mom's letter as his own to tell me how thankful he is for me, makes my heart thunder for a completely new reason. He might be a playboy but I doubt he has ever done something like this before. It feels too raw.

I can see so much of him in the words, he sees me in a way nobody else ever has. Not even Kayla or Mel saw me in the way he does. Like I'm worth something to him, more than just a fake wife and a way to fool his family.

Without taking a second to ponder what I should do, I take off out of the room and towards the front porch. Not bothering to slip on any shoes I swing open the front door. Aiden spins on his heels, looking at me with wide, expectant eyes. I fly towards him, jumping into his arms, curling my legs around his waist before I kiss him.

I kiss him with all of my gratitude.

I kiss him with all of my anxiety.

I kiss him with all of the feelings I have for him that have been bubbling under the surface.

We don't talk, there is no time because every time either of us tries to pull away the other chases their lips again. I kiss him until my lips are numb and, even then, I groan at the loss of contact.

Finally giving in to the need to breathe, I slide down his body, putting my feet back on solid ground, even though I still feel like I'm in the clouds. Words just seem unworthy of what is happening between us so we keep the silence. I wrap my hand around his, pulling us back through the house and upstairs to our bedroom.

We come together slower than before. I want to enjoy this, every inch of my skin is his tonight. My hands slip under his T-shirt and I try to whip it off for him, feeling like if I don't feel his skin against mine soon, I'll lose my nerve. Sensing my need, Aiden answers my prayers, lifting his own top off, revealing his bare tattooed skin to me.

He picks me up then, holding me close as he bends us over to lie on the bed. I pull back slightly, just enough to bring my hands between us to pull down his jeans.

Before he has spent time warming me up, but when he goes to fall to his knees at the foot of the bed, I pull him up instead. "I need you now, Aid, please."

"I'm here," he whispers against the skin of my neck as he settles his hips over mine. He brings fingers to my centre to see how wet I am. Even if I rushed him there is no way he would hurt me.

When he finds that I'm soaked and ready for him he groans, and my breath shutters in my chest. He takes my hips in his hands, flipping me over onto my knees. I gasp but still I don't hesitate to drop my weight down onto my forearms on the mattress. I sway my ass in front of him. Pulling my hips back, he uses one hand to notch himself at my centre before pushing in to the hilt.

"Aiden. Fuck," I moan, and when I meet his eyes over my shoulder again, I know he is mine.

Even if just for now. There is no way that I'll be able to let him go when we go home, I need to be his wife because I feel like he could really be my husband. If he feels the way I do right now and he isn't clouded by lingering grief then there could be something real here.

I'm a master at hiding behind walls. Walls he is trying everything he can to break through. As I moan louder his fingers sink into my red hair, I can feel myself tightening around him, bringing me closer to the edge with each thrust. Together we snap, our voices reaching a crescendo of moans that almost echo around the old house. Pulling out of me with a hiss he doesn't bother getting up; instead, he rolls us over so he is on his back and my head is resting on his chest.

I wonder what it would be like to have this every night. The man I'm falling for in my arms with nothing to worry about except what we will do tomorrow. I push away all my fears and anxieties about my texting terror and push my face further into Aiden's chest. I want to open up to him, the way he did to me in that letter, but there is still so much he doesn't know about me. It feels wrong to tell him I might love him when he only knows the parts of me I have wanted him to see.

It might be selfish to hope he keeps trying to get through my walls. I want him to know every part of me, I just need to find the courage to face him. The same courage he showed me.

Chapter Twenty-Six

Lyndsey

I could feel that last night was different. I saw the shift in Aiden's eyes before I got onto my knees for him but I chose not to comment on it. What could I say? I think he is falling for me but he doesn't fully know who he is married to. There is so much he doesn't know. Crazy texts aside, I have avoided telling him about my family. They are why I know he can't love me. If the people who are supposed to love me unconditionally find conditions and boundaries then he will too. In fairness, they pushed me away for being queer, and Aiden already knows that, but what does it tell him if even my parents see me as unloveable?

I could chalk it up to his grief. He is still overwhelmed by emotion and is clinging to the idea of a happy marriage. I don't know what a happy marriage even looks like. If I asked my mom she would tell me that she loves Dad and he loves her and maybe he does but he doesn't respect her. Aiden respects me, I can see the difference. My mom is the scapegoat in my childhood home. If anything goes wrong it is because she isn't working hard enough. If dinner is cold because Dad came home late then she should have known he would be busy and accounted for it. If he didn't get a good sleep it is because she bought a cheap mattress.

When I came out to them, he blamed her for sending me to school and letting them indoctrinate me.

I know that he is full of shit. That isn't love. Aiden doesn't treat me like that. He sees me as an equal even though we both know I'm not. He is superior in every way. He makes more money, he has more friends, he has a loving family.

I'm glad he didn't say the words. That he loves me. If he did he could make me believe it. It would just hurt all the more when he realises that I'm lacking. I can't cook for him when he comes home from a game and I turned all my white shirts pink with a red bra. I'm good at supporting him here. Supporting him emotionally. But when it comes down to the little things, the things that keep couples happy for decades, I'm not the cream of the crop.

We are lying together in bed now. Aiden is scrolling through his emails as my mind cycles through every eventuality that could come when we get back to Seattle. We only have a few more days here and even though I'm tucked against his side I can feel myself creating distance. Knowing I won't survive when he realises how much better he can do.

My phone buzzes beside me, pulling me from my thoughts. Absent-mindedly, I reach out to the nightstand, not rolling out of Aiden's embrace. When I see the message, I wish I had.

> You have seven days. I have been generous enough. Get me $10,000 or I tell the world the gold digger you really are. A fraud. What will your little husband think of you when the whole world sees you for the whore you are?

Bile rises in my throat and I jump out of the bed, ignoring the dizziness coming over me. Throwing open the bathroom door, I fall to my knees, hunching over the toilet as I wretch. It is still early morning so there is no food to throw up, instead bile burns and my abs clench over and over. Aiden comes up behind me and lifts my hair off the back of my neck, holding it for me while using his other hand to stroke down my back.

"Darlin', are you okay?" he asks, clearly concerned, and I don't know what to say to soothe him. Instead I just hum. Hoping he will think it was something I ate.

"Um-hum."

"I'll go get you some water. Why don't you jump in the shower?" he offers after the retching stops.

I slump against the rim of the toilet, but as soon as he is out of sight I throw my clothes off and jump in the shower, not even giving any time for the water to warm up. This is an older house and it can take a while for the water to get to heat but right now I don't care. I just need to be under the stream. I need the water to hide my tears.

Once they start, I don't think I'll be able to stop them. Tears stream down my face but as hard as I try to swallow my sobs they burst out anyway. I wanted to use the sounds of the shower, the anonymity of the curtain, to hide from Aiden, but to do that I need to be quieter. The harder I try, the harder it is to breathe.

"Darlin'?" I'm trying so hard to catch my breath that I must have missed him coming back in. Another sob slips past and I whimper as the curtain slides back. At the sight of my arms wrapped around my body and tears streaking my cheeks he gasps, "Lyndsey!"

"I'm sorry." I struggle to catch a full breath and I can't look him in the eyes, but the sound of my voice pushes him into action. Not bothering to strip, he steps into the shower with me, pulling my wet body against his chest.

"Shhh, you're okay. It's going to be okay," he says, a mantra against the crown of my head, but it doesn't calm my raging mind. My chest is still heaving and his shirt is soaked by both the shower and my tears. He holds me so tight I'm not sure where he starts and I stop.

"I ruin everything. Everything I touch." My voice is stuttered but he continues to soothe me.

"No you don't, you're okay," he says. Instead of fighting him I just let the water fall around us.

As my sobs slow I start to hiccup. No matter what happens I have found happiness this month. I have found a home in his arms. When he hears what has been happening, this is all going to be thrown away. I'm too much work to be worth all of this. I come with a damn stalker or blackmailer, whatever the hell they are. I won't ask him for the money though, because he would probably give it to me. He will try to fix this for me but I can't let him. I will not let him throw his money at some faceless entity to make my life easier. Not when I am making both of our lives easier by letting him divorce me. He only needs to distance himself and they will have nothing to ask for. I don't have $10,000 and without him they can't try to push it.

That settles it.

I have to tell him everything.

Even if it is going to hurt.

"What's going on?" Aiden asks as he guides me out of the water stream. Wrapping a fluffy towel around my body, he doesn't pull away from me. He uses an arm over my shoulder to guide me back into the bedroom and over to the bed. Instead of getting dressed, he sits down beside me, still dripping wet.

"Someone is threatening me. And you." Now that I have my breath the words come out more clearly but I can still see the confusion on his face.

"What?" His eyebrows furrow and he takes both of my hands in his, warming them from where they are chilled from the cold water.

"Since we got married, they want money." I wish I could drop my head into my hands but he keeps tight hold of me. My truth makes his brows drop further somehow, as though my words don't make sense to him.

"Why didn't you tell me?" he asks, offended. I can hear it but I know my reasons are solid. He had too much going on. His damn grandfather just died and he expects that I would pile on top of that? Never. It was the right thing.

"I thought I could handle it. You had enough to deal with." My eyes sting as tears come again. This time it is a release. Everything I have held in, every worry pours out of me. Instead of arguing about what I did, Aiden pulls me tight to him.

"I've got you. Shh, I've got you," he tells me. Standing, he brings me with him.

Unwrapping the towel from around me he uses it to dry me off. After using it to squeeze the excess water from my hair he discards it and leaves me standing naked in the middle of his bedroom for a second. Just as quick as he left he is back with a pair of his sweats and a Spears jumper. Dropping to his knees in front of me, he helps me step into some underwear and then the pants. Next, he lifts my arms over my head to pull the sweater over me, skipping a bra. Silently he turns and strips out of his still wet clothes. Together we crawl back into the bed where he wraps me in his arms and the blankets, knowing I need the comfort. We don't talk, though I swear if I listen hard enough I can hear his thoughts.

Too tired to argue I let my eyes drift close as he holds me. I'm suddenly exhausted from the stress of the morning and even though we should probably eat we just lie there together instead. I let him be my rock, knowing he is good at being that support. I have seen him do it for others and now it is time to let him do it for me.

Chapter Twenty-Seven

Aiden

I can't settle. I wish I did have a private jet for this journey because everyone on board keeps eyeing me out of their peripherals. I understand why. I look like a man on the edge. That's because I'm on the edge. My knee is bouncing non-stop and Lyndsey keeps looking at me with her big, sad eyes. It just makes it worse. For weeks I have dragged her through my family drama, forced her to pretend to love me and attend a fucking funeral, and the whole time she has been suffering. Without feeling like she could tell me.

That's what hurts the most. The fact she didn't share with me. I have opened up to her so much and still she doesn't trust me. Hell, she only told me when it got so bad she physically couldn't hold it in any more. I have been so wrapped up in my own problems that I didn't see. I've spent weeks with this woman. Every night alone with her. And someone was threatening her the entire time. While she was under my roof.

My fingernails are worn down from biting. I haven't bitten them this bad since the week of my parents' funeral. I thought I had grown out of this but, clearly, I just haven't had a situation hit me hard enough to trigger it again until now.

"I'm so sorry." Lyndsey's voice cuts through the tension. We are sitting beside each other but we feel hundreds of miles apart. I want to reach out my hand and hold hers but I don't, instead I ball my fists on my knees.

"Stop apologising," I tell her for the hundredth time since yesterday. We rescheduled our journey home and are now sitting on an earlier flight than expected. We needed to be back in Seattle to fix this. Lyndsey has apologised over and over no matter how much I tell her to stop. My clear distress is weighing on her.

"I don't want you to hate me." She sighs. This time I don't hold myself back, I reach my hands out until my palms frame her face.

"Hate you?" I shake my head, needing her to understand. "I'm not mad at you, I'm pissed at myself."

"Well, you should be mad at me, it's my damn fault." As she speaks, she pulls her face out of my hands. I want to pull her closer but I let her have some space. I can only tell her so many times that she is wrong until she believes me. Or at least I hope she will eventually believe me.

"No." My voice is strong. It is the thing I feel most certain about. There are a hundred anxieties in my mind but the one thing I know is that Lyndsey does not deserve this.

"Aiden," she tries to interrupt, probably to apologise again, but I don't let her.

"No, Lyndsey, you did nothing wrong. But I'm going to make it right, I swear." And I mean it. I'll do everything in my power to make this go away. I offered to just pay them the money, but Lyndsey would hear none of it. I guess she is right. If we give in to them then it will encourage them to do this again.

How could I not see her struggle? I noticed her anxiety around her phone, but I thought she was just reading hate comments from our wedding announcement, which is why I did my best to reassure her otherwise. How egotistical of me. I'm so famous that everything must be about *me* apparently. I was so self-focused that it never crossed my mind that she could be really suffering silently.

I should have learned from Liam and Ellis: he tried to keep her out of the limelight and that only ended with her crazy ex confronting them in public. Cassie is going to kill me. I'm going to need her expertise here, because if I try to do this myself, I'll probably make it worse.

As soon as the plane touches the tarmac, I'm already calling Cassie.

"Cassie, I need your help with something." I tell her as soon as the call connects. Lyndsey looks up at me, nibbling on her lower lip. In the last few hours she has gone from dealing with this alone to suddenly more and more people knowing.

"Oh hell, Anders!" I can almost imagine her dropping her head onto her desk in exasperation. "Whatever happened to saying hello?"

"Hello, Cassie, did you know you're my favourite Spears employee?" I tell her with a sickly-sweet voice. I mean it though. I love everyone who works for the Spears, but Cassie is the one I talk to most after Coach Mitch.

"Good try, what did you do? Am I going to want to kill you?" She laughs. Cassie is a very straightforward woman. She is always using pens as projectiles when people cause problems, but I know how much she cares about us.

"No, but you might have to stop me from killing someone else," I tell her honestly, refusing to look down at Lynds as we start to collect our bags and disembark the plane. I don't want to see if she is disappointed with me. It's why I don't want to deal with this alone. I don't know how I will handle it when I find out who has been harassing my wife but I doubt it will be sunshine and rainbows.

"What the hell? What's happening?" As calm as she tries to sound, I hear her fingers clacking on her keyboard furiously on the other end of the line.

"Look, we are going through the airport and then we will come straight to you. We are going to need a PI." It will be easier to talk to her in person, plus I don't want everyone in this airport knowing our business. My disguise of a cap pulled low on my head isn't exactly amazing. It would take one person recognising me and hearing what is going on and it would be all over the internet within the hour. This needs to be on a need-to-know basis.

"Are we in some kind of spy novel?" She laughs, but when I don't join her the laughter dies as quick as it started. "Fine! Okay, I'll be waiting, with a private investigator apparently." I can hear her keyboard going crazy again as she tries to get everything in order.

"Hey, Cassie?" I want to lighten the atmosphere before I end the call. I know this is a stressful situation. Especially as she doesn't really know what is happening.

"Yeah?" she asks, her voice quieter than before.

"Am I your favourite Spears employee?"

I hear her swear on the line before she ends the call without answering.

Lyndsey has been watching me. When she sees my smile at Cassie's outburst, I see tension flow out of her. I know that as long as we are honest with each other from here on out, we will be able to get this sorted. There is still a lot of work to do. After Lyndsey fell asleep last night I thought of a million questions I still have but I don't want to ask. I'm scared of her answers. I want to know what they have on her. Does she have any idea who it could be? My front runner is her ex. She told me to stay away and a few months later Lyndsey and I were married. That would be enough to anger anyone. Still, I don't want to know the truth. Because it could be so much worse. If Lyndsey has no idea then it means we are at square one. This person has given her two weeks so we have to find them before then. I can't risk letting them get away with this. Not without some repercussions.

Chapter Twenty-Eight

Aiden

As much as I wanted to go straight to the stadium to meet with Cassie, Lyndsey demanded that we stop by her place first because she wanted to change out of her plane clothes. I told her that Cassie wouldn't mind, but I think deep down she just wants to be in her own space for a minute. She has been surrounded by me and my family for weeks. If going to her apartment will make her feel better, then so be it. My car has been at the airport the whole time we were in Texas. Lyndsey was confused as to why I would do that, leave my car here despite the expense, but to me it's nothing. I love this car, I don't want to hire a driver to take me to and from the airport. And right now I'm glad for it, I wouldn't want to be in a random hire car right now while I feel so amped up.

"Maybe you should come and stay with me." I make the suggestion before thinking on the drive to her apartment. But given the threats, who knows what this person is capable of? I'll know she's safe if she is with me. I'd offer to stay in her place, but mine is closer to the Spears stadium – hell, it's even closer to Bloom and Blossom for her. It sounds like a win-win.

"Not happening, cowboy." She half chuckles.

"It would be safer if you stay with me," I try to urge her.

"They haven't made any physical threats, maybe they're all talk." Before I can tell her that they might escalate she says, "Besides, I live in a second-floor apartment where you need a key to enter the building. That sounds safe enough to me." We pull up outside of her apartment and, as much as I don't want to fight, it doesn't look safe to me. The front door is old and rusted, one of the windowpanes is covered with a piece of board where it has been smashed.

"Safer than my fully fledged security system?" I point through the car window at the clearly not secure building but she just rolls her eyes before climbing out of the car, not waiting for me to open her door for her. The honeymoon period is clearly over. Despite her attempt at deflection, I see the way her eyes scan from side to side as I come to stand beside her outside of her building. She is trying to soothe the protectiveness in me but I can see through that. She is scared, even if she wants to act as though she's fine.

The building might be safer than it looks because it takes her a few tries to get the door open. In the end she bumps her shoulder against it to crack it. She turns to grab her bag but I give her my best glare. It works because she pulls her hands back in fake offence, laughing as she starts walking up the stairs. My muscles aren't just for show and I use a lot of them to pull her two suitcases up the flights of stairs, apparently the elevator is out of order. More and more I want to make her stay with me but I don't push it.

As I round the last corner I bump into Lyndsey's back where she has stopped suddenly. In a flash she spins to me, putting both of her hands on my chest.

"Don't freak out," she tells me. But it does the opposite of what she wanted. I can see fear in her eyes, they dart around, refusing to look me in the eye. Finally looking past her at her door, my heart stutters in my chest.

The door is already hinged open.

The handle is hanging by a thread. Whoever has broken in has used all of their force to get inside. There are splinters of wood on the outskirts of the door frame.

Not wasting a second, I push Lyndsey behind me and gently edge the door open, peeking inside with a small field of vision.

What I see makes my heart drop into my stomach.

Every single piece of furniture is flipped. Plates are shattered around the room as though they were thrown at the walls. Her sofa is overturned and there are deliberate slashes through every cushion, leaving stuffing sprinkled on the piles of broken furniture. A lamp lies shattered on the floor, the glass of the bulb scattered nearby. Her dining table is in pieces, the wood pointing out in different directions.

I hear Lyndsey taking a sharp breath as the door widens for her view.

There is nothing I can do to protect her from the sight. I watch my step as I move into the home. To my right the bathroom door is wide open, the mirror inside also smashed, and the contents of her medicine cabinet dashed across the room.

This wasn't a robbery. Her TV is on the floor, her pills poured around. No obvious valuables appear missing. When I make it to her bedroom, my suspicions are confirmed. Every drawer has been poured out onto her bed, her bed sliced up like her sofa cushions, but there is a letter perfectly placed in the wreckage. I open it before

Lyndsey follows me into the room. She has read enough of these terrible messages. This one will be me.

> A whore gets what she deserves. Your so-called husband has no idea the low life he has married. A fake. A liar. A nobody.

As I hear Lyndsey's slow, approaching footsteps, I quickly rip the paper into tiny pieces. A quiet voice deep down tells me I should have shown that to Cassie. The handwriting could have been a clue in itself. *Reckless, impulsive Aiden*. But I'll be able to tell her exactly what it said. I'll see that letter behind my eyelids while I try to sleep for the foreseeable future.

Hearing Lyndsey shuffle behind me I turn and pull her against my chest. She cries openly. Exhausted from everything.

"Why me?" She sobs against my top, soaking it like she did all those months ago when Ellis collapsed. Her whole body shakes in my arms, fear and intense desperation comes off her in waves. I knew when Ellis collapsed that I wanted to protect her and those feelings are stronger now.

"We are leaving all this shit here, okay? You are staying in my place if I have to carry you there." I mean it too. I would drag her kicking and screaming because I know it will be safer. I don't think I'll have to, I feel the fight leaving her body. All of her weight is in my arms, her ginger hair tickling at my chin.

"I'll come. My stuff…" She hiccups from the strength of her tears, her green eyes red as they look up at me, but I just shake my head.

"We can buy new stuff, darlin', but I can't buy a new you. You are more important than possessions." I will buy her anything her heart desires. My money means nothing if I can't keep her safe. She wants a new car I'll buy it. She wants hundreds of bags then I'll buy one in every colour, but I need her safe in my arms. I need her to stop crying. I never want to see her cry like this again.

Feeling another surge of protectiveness, I pull my phone out of my pocket, dialling Cassie again.

"Are you guys nearly here?" she asks, but I don't bother to reply. I'm not taking Lyndsey to the stadium now. No, I need her in my house, maybe even wrapped in a blanket because she is shaking in my arms.

"Change of plan, Cas, I need you at my place as soon as possible." My voice is hard, leaving no room for disagreement. Even before she speaks again I hear Cassie shuffling on the other end of the line, getting her stuff together.

"Aiden, what's going on?" she asks, rushing around her office. I even hear her locking her office door behind her as she comes to help me.

"My wife is in danger."

Chapter Twenty-Nine

Lyndsey

I haven't said a word since we left my apartment. I don't know what to say. There is nothing that can fix it. I'm scared. I don't like admitting that but I am. When it was just texts, I could compartmentalise that, but they came into my home. My safe place. It wasn't the best apartment in the world, it wasn't exactly safe even if I tried to convince Aiden it was. I just wanted a minute alone from him, I have spent every day surrounded by his presence since we flew to Texas but I won't be getting that space any time soon. I will be living in his house. It's a big one at least. If I tried hard enough, I could probably live under his roof and avoid him, but after that scare I don't think I want to.

I like the way it feels in his arms. I like how safe I feel when he is next to me. He might only be my husband on paper but it is nice to feel like I have a family on my side. I can tell that the silence is getting to him, he wants to ask questions, but either he doesn't know what to ask or he is scared of the answer. So we drive in silence until we pull up at his house. The large modern house is more like what I expect from an athlete. Of course, this isn't the first time I have come to his place, but for the foreseeable future it is my house too. It makes me look at it with a different lens.

The large entryway opens into an open-plan room. The sofas face one direction with the kitchen on the other side. It feels warm even with all the large windows looking out over his back garden. Though it is more like a field than a garden: a pool, trees and even a greenhouse dots the scenery.

"Cassie will be here soon." Aiden interrupts my perusal of his, our place. I don't answer him though. I need him to take the step, to ask what he wants to know because I don't want to pour myself out for him if he isn't ready to hear it. "Darlin', I need to know," he says after a moment of silence, then puts his arm over my shoulder and guides me over to his plush sofa.

"Did you know I've never seriously dated a man?" I tell him. My voice is quiet but I know he hears me because his eyebrows furrow.

"What?" He scoots closer to me so my legs are pressed against his. It isn't close enough, so I drop my head to his shoulder. It works for two things. One, I'm closer to him; but two, it means I don't need to look in his eyes.

"I have slept with men but I've never dated one. It felt wrong." I can hear my parents' voices in my head telling me that I'm a heathen. That I'm a disgrace, that being gay is a choice.

"Wrong?" He is confused. I don't blame him but when you have been told a million times that being bisexual isn't real, it gets to you.

"Like my parents were right." I take a deep breath and then I pour it all out. I tell him what happened when my parents found out I kissed a girl. The memory is still raw, as though it was only yesterday.

"Lyndsey Stone, you make me sick!" My father is red in the face. With every word spit flies out of his mouth, but I don't flinch as it hits my face. It will just make him angrier.

"You said God doesn't make mistakes!" I throw back. I should keep my cool but I can feel my family's judgement seeping into me. My mom stands at my dad's side, looking just as disappointed.

"Don't you dare use God against me, girl! You have no right. You have been touched by the devil," he seethes. My heart hammers in my chest. He might be right. I think Ellie is beautiful but I shouldn't have kissed her. It's wrong. But it felt so right. It made me so happy.

"Dad. Mom?" I look between them, but instead of coming to my rescue, my mom take a step back, and my dad just laughs in my face as tears start to stream down my cheeks.

"Don't look at her, she is with me. You will not live under my roof if you're out there acting like a harlot, I'll find you a good man to marry." He nods. As though what he said makes sense. He wants me to marry? He can't do that, it would be wrong. He can't just pass me over to somebody I don't love. That's not what God would want.

"I'm seventeen! I'm too young to get married," I gasp out, but he clenches his jaw before yelling even louder than before.

"No, you will do what I say!" He takes a second to breathe before he steps closer to me, lowering his voice to a deadly timbre. "You will never speak of this gay nonsense ever again, do you hear me?"

"Why don't you love me?" I sob openly now. God taught us to love. That a parent's love is unconditional. Why won't they love me despite what they see as my flaws? I know they love Peter more than me but I have tried to please them.

"Because you are a sinner, Lyndsey. Be a good girl and I might be able to look at you again." He turns away then, *storming out of the house, but before he can slam the door behind him, I call after him.*

"Please, Dad. I didn't choose this." I'm begging but it just causes him to sneer.

"Either you marry who I find or you get out of my house." With that the door slams behind him. The door officially closes on my childhood.

"That night I left, I haven't been back since. I try calling every now and then but… nothing," I tell Aiden, still not looking up at him. As I speak I feel the tension in his shoulders but once I started talking I couldn't stop.

"They just let you go?" he asks, still trying to wrap his head around their cruelty.

"Yeah. And now whoever this is, they're saying that they will tell the world that they have proof that I'm gay. That I don't date men, so I must be using you for your money." I hate that they might be believable. To someone looking in, they might think that is the truth. All of my public relationships have been with women and, suddenly, I have a rich, famous hockey player husband. It does look suspicious.

"Fuck, darlin'." He tightens his arms around my shoulders and it is only then I realise how much I'm shaking.

"I decided that if they thought I was evil, I'd show them evil. I dyed my hair fun colours, I'd get whatever piercings I wanted and wear whatever made me feel good. I drank and partied and dated around, trying to find some stability. Don't get me wrong, I like who it made me; I like this version of myself. But it didn't fix what was wrong deep down. The horrible, festering feeling of rejection." I sigh, it still hurts to talk about this part of my life. "Eventually I realised that I wasn't happy because I was still trying to prove something to them. I tried to give myself the stability I obviously craved. I got a job, I started dating a girl called Mel, but she wanted to settle down and I wasn't there yet. She showed me that I didn't need to be the opposite of my parents to be happy, I just needed to be me. Still, that internalised homophobia that I learned growing up was hard to shake. Whenever I tried to date a man, I would hear my parents in my head telling me that they knew being gay was a phase that I would grow out of."

Silence settles between us, a black cloud, before he finally speaks. "They made you think you were some terrible person because you like women? They don't deserve to call themselves parents." I can hear the genuine offence through his deep voice.

"The blackmailers are wrong though. You know that, right? I don't want your money, Aiden. I swear. Please don't look at me like they did." I feel like all I have done for days is cry, but there is no stopping it when the tears come again. Aiden has always looked at me with reverence and if he thinks less of me it would crush me.

"Hey." He tuts, pulling my head out of his shoulder so I can look into his stormy blue eyes. There isn't an ounce of hatred or disappointment there. He looks at me like I'm precious. "I know you. I know the truth. Nothing could make me hate you." He stares into my eyes, determined to make me see the truth there. And I do. I believe that he cares about me. That he is willing to accept me even with all of my pitfalls.

"The public don't know me though, Aid, they will believe that I'm some gold digger. They were rude enough when they found out you married an 'average woman', what will happen when they find out I'm queer?" It's a valid fear. If the blackmailers share proof that I have dated women, then the world is going to paint me with one brush: that I'm a liar, and it won't just be me that suffers. Every bi woman dating a man will suffer because people are always looking for a reason to invalidate them.

"I'll set them straight. You are my wife. That is the truth. You have dated women and now you are married to me, they don't cancel each other out, and if anyone thinks it does, well, that's their problem." I fall in love with him right there. With his arms around me and his words painting an armour around my skin. He must see the adoration in my eyes because before I can thank him he pulls me closer to him with a hand wrapped around the back of my neck.

He kisses me hard. His lips are soft but determined against mine. He is kissing me with everything he has. As though if he kisses me hard enough he can wipe away all of the hatred I have had in my life. I'm willing to let him try. He is my lifeline and I cling to his shirt.

A knocking on the front door pulls us apart. Cassie is here and now I'll have to do this all over again. I'm exhausted at the thought. I don't know who is harassing me but I won't let them win. I have let enough people make me feel like I'm lesser than them and I don't want to feel that any more. I can be both. I'm a bisexual woman and I'm married to a man. That doesn't make me any less queer than I was when I was dating Kayla or Mel. Aiden might want to divorce me one day soon but he has changed my life forever. He has shown me that I don't need to be scared to show who I am. All of it. The things that I hide behind masks. With his support I have finally found that I'm not that young girl begging for love. I'm a grown woman who won't be beaten by small-minded assholes any more.

I've suffered enough. I won't let them defeat me.

Chapter Thirty

Aiden

Lyndsey being so vulnerable with me, finally trusting me with what has been holding her down, has sparked something in me. There have been many half-truths and secrets between the two of us since we met and I would be a hypocrite to let her tell me her truth and hide my own. Besides, it might make her feel better to know that this wasn't a terrible thing to me when we woke up in Vegas. If it wasn't for her and Kayla's relationship, we might have been in this place a lot sooner. Probably not married, but together. A team.

"When I saw the messages, I thought it was something else," I tell her. We are alone again now. Cassie and her PI left ten minutes ago. It hurt to hear Lyndsey have to repeat it all again but I hope I was bringing her comfort by holding her close.

"What do you mean?" Her voice is tired from her tears but when she looks up at me her eyes are still bright.

"I thought they were trying to hold the fact that you were in a relationship when we got married over your head." I try to laugh to lighten the mood, but her face sours immediately, cutting off my chuckle.

"What?" She sounds confused and suddenly I feel uncomfortable. I twitch in my seat under her glare. My palms start to sweat and awareness that everything isn't what it seems creeps to the surface.

"Your girlfriend? Or ex-girlfriend, I guess," I speak. Her confusion mirrors mine. She knows I don't care that she has dated women so I don't know why she would be acting so shocked.

"I haven't been in a relationship since before Ellis was pregnant. What are you talking about?" She shakes her head lightly, but the blood drains from my face from the shock. I can hear my heartbeat starting to pound.

"Kayla." Her name is a whisper, as though my throat is closing around the sounds. I force it out anyway and Lyndsey recoils, pulling out of my arms, jumping to her feet before me.

"How the fuck do you know who Kayla is?" she asks, her voice rising in pitch. She starts to pace but I'm stock-still on the sofa. She stares at me expectantly and I know I have to come clean after months of running from her. I know I have to tell her what happened. No matter how ugly it sounds.

-

I rock back and forth on my feet as I wait for Lyndsey to come out of Bloom and Blossom. I have no news on my phone about Ellis collapsing but I think that might be a good thing. If something was wrong with Ellis or the baby I'm sure Liam would have let us know by now, it's been hours. I just need to get Lyndsey to Liam's so I know she can be surrounded by people, I'm sure little Jack will cheer her up. He has that effect on everyone. Having her break down into tears in my arms flayed me open. I felt like I wanted to fix it for her but there is only so much a well-placed joke can do. It's times like this I wish I was better with words but, unless I'm giving my teammates instructions, I never know what to say. I watch Lyndsey go into the back of the shop through the windows when a slim woman comes up beside me, trying to edge into the store.

"Sorry, the shop is closed," I let her know. The way her eyes snap to mine shocks me. There is a lot of anger there. She glares at me for a second but she doesn't try to go in.

"Who are you?" she snarls. Her thin lips curl up as her eyes scan me from top to bottom. I'm not used to women looking at me with such hatred. Granted, when women look at me a lot of them just see the captain of the Spears and not Aiden. This woman sees an inconvenience.

"Excuse me?" I ask, royally confused.

"Well, you aren't Ellis or Lyndsey so… who are you?" Her voice is laced with condescension and I'm taken aback. Her caramel short hair seems wild, like it hasn't been brushed in a few days, and her make-up is slightly smudged, but I can't tell if it's intentional.

"Oh, I'm Aiden. I'm a friend of Lyndsey's." I feel like a kid being grilled by a parent.

"Oh, you're my girlfriend's friend, are you?" the woman growls, and I'm stunned silent.

"Sorry?" My eyebrows furrow, I'm wondering if I heard her wrong, because I can't believe what's coming from her mouth. "Your girlfriend?"

"Yes, I'm Kayla." She rolls her eyes as if it's supposed to be obvious, but I'm floundering. I know Lyndsey is bi, I also thought I knew she was single. Apparently I'm wrong. "We were on a break, but we are back together now. So, are we going to have a problem?"

"Oh! No!" I try to keep my shock hidden but I do a terrible job. I'm not the type of man to try and break up a happy couple. If Lyndsey had told me I would have stopped flirting. God, I

feel like an idiot. No wonder she asked me to stop pursuing her. "Like I said, I'm just a friend. I'm giving her a lift somewhere after work, that's all." I choose not to mention Ellis. I'm sure Lyndsey will fill her in when she is ready. It's not my place to tell her girlfriend what happened. Kayla scans through the windows but when she doesn't see Lyndsey she huffs, turning to me.

"Look, I have to go, but remember your place. Friend." Her words are filled with poison but she's right. I'll remember my place. Lyndsey asked me to be her friend. I'll be her friend.

Kayla tries to bump my shoulder as she walks away, but because of her shorter stature her shoulder digs against my bicep. She hustles past me, not looking back as she leaves. A few seconds later the door opens and Lyndsey exits the shop, eyes still downcast. I don't know how to mention what just happened. Especially since Kayla is no longer in sight. Lyndsey doesn't linger though, as soon as the door is locked and the shutters come down she wanders over to the passenger side of my car. Now isn't the time to question her relationship, she has been through enough. Instead I open the door for her and go back around the front of the car to get in myself. The drive to Liam's house is quiet, nothing but the low songs on the radio fill the space.

—

"What?" Lyndsey's voice is dangerously low by the time I finish filling her in. Angry and rough, but I know it isn't directed at me. Well, at least I hope it isn't. Still, it's hard to look in her eyes because of the fury looking back at me.

I wish I'd never mentioned anything. Then I'm happy I did. A walking, talking contradiction, because if I hadn't mentioned it then Lyndsey wouldn't be so worked up. But if we never had this conversation she would never know the truth. That I never wanted to push her away.

"I'm sorry, I think I'm losing my mind." She drops back down onto the sofa beside me.

I watch her file through a hundred emotions as I talk. Anger and guilt. I also see her eyes flood with tears when she tells me about how she felt when I kissed her and walked away. No wonder she blocked my number. To her I looked like a giant fuckboy. And she wasn't wrong.

She has been through a lot today and I can see how much the weight is hurting her but I have to tell her everything. If this is going to work out between us the way I want it to then we need to be more open with each other. Not communicating is what hurt us back then, I won't let it happen again.

"Wait, why did you think I pulled away from you?" I ask. It hits me now that if she was single the whole time then I all but led her on just to drop her. I need her to tell me how much it hurt so I can make it up to her.

"I thought that me crying on you that day, that being vulnerable with you just turned you off. That's why I was so confused on New Year's." Her skin flushes pink as she talks and a stone settles in my chest.

"Nothing you could do could turn me off, darlin'. You could kick me in the balls and I'd still be crazy about you." She laughs at that but I mean it. From the first time I met her at Liam and Ellis' barbeque I have known she is the most beautiful woman I have ever seen.

"Okay, cowboy, that was cute." She is still laughing but when I pull her against me again, placing a chaste kiss on her smiling lips, she lets out a happy sigh.

"I have to ask. Could it be Kayla blackmailing you?" I can pray it will be this easy but I'm also sure that if Lyndsey suspected her she would have told Cassie when she was here. Still, a man can have hope.

"I thought so at first but the texts are too coherent. Her texts are always just drunk ramblings, plus her family is rich as hell. Ten thousand is a blip to her." She lets out a bone-deep sigh and I wrap my arms around her shoulders, pulling her tight to my side.

"Jesus." I laugh, I can't help it. I do refrain from telling her she has a type for rich people. That probably wouldn't make her laugh right now, especially with what she is being called in those disgusting texts, but I do want to make her laugh. I hate seeing this beat-down version of her. The Lyndsey I know is filled with fire and sass. She has been kicked when she was down but she has never let it defeat her. I won't let it beat her now.

"She comes from some old-money oil family. I just don't see her being this consistent with it." She throws her phone down onto the coffee table, the sound echoes around the room. I want to get her a new one but when I mentioned it she told me it was no use. She has already tried so much to remove herself from this nightmare but she tried to do it all alone. Now she has a force behind her.

"I'll let Cassie know anyway, it's worth it even if it is just to rule her out." I place a light kiss on the crown of her head. I never want to stop touching her. When I can feel her skin against mine, I know she is safe. When I kiss her I know she is here with me. It is selfish but she doesn't complain as I all but haul her into my lap. Next to me isn't close enough any more.

"You're right." She giggles as she settles her weight on my thighs, but I gasp dramatically at her words.

"Oh, I'm sorry, I need my phone. I need a recording of that. Can you say it again?" I fumble for my phone but Lyndsey just laughs harder, slapping her hand on my chest.

"Oh fuck off, cowboy." She smiles up at me despite her biting words.

"There's that smile." I trace the curve of her bottom lip with my thumb. I want to make her smile like this every day.

We haven't really discussed what will happen with our marriage now that we are back but I'm not going to ruin the mood by bringing it up now. The past few days have been heavy for the both of us and I won't let the blackmailers win by divorcing her now. I won't let them believe that they got between us. At least for now I know I can keep Lyndsey safe by keeping her my wife. Hopefully by the time I have fixed this she will be ready to accept my love.

Because I do love her. Even with all of this it has not altered my feelings for her. Quite the opposite: it has made them stronger. Her strength floors me. If I have my way I can be her soft landing and she will finally start to lean on me as her husband. I have leaned on her since Pops died but now it is my time to be her rock. As long as she has my ring on her finger, she will have a support system in me. Hell, even if she wants a divorce one day I will always only be a call away.

That's the thing you do for the people you love.

Chapter Thirty-One

Lyndsey

Being back from Texas feels like my life should be back to normal. It isn't. And yet Aiden and I have found our own version of normal. His house is a dream and living here is like a vacation, with beautiful views of the land around the back of his house and the large tub in the spare room I have moved into.

Plus I get the great view of Aiden working out. His home gym is my favourite part of the house, for sure. Do I work out? Hell no, but I'm going to do yoga in the corner while I watch Aiden lift weights and run on a treadmill. I have to stop myself from drooling while he runs shirtless, the sweat dripping between his abs drives me crazy. I want to lick it up and then I gross myself out. Still, I'm there every morning waking up earlier than I would like to just to get a glimpse of my husband's tattooed torso and arms pulsating.

It adds a new layer now that I understand some of his tattoos. A pair of angel wings to represent his parents. A small flower to represent Eden. The Shakespeare quote "That as fast as you pour affection in, it runs out": a line said by Celia in *As You Like It*. The matching tattoo he has with Alice. Each one tells the story of his family and his love. Seeing what his body can do is art.

The way his muscles clench, the skin tanned and reddened, makes me understand how people write sonnets. If I could carve him out of marble, I would never be happy with my work because nothing could come close to emulating his perfection. Damn, I need to get laid. I want my husband to take me to bed and show me the stars but we aren't even in the same bedroom right now.

For all I know, most married people might not share a bed. The closest to a conventional relationship I have ever seen is Liam and Ellis and they aren't even married yet. Plus they were apart for ten years and got pregnant from a one-night stand and that is the closest I have to healthy love. It wasn't even until I saw how devoted Liam is to Ellis that I realised how fucked up my parents' marriage is. The arguing and the passive-aggressive silence shouldn't be normal. Whenever my mom made my dad mad, he would act like a petulant teenager, slamming doors and icing her out until she would beg for his attention and affection.

I thought that was normal because it was how I was raised. I would follow her, I did everything I could to keep my dad happy. I would make sure he ate first and that I didn't bother him in the mornings because he was a monster before coffee. I learned to tiptoe around my own house and growing out of that was hard. Then I saw how Liam worships the ground Ellis walks on and it showed me that men can love their partners. Truly love them. Not love them for cleaning and cooking, but love them because they exist and that is enough. Hell, even in most sitcoms the husband hates his wife, she is always the butt of the joke. But it doesn't have to be that way. It shouldn't be that way. I'm finally figuring that out.

Even while dating a woman I never really considered marriage because I thought there was no affection there. If I tied the knot, that would mean that I was giving myself over to my partner and telling them they could stop caring. They would have got me and not needed to try any more. It was irrational and I even knew it then but deep down I thought that would be my future no matter who I married. So I told myself that would never be me. I would never marry and give someone that power over me. Now here I am. Married and sleeping apart from my husband.

Granted, he isn't my *chosen* husband. Unless you count drunk me making the decision for sober me. Still, I have managed to become what I was scared of. And yet I'm happy. There is so much quiet affection between us. We have a routine. One we never even discussed. After he works out and I pretend to work out while ogling him he makes breakfast. I was worried he would try and push me to eat a bunch of healthy food but my husband has a sweet tooth. We have waffles – yes, they are protein waffles but I can lather mine in maple syrup to make them more enjoyable. While he makes those, I make us coffee so we can eat together.

We talk about anything. About our weird dreams the night before. About our families. About what our plans are for the day. After breakfast he runs upstairs to shower while I clean up the mess. Seeing how he cooks, it's only fair that I clean up. Even if he tells me every day that I don't have to do it, I do anyway. He is refusing to let me pay rent so I have to pull my weight somewhere. It also helps to keep me busy instead of picturing him shower. I have to stop myself from imagining the way he suds himself up, his large hands rubbing over the expanse of skin.

Then I jump into my own shower to cool my thoughts. As much as I try to resist I touch myself picturing him joining me. Pinning me against the cold white tiles, taking me hard and quick, needing to fuck me one last time before he has to leave for the day. It's a great way to start my day, up until I remember how I'm still in the shower alone. That is a sharp comedown. By the time I'm clean and dressed Aiden is waiting for me downstairs with lunch he made for me to take to work. Ever since I got here, he has driven me to Bloom and Blossom. It is on his way to the stadium but I know he should probably leave earlier to beat the traffic, though he has never complained.

We drive together with the radio low to fill the silence in the car. At first it felt awkward. I had so much guilt about all the drama I have brought into his life, I was constantly waiting for the other shoe to drop and for him to snap at me. Every day I become a little less on edge and am starting to enjoy our quiet drives. Knowing that no matter how busy our day gets we've had this time together. Just enjoying each other's company.

On the days when he has a game I come home to an empty house. It still feels wrong to be in the house alone but Aiden has told me a thousand times to make myself comfortable. I make some food and I always make enough for two. Even if I tell him I did it accidentally he knows I'm lying. I just hate the idea of him coming home hungry and having to make himself something when he has already worked so hard all day. The difference between me and my mom though is that I'm doing it because I want to make his life easier, not because if I don't he will make my life harder. Plus my husband always gets hungry at night. He calls it his midnight munchies, so having leftover food means he doesn't wake me up cooking something for himself in the middle of the night.

My favourite nights are the ones when he comes home early. The nights we eat together and sit in the TV room. He watches game tapes and I read my Kindle and again there is quiet between us but I love it anyway. It makes me feel incredibly domestic. Sometimes he pulls my feet over his lap, digging his thumbs into the arches of my foot. Neither of us mention it, too scared to ruin the moment. When he gets through his tapes he sits with me anyway.

After a few nights of this I convinced him to watch some *Real Housewives* with me. If any of his teammates asked he would tell them that it is stupid, but I know the truth. He is outraged about their in-fighting and is fully invested in them. I caught him looking them up on social media, he denied it but I know what I saw.

He told me one night that he never really watched a lot of TV growing up. He was always too busy training or keeping his sisters entertained, so that even when he had time for himself he was working on his form. Looking up the best skates or the newest teams in the NHL, it was his entire life. Now he enjoys that I force him to stop. To take time for himself where he isn't beating himself up for things he can't control.

Even after spending our evenings together, once it is time for bed we go into different rooms. I shouldn't complain. The room I'm staying in is beautiful, the bed is huge and comfortable, but it is oh-so lonely. After spending every night in bed with him in Texas, now the bed just feels cold and empty around me. Every morning I wake up in the centre of the bed holding a pillow to my chest after dreaming that he was holding me close.

The master bedroom is just next door and every night I think about knocking on his door. I imagine walking in there and crawling into bed beside him, demanding that he hold me. But I don't. If he rejected me I don't think I would survive the embarrassment. I definitely wouldn't be able to stay in this house and, as much as I love Ellis, there is no way I'm crashing at her place. I love her kids but I love them when I get to come home to the quiet at the end of the day.

My sleep is suffering. If I'm not dreaming about him holding me then I'm dreaming about whoever is texting me showing up here and demanding the money. I wish I could find comfort in Aiden's arms but he has never mentioned us sleeping in the same bed. When he first moved me in here I don't know why I assumed I would be sharing his bed. I disappointed myself because when he brought my stuff up to this room I was close to tears. It was him drawing a line in the sand.

There is in Texas and there is after Texas. I'm just struggling to separate them. I remind myself that originally he thought he would be divorced from me by now. The plan was only to be "married" for those few weeks and now here we are still married. We have to continue the ruse until we figure out what to do about the blackmail. I thought he might want forever but I was just caught up in being his wife. He was overwhelmed with his emotions, his grief. I confused that for real feelings. That is on me and I have to remember that. Because of his letter I thought he might have feelings as deep as mine, but then I remind myself the number of emotions that were in the air. He saw me as some kind of light in his darkness, but now he isn't surrounded by grief and expectation he must have realised having me around doesn't make his life better. If anything, I make it worse. I have an airplane worth of baggage and I'm pulling him through it with me. Every morning that I wake up alone I hear my father's taunting voice in my head reminding me that I'm not worthy of love. And each night I go to sleep remembering that I did this to myself. I fell for my husband and fooled myself into thinking he wanted that too. Him shoving me into a spare room is proof enough that I'm a burden to him the same way I was to my family.

It's not that I think he was lying to me, he probably really did feel those feelings, but I know I'm not enough for him. Now that we are out of that Texas bubble it has only proved me right that I'm not worthy of a happily ever after. Maybe my parents are right, maybe there is a God up there, mad at me for my sins, or maybe I'm the one punishing myself. All I know is that Aiden Anders should be with a woman who can give him the world, not just the broken pieces I have to offer. And still every day I get my hopes up that today is the day he will show me he loves me – he doesn't even have to say the words, just show me that what happened in Texas wasn't a mistake.

Ellis has had enough of my brooding. I'm putting together a bouquet for a first date when she lets out a deep sigh beside me.

"Okay, Lynds, I'm done," she tells me, glaring at the side of my head. I have been waiting for this. I have kept her pretty in the dark about everything. She has enough going on in her life without me piling on as well. But she is my closest friend, it is unfair of me to keep her out.

"Nothing is going on," I lie. I know it, she knows it. My voice doesn't have any conviction and Ellis reaches over to pull the flowers out of my hands, putting them back on the table in front of us. Taking my hands in hers, she turns me to face her.

"You're married and are living in his house but you won't tell me about anything the two of you are up to behind closed doors. Cassie keeps turning up asking questions about you. You are avoiding me. Your time is up. Talk to me." I know she won't take no for an answer. She looks down at me with determination in her eyes.

"Okay. Fuck! Someone is blackmailing me." I sigh, slamming my eyes shut so I don't see her reaction.

"What?" she yells. Every one of my muscles clench and I screw my eyes closed even harder, refusing to look back at her.

"Cassie and Aiden have contacted a PI but while we were in Texas someone broke into my apartment so Aiden doesn't think I'm safe there. That's why I'm living with him but that's all," I rush out, barely taking a moment to breathe. I try to pull my hands out of hers but she holds them tighter, shaking them until I peek at her through one eye.

"That's all, she says! Lyndsey, why didn't you tell me?" She pulls me to her until she can wrap her arms round me. Her five-foot-ten frame swallows up my five-foot-four and when she holds me to her I feel protected.

"I'm sorry, it's just I thought I could deal with it and then it got scary and I didn't want to pull you or the kids into my drama." It's the truth. If she or her beautiful kids got hurt because of me I'd never forgive myself. I don't know if whoever is after me is dangerous but I wouldn't risk her safety.

"Liam said Aiden has been a bit distracted but I just thought he was lovesick," she says absent-mindedly while rubbing a hand up and down my back. I freeze at her words. Feeling the tension in me, she pulls back slightly, putting her hand on my shoulders so she can look in my eyes.

"Yeah..." I cough back the lump in my throat. "He isn't lovesick," I tell her, but her face scrunches in confusion.

"Do you love him?" she asks gently. I'm glad there are no customers because I would feel embarrassed if anyone else saw the way I'm blushing. I know I have strong feelings for Aiden. It would be impossible not to. He is kind and loyal and great in bed, which is always a bonus.

"I don't know. I think so. Maybe," I grumble, wiping my hands down my face. "It's just so complicated. It was all fake and then suddenly it was real. Then when he moved me in he put me up in a guest bedroom and I don't know if that was a message, you know?"

"Have you asked him?" she asks, and I let out a laugh so loud it surprises both of us. The loud sound causes Ellis to giggle and we both laugh together for a second.

"No." I shake my head. Of course I haven't asked him. If I ask him then he will give me an answer. If I never ask then I never have to know the truth. Never have to have the memory of him telling me that I'm too much work and that he actually does want a divorce.

"So let me get this straight." She crosses her arms over her chest, giving me her best mom glare. "You are in love with your husband but you're scared he doesn't love you even though he has always been crazy about you." I can hear the accusation in her voice. She says it like it's so simple. That because he finds me attractive that must mean he is madly in love with me, but that just isn't realistic. Just because Liam was obsessively in love with her from the start, that isn't how everybody's lives go.

"Pretty much." I try to turn back towards the flowers but she twists me by the shoulder so I'm facing her again, not letting me hide.

"I love you, but sometimes I want to slap you." She shakes her head slightly, clearly disappointed by my refusal to talk to Aiden. Still, she makes me laugh again.

"Oh thanks!" I say between giggles. I know she means nothing but love with her words, El doesn't have an aggressive bone in her body.

"You're welcome. Talk to him, Lynds, you both deserve to be happy." Clearly happy that she has made her point, she leaves my side. Walking back into the office to fill out more paperwork, she leaves me reeling.

Ellis has always been wiser than me. She had to grow up early because her mom was terrible and she has been suffering with a chronic illness since she was a teen. We aren't that far apart in age but still she has always felt like a guiding figure for me. If she seriously thinks I should talk to Aiden then I know that I should. That doesn't mean I will, but I'll think about it.

I'm still thinking about it when my taxi pulls up outside of Aiden's house after work. Actually it is all I have thought about all day. Every little moment we have shared over the past year and a half. Every little glance and lingering touch. All of the miscommunication between us. Not talking is how everything fell apart at New Year's and we told each other we would share our truth.

When I walk inside, I'm shocked to hear music coming from the kitchen. Following the sound, I find my husband cooking dinner. I stop in the doorway and when he turns to look at me his face lights up. He opens his mouth to greet me but I don't give him a chance. I wanted him to show me his feelings and this feels like a good indicator that I was wrong. Maybe he does want me. Instead of asking, I take action. In two large steps I'm in front of him and throw myself at him. Wrapping my arms over his broad shoulders and jumping so my legs wrap around his trim waist, I kiss him. Aiden groans against me but he kisses me back with fever. Gripping my ass with his callused hands, he pulls me tighter to his body.

I might not be good at communicating but I can't fake this any more. The way his lips feel on mine, the fire that thumps through my veins. I can't hide from him when his tongue plunges into my mouth. The groan I let out echoes around us but we don't pull away. I hope he never pulls away.

If this doesn't show him where I stand, I don't know what will. But I do know that Ellis is right.

I love my husband and I want to know if he loves me too.

Chapter Thirty-Two

Aiden

I love driving my wife to work. Hell, I would drive around the block one hundred times if it meant I got more time with her. We might not be talking the whole time but, in a way, I like that more. The comfort and ease we feel together. Being in her aura is calming, it really sets me up for success every day. Knowing that there is someone willing to support me takes away anxiety I had pushed down, trying so hard to be dependable that I couldn't even support myself. Now, because of Lyndsey giving me the room to express emotion openly, I feel stronger both mentally and physically.

After dropping her at work each morning I have to get into focus mode on my way to the stadium. I have to take off my husband cap and put on my captain cap. I love my job. The feeling of knowing every man on my team respects me and sees me as a guiding light is proof to me that this is where my life was supposed to go.

For a while I doubted that. When Pops asked me to come home after my parents died and step up for my sisters I wavered. Alice gave me the strength to fight for what I needed and she was right. I needed this more than I think I ever would have guessed. When I step out onto the ice, I feel the weight of expectation, but it just makes me want to push harder. Now I also have Lyndsey's strength behind me.

It's why I won't let her go. I'm giving her time to come around to it, I would hate to push her when she isn't ready but I know in time she will find what I have. That we are better together. I want her to come to me, it's why I offered her the guest room. Now that we are no longer pretending for my family, I wanted to give her space to work through her emotions, but that doesn't mean that I'm giving up on us. Plus, there is the problem of our divorce papers hidden in my nightstand. When Cassie brought her PI over, she also had the papers in her bag from the lawyer. I haven't signed them yet, and frankly I still don't feel ready to give them to Lyndsey. What if she wants to file them right away? I don't think she would really want to, but there is always that tiny bit of doubt that she might truly want rid of me.

She is my wife and I want it to stay that way. It might not have been our life plan but I'm so much happier with her by my side than I ever thought was possible. I understand why my dad wanted me to get married so badly. Having the support of a good woman makes life greener.

I think my darlin' might be willing to stay married. She hasn't brought up getting divorced once in the time we have been back. She stopped mentioning it in Texas and I refuse to utter the words. I won't put the idea in her head that I want her gone. That could never be the case. I sense her anxiety around her blackmailer and I know she thinks I'm going to abandon her.

Why wouldn't she?

The people who were supposed to love her unconditionally gave up on her; of course she expects the same from me. Her parents scared her in a way she tries to hide but when you brush just below the surface, she has so many bruises still to this day. Just because things aren't easy that doesn't mean I'm going to leave. If anything it makes me want to stay even more. To show her that I will always be by her side no matter what fate throws at us. I hope that with time she will see that I'm not going anywhere. I'll make her breakfast and drive her to work, I'll take on any weight that is on her shoulders, all until she realises that I'm right here. Not planning on going anywhere without her with me.

I'm on autopilot as I make my way through the training rooms at the stadium. By the time I make it to the locker room I can't drop my small smile as I think about Lyndsey. Based on the sound leaking from under the door it is clear I'm one of the last few guys here but it has been like this for days. I refuse to stop dropping Lyndsey off at work, even if that means they have to wait for me. It's only a few minutes, I deserve that grace. For years I was the first guy here and the last one to leave so I have done my time, they can give me ten minutes every day to spend with my wife.

"Mornin', boys!" I holler as I enter. They all call back their hellos, patting my shoulders as I walk through them to my locker.

"Anders! How is domesticated life?" Rook yells. He isn't even the rookie on the team any more and yet I can't imagine calling him anything else.

"Life is sweet," I tell him honestly and the dramatic sound of him gagging fills the room.

"God, everyone is getting tied down. First Ruin and now you. Hell, even Felix is married." He might say he hates it but I see the truth. He wants what we have. Seeing

Ruin find love with Ellis and have a family with her affected us all. I always thought I loved the single life but I think I was just complacent in my loneliness.

I just laugh at him and Felix the goalie throws a pair of socks at his head, making us all laugh harder. Edge is quiet but that isn't strange. Jay Brink is a brooding observer. He will wait until he has something substantial to say before he interjects, but he eyes me from across the room.

"So Anders... you going to be a dad next?" Felix asks, clearly teasing, nudging me with his shoulder. Images pop into my mind of Lyndsey carrying a baby but I push them away as quickly as they came.

"Slow down, she might not even stay married to me." I don't know what else to say. I don't want to think far into the future with Lyndsey when everything is still so uncertain. Still Felix just rolls his eyes at me, clearly unimpressed.

"You aren't getting divorced. She's always been into you. It's the reason she never tried to flirt with me," Rook says from the bench where he is lacing his skates. His voice is confident but he very rarely sounds unsure.

"Oh, is that the only reason a woman wouldn't want you?" Edge shoots back, voice dripping in sarcasm. The relationship between those two is strange. They do nothing but bicker but they also care deeply about each other. It is a true sibling relationship, with Rook being the cocky younger brother always needling Edge.

"Obviously, I'm a perfect human specimen, eh," he replies, flexing his arms like a bodybuilder, but Edge looks unimpressed. I can see him trying to smother a smile though. If I didn't know him as well as I do I would probably miss it. Rook does, too busy flaunting his biceps.

"How about you put those muscles to work? We're running drills," I yell, clapping my hands to grab everyone's attention. Groans ring out around the room but I feel excited to get out there. I prefer being on the ice over being in the gym any day.

"Anders." Edge grabs my shoulder, pulling me back into the room. Neither of us says anything until we are alone. Waiting patiently for the rest of the team to trickle out, Edge stands at my side, tension marring his face.

"You good?" I ask when the door clicks closed behind Felix.

"Look, I'm not trying to stick my nose where it doesn't belong but, I know about the PI Cassie had to hire. I don't know everything but if you need support I'm here, yeah?" He rubs a hand on the back of his neck, refusing to meet my eye. I appreciate him not mentioning this in front of the team, but I want to know how the hell he found out about it.

"How do you know?" My voice is a dangerous growl, needing to protect my wife's privacy.

"I overheard Cassie when Coach Mitch sent me to ask her something. She didn't breach your trust or anything," he rushes out, almost too quickly, but I know he isn't coming from a bad place. Still, I find it hard to cool my blood.

"Can you keep this quiet, the less people that know the better." My voice stays slow, someone could walk in at any minute and I want to keep this as far away from the team as I can. If Lyndsey wants them to know she will tell them herself. I won't disrespect her by telling them all her business. She has never had anyone she could depend on to keep her secrets for her. I'll be that even if she doesn't know it's happening.

"Of course, it's just... Look, I like Lyndsey, she is a great girl, I just want you to know that I'm here to support you both." Both he and Lyndsey are Ellis and Ruin's baby girl's godparents and it's given them a special bond. I love seeing how my team cares about her. Putting a hand on my shoulder, he continues, "You might be my captain but you are also my friend. And so is she."

"It's a shit situation but I think we are going to be okay." I sigh. I wish I could make it all go away but I know that isn't realistic. For now being by her side has to be enough. Keeping her safe is my priority and the only way I can do that right now is to leave her alone as rarely as I can.

"What are they blackmailing her with?" The words tumble out as though he knows he shouldn't ask but the curiosity got the better of him.

"That's between me and her. All you need to know is that I trust her with my life and if anything comes out in the press about her it's not the whole truth. She is my wife and that is what matters." My tone leaves no room for argument and he just nods, his eyebrows lifting in acknowledgment.

"I respect that. Married life looks good on you." He laughs, walking past me and out of the room to get himself on the ice.

I take a second before I follow after him. I do love my job but I love my life off the ice too. The small moments just between Lyndsey and me on my sofa, the quiet moments as we eat together. I want to make sure I have a good balance between both parts of my life. I have worked hard enough the past few years and I think it's time I gave myself some slack. I don't need to be the last man here to be a good captain. I can support my team and my wife, neither needs to suffer.

With that thought I flick off my skate guards and step out onto the ice, taking a deep breath of the cold air. Yelling formations at the team, we run drills together, Coach Mitch watching us from the sidelines. Sweat drips from my hair but I smile anyway, a plan forming in my head as we start practising slap shots. I'm going to be home when Lyndsey finishes work today. Make her a romantic meal, buy a nice bottle of wine and maybe even a fancy chocolate dessert to share.

I can see it now: the candlelit table and the perfectly cooked steaks. I would buy her flowers but buying them from anywhere other than Bloom and Blossom feels wrong and that would ruin the surprise.

-

It's a few hours later and my plan is forming in front of my eyes. I'm almost giddy as I wait for her to arrive. I haven't had a serious relationship before so this is probably the most romantic thing I have ever done. I have taken women to fancy restaurants but turning my own house into our own private dining experience with myself as the chef? That one is new to me.

There are candles on the table ready to be lit when I serve the food but, for now, I'm making a salad to go with our steaks. I hear a car door closing outside and know it must be her, she gets a taxi home most days. I love calling this house her home, I hope she feels like it is her home. I want her to love it here – if she wanted to move I would follow her anywhere, but this is the house I pictured starting a family in.

The front door clicks open and I turn to pull two glasses out of the cabinet to pour her some wine, but she stops in the doorway. Turning, I see my wife reacting to the scene in front of her. Emotion flits across her face. Excitement. Lust. Happiness.

Then her eyes flick up to me, the intensity in her gaze makes me put the glasses down on the side and walk towards her. Before I can get too close though she is flying across the room and jumping into my arms. Instinctively my hands band under her thighs, pulling her tight against me as her lips press against mine. Not waiting a second, I kiss her back. It is not often that Lyndsey initiates affection and I won't look a gift horse in the mouth. My wife wants me to kiss her, she will be kissed.

Spinning her around I settle her on the kitchen counter, kissing her harder. Leaving no space between us I push my chest against hers, moaning while her fingers weave in my hair. I'm glad I bought steaks because I don't think we will be eating any time soon. I'm too busy enjoying the taste of my wife.

Our tongues battle against each other, almost fighting with the need for more. I want to imprint myself into her skin, my fingers dig into her soft curves. Her legs tighten around my waist, pulling me impossibly closer. We barely come up for air before I realise this will not be enough.

Finally pulling away from her I nip at her bottom lip, nudging my nose against hers lightly. Our breathing is laboured but neither of us tries to create space. Sliding my hands further under her ass I lift her from the counter and move towards the stairs. I want my wife and I want her now.

I want my dessert before my steak.

Chapter Thirty-Three

Aiden

It's later that night when we sit together on the sofa, just like we have every other night. But this isn't like every other evening, tonight I'm done with tiptoeing around my feelings. I gave her space and she did what I'd always hoped: she came to me. Lyndsey kissed me. Hell, she kissed me as though it was the last thing she would ever do.

Another episode of *Real Housewives* plays on the TV but I'm not keeping up with the drama. My eyes keep slipping to my wife. Her satin PJs and hair thrown into a bun, she looks so at home and comfortable. She looks breathtaking. I love her more like this than when she is all dressed up, not because I don't appreciate the effort but because I know she doesn't let everyone see her like this. When she is around other people there is a mask in place, armour to protect herself from scrutiny, but with her sitting on the other end of the sofa she is completely at ease.

I hate that I'm not touching her. So I do. I reach over and pull her hand into mine, twining our fingers together. I don't know what Lyndsey sees when she looks over at me but her brows furrow in confusion.

"You okay?" she asks, rubbing her thumb over the back of my hand. I notice the size difference, how small and delicate her fingers seem compared to my callused hands.

"Can't a man admire his wife?" I ask, laughing and pulling her hand up to my lips, leaving a kiss on her pale skin. She laughs then. A beautiful sound full of light.

"I love it when you call me that." She sighs when her laughter fades, squeezing my hands tighter.

"What? My wife?" When she just nods, I pull her along the sofa until I'm sharing her space: cuddling her into my side, throwing my arm over her shoulder and kissing the crown of her head. The little sigh of contentment she releases paints a smile on my face. "I never thought I'd get to kiss you, never mind call you my wife. I'm going to say it every damn day."

Her head whips around so she can look me in the eye. I think she is looking for a lie but she won't find one. Even if she wants a divorce, I'll always think of her as my wife. After a moment her eyes melt and her lips split into a coy smile.

"That's really sweet," she whispers. Needing her to know how serious I am I pull her up onto my lap. She straddles my thighs and links her hands over the back of my neck so we are eye to eye.

"Why are you still sleeping in the guest room?" I do what I can to keep my voice light, but with her sitting on my lap this way there are a million dirty thoughts racing through my mind. That's why I want to know why she isn't sleeping with me, I want to wake up with her in my arms. If that leads to some great morning sex then that's a bonus.

"I didn't know I had another choice." She shakes her head slightly, but I see every emotion in her wide eyes.

Her confusion is obvious and it makes my heart stutter in my chest.

"You should be sleeping in my bed, our bed" I tell her, cradling one side of her face in my hand. I want to be connected to her in every way, each inch of my skin that isn't touching her feels like a waste.

"You never asked." She shrugs, but there feels like there is something she is holding back. There is a wall coming between us but I refuse to let it, I want her to know exactly how much I want her.

"Darlin', you're going through a lot. I'm not going to push you to sleep beside me if you need space." I bring my other hand up to her face so she is locked in with me. I want her to look into my eyes and see me completely. "You were basically forced to stay married to me, a guy you weren't even dating; then all the blackmail stuff. I wanted you to have a choice. I wanted you to choose me, not because of circumstance but because you wanted *me*."

I won't be another example of someone demanding things from her.

"Aiden…" She pauses, clearly not sure if she is ready to give a voice to what she is feeling. I give her time and after taking a deep breath to steady herself she continues, "I thought you regretted it. That you only wanted me in Texas because of the high emotions."

"Fuck, darlin', does this feel like I don't want you? Does the fact I've had the damn divorce papers hidden in my drawer for weeks feel like I don't want you?" I pull her hips down so she sits tighter against me, my hard cock pressed against her centre. Her eyes widen, her breath hitches and she bites her lip, not looking away from my face. The sight of her so flustered makes me even needier for her. I let her take in what I have just said, let her come to terms with the fact I have been keeping a secret from her. But instead of getting mad she looks at me with tears in her eyes. For a second I panic, but she grips my face in her hands, smiling at me.

"You have them? But you didn't make a move. I was scared you only wanted me because I was there at the right time." Her breath hitches and her voice goes up a notch. Still she holds me tighter, and I can see a little bit of hope behind her eyes, as if she was worried that I still want out of this marriage.

"I won't make that mistake again. I didn't tell you about them because I didn't want you to sign them. You are who I'm choosing, only you. Always you." This time I kiss her, sliding my hands around until they are buried in her hair. I'm hungry for her, it has been days of her being in my space without actually really having her.

Lyndsey pushes down even harder against me and we both groan at the contact. I'm so desperate for her that I might come in my pants like a damn teenager but I can't find it in me to slow down or to care. She must not care either because she rocks herself back and forth, rubbing her pussy over me, not stopping to break our kiss. Our tongues battle but we are too wrapped up to care when our teeth bump against each other. I bring one hand down onto my wife's hip, guiding her over me. Her fingers pull at my hair, making me moan, and I feel her smile against my lips, happy with how crazy she makes me.

I'll show her just how crazy I am for her. Lifting my hips, I push our bodies closer together and finally pull my lips from hers. She pouts but I ignore it, dropping down to the soft skin on her neck. Her pulse thunders under my kiss and it is my turn to smile. Taking one of her hands out of my hair she takes her breast into her hand, massaging and squeezing the soft flesh. God, she is so fucking hot, taking what she needs from me. With my lips on her neck and her hand on her tits she starts to shake above me. Gasping out my name, all of her muscles stiffen and even through our clothes I can feel her orgasm.

Once she catches her breath, she drops her head onto my chest but we aren't done yet. Standing with her still wrapped around me Lyndsey squeals, making me laugh. I carry her up the stairs, not stopping until I get to the foot of my bed, but she keeps her face buried in my shirt until I drop her onto the mattress.

"God, you are so fucking sexy," I groan. She lies out in front of me with a dark wet patch on her satin PJs. Evidence of how much she enjoys what we just did. When realising where I'm looking, she tries to bring her legs together. I put one knee onto the edge of the bed, using both of my palms to open her up again. Sliding my hands up the shining fabric I run my eyes over her flushed skin and I don't think I'll ever let her sleep in a different bed again. If she wants to go to the guest room, I'll be going there with her because the image of my wife flushed and ready for me on my sheets is a masterpiece.

Hooking my hands into the top of her trousers I pull them down to find her naked underneath. No panties to hide her swollen, wet skin. My tongue darts out to wet my lips but I must be going too slow for my darling wife because she whips off her shirt to bare her completely naked body to me.

She needs to find a way to have some patience, and an idea pops into my head. My wife wants to come, I want something in return.

"Here's how this is going to go, darlin', I'm going to eat you out. But you can't come," I tell her, and instantly I see anger race through her.

"What? Why not?" She gasps when I grip her waist and pull her down to the edge of the bed, her ass hanging over the side slightly.

"I had to wait for you to be ready to share my bed, you have to wait until I'm ready to give you pleasure." Ignoring her protests, I settle on my knees before her. Placing her legs over my shoulders, I look up at her one last time. "And when you do come, when I make you see stars, you are going to scream out for your husband."

I start slow, lapping at her soft skin. Not staying in one place too long, I lick and kiss the inside of her thighs, nipping the skin and rubbing my stubble there. She writhes below me, trying to get me to move where she wants, but I keep my cool. My dick strains against my sweatpants but I ignore it for now, needing to bring her to the highest heights. My fingers dig into her soft hips hard enough to bruise but it is one of the ways I'm keeping myself in check. I won't give her what she wants, not yet. I need her to be weak for me, completely at my mercy. Show her exactly how she makes me feel every day just by existing.

Moving my lips back over her centre I lick her from top to bottom, tasting the proof of her earlier orgasm. The tangy taste makes me moan. My tongue pushes inside her and I hear her breath shudder above me. She weaves her fingers in my hair, holding me tight against her, but I'm stronger than her. I pull myself away completely, much to her dismay.

"Please, Aiden. I need it," she whines, and her hands flop at her side.

"I know you do, darlin', but you can take more," I tell her, keeping my hands on her calves. I massage the muscles then inch them up higher, slowly massaging her legs until my fingers skim her pussy again. She flinches under me, so tense with anticipation, but I keep moving upwards until I'm massaging her breasts, ignoring the way her thighs push together trying to find release. I settle my weight over her to kiss her lips, red from where her teeth have dug into them.

She always looks so worked up and it hits me that it hasn't just been me waiting for this. Lyndsey has wanted me just as much as I want her and we have been denying ourselves for no reason.

That won't fly any more.

"Tell me you'll move into the master suite with me," I whisper against her lips, and instantly she starts nodding, not leaving any room for confusion.

"Yes, God, just please let me come," she moans, and I smile down at her with a wolfish tilt.

"Tell me I can throw the divorce papers away." I nudge her nose with mine, ghosting my lips over hers but refusing to kiss her yet.

"You can burn them for all I care. Please, Aiden."

My smile is blinding as I fist my fingers into her hair, kissing her with reverence.

Kissing down her body again I don't stop until I'm between her thighs. This time I don't hold anything back. Using two fingers I push inside of her and curve them until I hit that spot inside, making her moan out louder than before. Taking her clit between my lips I suck lightly, keeping steady pressure until she yells out my name. Moving between kissing and sucking at her skin I slip in a third finger, stretching her around me. Her wetness soaks my hand and I know she is close.

My dick leaks in my pants and I can't put myself off any longer. Pulling myself out I wrap my spare hand around my length, pumping in time with the way my fingers pump into her. The fact I held off this long should make me a saint but with the feeling of need I'm experiencing I may be going straight to hell.

With every swipe of my tongue her voice comes out louder and louder until I'm sure, if we had neighbours, they would be calling in a disturbance. Her body thrashes under me and my dick throbs in my hand. I know she is close and I want to come with her, tightening my fist around myself I pump harder as I suck her clit between my lips again.

With a final loud scream Lyndsey comes with my name on her lips, just like I told her to. She can be so obedient when she wants to be. The taste of her and the sound of her wetness around my fingers is what pushes me over the edge. We come as one, me on my own hand and her against my face. It is the best meal I have ever and will ever eat.

Using all the energy I have left, I heave myself onto the bed and pull her pliant body up with me until we are settled against the pillows. Lyndsey throws her leg over my hip and her warm breath puffs against the sweaty skin of my neck.

It doesn't take long until her breath evens out and she falls into a deep sleep against my bare chest. This is how we should have ended every night since we came back and I won't make that mistake again. If she needs space, she will tell me, but until she does, I'm going to make my wife happy in every way.

In bed but also in our day-to-day. I'll continue to drive her around and make her breakfast, I'll listen to her stories about work and I'll show her my love in a million little ways.

I fall asleep with one last thought in my head: I will prove to her that this is it for me. She is it for me.

Chapter Thirty-Four

Lyndsey

I don't know how the only ice hockey game I have been to has been Jack's, Ellis' son. I'm married to the captain of the Seattle Spears and I have never been to a game. Granted, a lot of the time we have been "married" has been spent in Texas during the off-season, but he has played a few games since we came back and I have been putting it off. Doing something so publicly when I was still getting blackmail texts felt unnecessarily dangerous. But the two weeks they gave me to get them the money has passed; I haven't received any more texts and nothing has been leaked to the press. Or if it has, maybe they haven't cared?

I could only hide away for so long until Ellis came and demanded I go to a game with her. It has been a long time since we had any girlie time. Between her pregnancy and my shock marriage we have struggled to see each other outside of work. We gossip and talk there but there is something more freeing about knowing she likes spending time with me outside of being her employee. We decided to surprise Aiden with coming to their game against Toronto tonight, even bringing Ellis and Liam's little girl Charlotte with us. As soon as he left the house, I got a taxi to her and Liam's place to get ready.

"I'm proud of you, you know?" I tell her, sipping some of the cocktail she made for us. She sits behind me curling my hair because she is just better at it than I am.

"Proud? Of what?" She laughs, rolling my hair around the barrel.

"Jack is at a sleepover and you haven't been checking your phone every five minutes." I laugh. Before she met Liam you had to pry Jack out of her arms. They were all the other had and opening herself up to needing support was a struggle. She fought hard enough to let me look after him the night she went to a bar and bumped into Liam.

"He is growing up." She sighs. "I won't smother him, I don't feel as much guilt about being apart from him any more, plus I still have Charlotte to keep me busy. It's nice having support, isn't it?" She laughs, nudging my shoulder with her knee. I know she is talking about Aiden, the support he has shown me since he found out about everything is more than I could have expected.

"Yeah, it's not bad, I guess." I roll my eyes, trying to downplay how much I like leaning on him. Falling asleep in his arms. I never thought I would be this domestic woman but I feel safe with him.

"Oh, give me a break, Anders is loving his new job as your husband." She laughs, not believing my shit. She has always been hard to lie to, I think it's because we were both at our lowest when we met. She was living in the back of the shop pregnant with Jack and I had just split up with Mel, my first real girlfriend, and didn't know where to go from there. She took me in and since then we have had a way of seeing behind the bullshit.

"I like having a husband, I like being a wife," I tell her with a deep sigh. It's a weight off my shoulders to admit it out loud. I know I should tell Aiden before I tell her but she knows what it's like to fall for a hockey player.

"If he is anything like Liam, he is going to go crazy seeing his name on your back. He is going to want it to be your name too," she teases, but she is probably right. Apparently, it's a thing for sportsmen seeing their woman in their jerseys? I'm not sure why but I'm not going to argue because it's comfortable. Plus it can be chilly at the side of the rink and I won't stick my nose up at extra warmth.

Images flash through my mind of actually being Lyndsey Anders instead of Stone. Having that connection to my family has always been painful but I also thought Aiden and I would get divorced. I never imagined actually taking his name, but I don't think it's a bad image.

"I don't think I'd hate that," I say, quickly taking another sip of my drink and rolling my eyes when Ellis cheers behind me.

"Lyndsey! Now I'm proud of you!" She puts her hands on my shoulders, shaking me lightly, and when I don't respond she runs her fingers through my curls to break them up. "Okay, enough lovey stuff, drink up. I'm going to wake Charlotte up, we have a stadium to get to."

—

Stupidly, I thought that the friends and family of the players sat in a box at the games. Ellis laughed at me and asked why they would spend that much money on commoners like us. I guess she has a point. It worries me a little being so out in the open: my anxiety about being confronted by my blackmailer tickles at the back of my head, but I push it away. Instead of being in a box all of the friends and family have seats a few rows back behind the glass.

Our view is amazing and when the boys come out onto the ice for warm-ups, Ellis jumps up with Charlotte wearing a Brink jersey for her godfather instead of her usual Ruinsky jersey. Liam was happy to stay at home and watch the game on the TV. I think a part of him wanted to be free in case Jack wants to come home. He has been an amazing stepdad to that little boy. Charlotte has baby jerseys for every player. They all think they're going to be her favourite uncle and they try to buy that affection with gifts, but I think Edge might be her favourite. That giant man is wrapped around her tiny little finger.

I jump up to wave with her and Aiden's eyes light up when he comes out of the tunnel and sees me. His eyes run all over me as though he thinks I'm going to disappear. The smile that spreads across his face will melt panties around the world but it is just for me. Not stopping until he is right at the glass, he taps his gloved finger against it and spins his finger around, making me roll my eyes knowing exactly what he wants. Slowly, I turn my back towards him so he can see Anders printed across my back, his number 3 across the centre.

I turn back around and he taps his hand against the C on the front of his jersey and I copy the motion. Taking two fingers I tap the C over my heart. With that his smile splits even wider and he starts skating backwards away from the glass with a parting wink.

"Oh, you two are in deep," Ellis says in a sing-song voice as Charlotte waves at her uncles through the glass.

It's a long time later when I wait outside the locker room. Ellis left after the game to get Charlotte home and in bed, plus she knew I wanted to see my man. Especially after the game he had. It was close, too close, but they pulled off the win and we are planning on going out for a drink with some of the guys.

Knowing I'll have to tell him, I pull my phone out, loading up the message that came through during half-time.

> You're bold I'll give you that. How long do you think you can hide behind him? I gave you grace and you spat in my face. Next time I won't be so nice.

As soon as Aiden comes out of the door the smile he is giving me drops; instead of speaking I just give him my phone. He frowns down at the screen before flicking his eyes back up to me. He grabs my shoulder and pulls me into his arms, my face buried in his neck. I didn't tell Ellis about the text. I knew she would just worry and want to leave. I didn't want that. I didn't want to let it ruin our night, but I won't keep it from Aiden.

"I'll forward it to Cassie and then we forget about it for tonight, okay? We are going to keep our chins up, go for a drink and not let them get us down." His voice is low but determined as he rests his chin on my head. I can feel him fiddling with my phone behind my back but I know he is just contacting Cassie – hopefully her PI has some information because this is becoming a nuisance.

"Okay." I sigh, tightening my arms around his trim waist, my arms linked under his suit jacket.

"I'll keep you safe," he vows. Knowing we are going to be with a lot of big hockey players calms me too. With them around nobody would dare try to approach me.

"I know," I tell him truthfully. As long as I have him by my side, I know whoever this is will keep their distance. They are a coward. They want to scare me but I won't let them, Aiden is right. I lift up on my tiptoes to plant a light kiss against his lip. He tries to deepen it but just then Rook comes barrelling out of the locker room.

"Come on, Anders and Mrs Anders, we have beer to drink!" Linking his arm through mine as he talks, he pulls me away from Aiden and down the corridor, making me laugh over my shoulder as my husband looks after me, smiling.

Jogging after us until he is right there, Aiden pulls me away from Rook and swings me so I'm over his shoulder looking down at his trouser-covered ass. Rook whoops beside us and I lift my eyes to see the rest of the team trickling out of the locker room, joining us without even mentioning the scene in front of them as though this is completely normal. Instead of fighting I slap my husband's ass and he smacks mine right back.

—

By the time I'm two drinks in I have successfully pushed all thoughts about the text away. Mostly. With the guys entertaining me and plying me with alcohol they have kept me distracted.

"How have I been married for months and not one of you has told me any embarrassing stories about my husband? What kind of family are you?" I ask, dropping my glass to the table and cuddling in to Aiden where he sits on the lush velvet sofa next to me.

"Oh, I have one!" Rook's Canadian twang is strong from the alcohol and his voice is loud over the low music in the bar, a private room in a speakeasy the guys found earlier this year. "Alice came to a game once, eh, and she came to training right?"

"Oh God. You came on to her, didn't you?" I guess, my face scrunching in disgust.

"Of course I did, she is a smokeshow," he laughs, and Aiden's shoulders shake next to me, clearly knowing where this story is going. "But before she could fall in love with me your dear husband here threw a puck at my head. Well, he tried to, didn't you?"

"What does that mean?" I ask, looking up at him.

"I missed." He closes his eyes while he admits it.

Rook laughs loudly, struggling to catch his breath. "He didn't just miss, he hit Coach Mitch!" he yells, throwing back the rest of his drink. Aiden drops his head to my shoulder but I burst into giggles myself. Everyone jeers and laughs as they move on to the next thing.

Seeing them like this, so open with each other, I know what Ellis means when she says the guys are a family. They all see Aiden as the team dad who they can depend on. Edge is the grumpy uncle. They all have their roles. It makes me miss the idea of family. We were never like this but I wonder if we were ever happy. If all my bad memories are overshadowing all the good. I know my mom loves me, even if she has a hard time showing it. My dad, I'm not so sure.

Still, it makes me wistful. I don't know if it is the alcohol clouding my judgement but I pull my phone out of my purse to fire a message off to my dad. He is proud – even if he has come around on my sexuality, I doubt he would reach out. I want to take that step. If Lyndsey

Stone can end up married to an ice hockey player, I guess anything is possible.

> Hey, I hope you're good. Can we get together one day, talk. I think it would be good.

I type quickly and hit send before I can regret it. It's only a few minutes later that I get a reply. It's not the one I want.

> Who is this?

Instantly tears spring to my eyes, but I blink them away. I don't know what I was thinking. I guess having so many loving people around me confused me. Made me realise that I'm loveable, so my parents must love me deep down. I'm wrong. How can he not have his only daughter's number saved? How soon after I left did he delete me from his life?

Sensing my distress, Aiden hooks a finger under my chin, pulling my attention from my phone to him. "Hey, what's wrong?" he asks, his eyes suddenly blazing. He looks down at my phone but the screen has turned dark.

"My family hates me, nothing new," I tell him around the lump in my throat. I see pity in his eyes but he quickly replaces it with burning determination. Keeping his finger under my chin, he nudges my head so I can see the laughing guys all talking and joking together.

"You have a new family now," he tells me, his lips close to my ears, his words just for me.

"I have a story." Edge's voice splits across the room, shocking me. My eyes fly to him and his eyes shift between me, Aiden and my phone. I think he sees my distress because he puts his own drink down in front of me, offering it to me. Picking it up with a soft smile I sip the room-temperature beer. "Did you know I have an A tattooed on my ankle because of your husband?" he tells me, and clearly Rook didn't know this nugget of information because his head snaps to Edge with wide eyes.

"What?" Rook and I say at the same time, both with the same level of excitement.

"Oh yeah, we were both drunk and playing pool. He said if I won he would get a J tattoo but if he won I had to get an A." He nods like it is the most normal thing in the world and I shake my head at their antics.

"And you lost?" I laugh, thinking that is the whole story. I'm wrong though because Edge glares at Aiden and shakes his head.

"Yeah, but only because he cheated," he accuses, and I look up at my husband to see him smirking. Oh God. What did he do?

"How?" I ask, swinging my attention back to Edge. Rook is on the edge of his seat and everyone else is starting to pay attention now too. Looking at their captain in confusion.

"It was only while I was halfway through the tattoo that he dropped the act, the fucker wasn't drunk." My jaw all but hits the floor but Edge is smiling, if he was mad about it, I guess that has passed by now. "He hustled me because I was the new kid on the team."

"Holy shit! Let me see!" Rook says, jumping up and lifting Edge's pants leg. Shaking him off, Edge rolls up his other pants leg and pulls down his sock and right there, just above his ankle, is an intricate A permanently etched in his skin.

Even though I'm laughing, I turn to Aiden and slap him on his broad chest. "That was mean!"

"Yeah, it was also fucking hilarious," he tells me, laughing and pulling me even closer to him, laying a kiss on my head.

I know why Edge did what he did and I'm so thankful. As Edge demands a rematch I put a lock on thoughts of my family. They have blocked me out of their minds and I guess it is time I do the same. At least now I'm not facing that daunting task alone. I doubt I'll ever be alone again.

Chapter Thirty-Five

Lyndsey

I'm awoken to the smell of coffee and Aiden lightly nudging my shoulder. The only problem with that picture is that it is still dark outside, way too early to be awake. So I try to roll back over.

"Darlin', I need you to wake up." Even through my sleep-fuelled haze I can hear the tightness in his voice. I roll back over so I can see him and I'm shocked to see him already dressed.

"What's going on?" I bolt up in bed, sleep fading away every second. His jaw is tense but he is still looking at me with softness in his eyes. Like he is genuinely rattled. Even the day William died he was more balanced, he started looking after his sisters and pushed his own emotions down. Right now I can see every worry and bit of anger he is trying to suppress.

"Cassie called. The PI has something for us, they are waiting at the arena." My whole world stops. Then everything starts spinning. My heart pounds in my chest as the room shifts under me. Aiden slides into the bed, his jeans hard against my naked legs but there is nothing sexual about it. He pulls me to his chest and it is when I feel the wetness on his oversized T-shirt that I realise I'm crying.

I'm relieved that this might be over. But more than that, I'm scared. Scared that someone really hates me this much. Scared of actually facing whoever has tried their best to pull me down. Scared that I might not even know them. That there might be a person out there who hates me even when they don't know me. There is the other option: that I do know them. That someone I might care about wants to ruin me. Another fear starts to rise. The fear that if this day goes the way I want it to, that we catch whoever this is, that I won't get to live with Aiden any more.

We haven't discussed divorce and I know he cares about me. We sleep in the same bed, fuck every chance we get, and he even made me *a private dining experience* – I never knew Aiden was capable of thinking about such things. But we were pushed together through circumstance and lies. I don't want it to unravel. This whole relationship, this love I've fallen into, could be hanging by a thread.

I push closer into his chest, needing the comfort only he can bring me, and he lets me cry. Slowly rubbing up and down my spine until I'm able to catch my breath. Still my mind runs a thousand miles an hour, trying to figure out who it could be.

Then there is the idea it might be a crazy Spears fan. Someone who thinks I'm not good enough for Aiden. But how would they get my number? How would a stranger know about my sexuality? I can imagine people being jealous that I'm his wife but doing all this just seems silly. Then again, when people are caught up in their emotions, they do crazy things. Fans have killed their idols before so blackmailing their wives isn't completely out of the realm of possibility.

I dress in silence, not ready to voice all of my anxieties. Aiden already looks on edge: his jaw clenches and he keeps mumbling to himself. The tension in the room is so thick that it feels hard to swallow. Not wanting to push him, I stay in my own world, imagining every possibility as we make our way to the stadium.

"Can you promise me something?" My words are a bullet through the silence. Aiden's eyes dart from the road to me as we pull into the staff parking at the arena.

"Anything," he tells me, taking one hand from where he is white-knuckling the wheel and lifting my hand in his, weaving our fingers together.

"Don't let whatever happens in there change the way you look at me. Don't hate me." My chest feels tight and it's hard to hold his gaze but I try.

"Darlin'... I'm doing everything I can to keep my anger in check. Half of me wants to find whoever is doing this and beat them to a pulp and the other half wants to take you home and lock us away so we don't have to face this." His chest heaves and his fingers tighten between mine. I go to comfort him but before I can he continues, "I'm not mad at you, Lynds, I'm pissed that you had to deal with this and glad that it might be over. I'm just trying to keep my emotions in check so I can support you."

"We can do this." I don't know if I'm trying to convince him or myself but he nods at me anyway, leaning over and taking my jaw in his hand.

"Together," he whispers against my lips, kissing me lightly.

By the time we make it to Cassie's office she is waiting with the PI behind her desk, a manila envelope waiting in front of her.

"Thanks for coming, guys, how are you holding up, Lynds?" she asks with a sad smile. My hands start to sweat and I can't talk through the lump in my throat. Instead I just nod.

"What do you have?" Aiden asks Lewis, the PI. This is the second time I have met him, the first being just after Aiden demanded I move into his place, and he looks exactly like I imagined a PI to be. He is a short man, not much taller than me, with thinning hair. Frankly he could be green with spiky purple hair for all I care, as long as he has found the culprit.

"Mrs Anders, this isn't going to be easy to hear." He pauses before picking up the envelope and passing it over to me. "I traced the number, it was a burner but he used his credit card to buy it. I followed him for a few days and he has been in and out of poker rooms. My guess is that he is deep in debt."

My hands shake as I open the folder. There are a few pictures inside, different angles and different shady bars in the background. The man in the pictures, though, he looks the same as I remember him. Just more tired and thin.

"Him? Who is it?" Aiden asks from beside me, but his voice sounds like I'm underwater. My shaking hand comes up to cover my mouth, tears streak down my cheeks.

I manage to push out two words before sobs rack my body. I almost choke on them.

"My brother."

Chapter Thirty-Six

Aiden

Seeing my wife break in front of me, knowing there is nothing I can do to fix it, wrecks me. Lyndsey heaves, gripping the pictures hard against her chest. Her shoulders are curled in on herself and her hair falls over her shoulders. I would do anything to take this pain from her. Anger rises in my chest, hating to see her pain. I want to rage. To demand that her brother is arrested. I want to yell at Lewis for showing her these pictures, as irrational as that is. I knew when Cassie called this morning that it would be the reckoning but I never imagined it would be her own flesh and blood. I was so certain that it was Kayla that I didn't really think of another possibility.

I love my sisters so much that I can't imagine causing them harm. Of course we argue and have had our fair few fallouts but to hurt them this deeply? I don't know what kind of person could do this just because of who she loves. Lyndsey is an amazing woman, smart and kind and still, just because she doesn't fit with their religion, her family have written her off. Treating her so badly that her brother felt confident enough that he won't face any consequences. But he has never met me. I'll make sure he pays for hurting her this way.

"Why does he hate me?" Her voice is filled with anguish and I wish I had an answer. "What did I ever do to him?"

"Can we have a moment alone?" I ask Cassie. Her eyes are filled with tears, her hand covering her mouth to repress her own sadness. Giving me a stiff nod she stands and leaves the room, Lewis following behind her with pity in his eyes.

As soon as the door closes behind them, I fall to the floor in front of Lyndsey, kneeling between her legs, and pull her to me. Holding the back of her head to my neck I whisper reassurance into her ear.

"We can fix this," I tell her, but I'm also comforting myself. "You don't deserve this, darlin', you deserve to be happy." I mean it. Nobody should be treated like this, especially by their own family.

It takes everything in me to stay calm. She needs my gentleness right now but there is so much anger pulsing through my veins that it is making me shake. I hold her with soft hands, the hands I know have seen so much violence. As a hockey player I know how to work out my frustrations on the ice, if someone is playing dirty, I push them into the boards. If someone hurts my teammates, I take off my gloves and start swinging.

I have never been this deeply mad on the ice though. I have only been this angry once before and that was when someone was bullying Cece when she was younger. Someone pushed her down the stairs in school because they were angry she got the highest grade. Pops had to hold me back from driving to the school and yelling at a kid. But now I don't have a wise person here telling me how to focus these emotions. There is no one to hold me back from the blinding anger. I have to do it myself. I have to rein my rage in so I can be what Lyndsey needs.

My wife needs my heart not my fists. Still, it makes me sick to do nothing. But I would do anything to keep her safe, even if that means keeping her safe from me. Not that I would ever hurt her. I would walk to hell and back barefoot if it meant she would be happy and protected.

-

By the time we have made it back into the car, Lyndsey has stopped crying but I'm not much calmer. My hands are sweaty on the leather steering wheel and I can feel Lyndsey's eyes on me from the passenger seat. I don't dare look over at her though, knowing I'm still on the edge. I know she won't think less of me for being emotional but right now is her time to lean on me, not the other way around. I need to be the strong one. Hell, she just found out her damn brother has been the evil following her for the past few months, she shouldn't have to be walking on eggshells because of me.

I need to pull it together.

"You need to calm down, the police will deal with it," she tells me. Lewis informed us that the police have been sent all of the evidence he has collected and a restraining order is in the works. The Spears lawyers have already drafted a cease-and-desist that is being delivered this afternoon, informing Peter that if he continues with this, we will come down on him with the force of a thousand suns. And for now that is all I can do.

"I'll be calm when I know he can't contact you any more." It probably won't actually fix my anger but it will take a weight off my shoulders, that's for sure. There is also the bonus that if he does decide to go to the press in some last-ditch attempt at a money grab, we have a paper trail showing how erratic he is.

"I know you're angry but if you go and do something stupid, he will get you arrested to make you look like the bad guy." She sighs, and I know she is right in theory. Still, I think the satisfaction of breaking his nose might be worth a night in a cell.

"I just want you to be safe." And as long as the police do everything they can to keep her that way then I won't take matters into my own hands. But the police aren't always the most helpful with things like this. I don't like using my name for preferential treatment but if I have to sign a few pucks to hand out I'll do what I have to, to get her the protection she deserves.

"I know, cowboy." She pauses, clearly weighing up if she wants to say what is on her mind. "Do you think they know? My parents, I mean." Her hands wring in her lap, too anxious to stay still.

"Honestly, I don't know." I want to yell at her parents for treating her the way they have, it seems unbelievable to me to love your child under so many conditions. "I'd like to think they don't but I can't imagine kicking my kid out either so who knows?"

"I know they don't agree with my sexuality but they are still my family." She nibbles at her bottom lip, pushing her fingers through her ginger locks. "I wish I could say I don't care about them but a part of me still does. If they do know and didn't try to stop him, what kind of parents can do that to their own family?"

"Either way, I'm your family now. You don't need them, you have so many people that love you for exactly who you are." I hope she hears what I'm saying. That I love her. I don't want to give her those words when they are being overshadowed by all of the bad of the day. Still, it doesn't make it any less true.

I love Lyndsey. And I'm going to give her the family she deserves.

Chapter Thirty-Seven

Aiden

I'm doing something stupid. I know I shouldn't but I can't get the image of my wife sobbing, asking why her family hates her, out of my head. Every time I close my eyes, I see her tear-stained cheeks, her eyes filled with anguish. I think about her as a child doing everything to earn her parents' love, for them to throw it back in her face when she didn't conform to their desires and beliefs. I have to do something to wipe that picture from my head.

So I'm driving to her childhood home. I dropped her off at Bloom and Blossom and as far as she knows I'm on my way to the stadium for training. Actually, I called Coach Mitch and told him I'm going to be late. He knows what has been happening through Cassie and he was willing to give me a few hours as long as I work my ass off when I get back on the ice.

I didn't tell anyone on the team about Lyndsey's brother. It isn't my story to tell, but it's probably a good thing I didn't. I know that, if I did, most of them would be in this car with me ready to confront the Stone family. By the time I make it to Blue Ridge where Lyndsey grew up, I question coming alone. I don't know much about her dad. I could use some support but I'm so fuelled by my emotions that I push through.

Parking my car outside of the small family home, it looks incredibly normal. I don't know what I expected but I know what has happened behind those doors. The hatred and anger. To a passer-by nothing would flag this house as out of the ordinary. The lawn is trimmed and the car in the driveway is clean. There is not a single thing out of place.

I walk up to the front door of the light blue single-storey house and take a calming breath before I knock on the door. Probably harder than I should. It takes a lot not to pound on it and demand entrance; whoever is inside should be thankful I'm holding on to my emotions.

The door swings open and my eyes drop to the man in front of me. If it wasn't for his ginger hair, the same light strawberry shade as my wife's, I wouldn't know that this is her father. His hair is cut close to his scalp, his face is clean-shaven. His eyes, a much darker hue than his daughter's, look up at me with surprise.

"Ah. Aiden, come to visit your father-in-law, I see. Would you like to come in?" His voice is prim and proper. He drops the surprise from his face, trying to appear at ease, but I see his eye twitch slightly as I stare him down.

"Are you kidding?" I laugh at the absurdity. He is inviting me in like we are old friends. This is the man who kicked his daughter out for being gay and he expects me to be chummy with him. The level of delusion is diabolical.

"Excuse me?" he asks, incredulous. He even puts a hand to his chest as though he is offended. If that has offended him then he has no idea what is coming.

"How can you stand there and act like this is a normal occurrence for you? You are a disgrace." I spit down at him, truly disgusted by him.

I see Lyndsey in my mind wishing for this man's affection. Just wanting her dad to hold her and guide her through life, and instead she was given scraps of affection from this man who thinks he is so morally superior. My dad would be sick to see a man treating his children this way and my mom would be devastated to know how Lyndsey's mom never stood up for her daughter.

"How dare you!" he splutters, but I refuse to let him try and excuse his behaviour.

"No! You are going to listen." I put one hand on to the side of the door frame beside his head. His beady eyes flick back and forth between my eyes and where my fingers dig into the wood. "Your daughter has found people who love her and she doesn't need you or your shit attitude any more. I'm here to give you a warning. I hope you have nothing to do with what your son has done to my wife because if I found out you have been involved, hell, if I find out you even knew it was going on, I'm going to rake your reputation through the mud. What will your church friends think to know your son is a criminal? I don't think that would be good for you." I mean it too. It would be nothing to add him to the restraining order if it came out that he knew about his son's harassment. Having a record when you are such a respected member of the community – well, that would ruin his squeaky-clean facade.

"Are you threatening me?" His skin flushes red now when he starts to shout, his eyes bulging.

"No, sir, I'm telling you. If Lyndsey gets one more text from anyone in this family, I'll file a harassment suit. I will throw everything I can at you until you are ruined. Do I make myself clear?" I have money to spare and I'll use it to bury this man in litigation. Even if I know that no charges would ever come from it, I'll hire the best lawyers to make sure he never financially recovers if I have to.

"It's not my fault she is sick in the head. She let the devil in. She has always been a problem," he sneers, spitting as he rants, but then his lips split into a sick grin. "Maybe marrying a good man might fix her sinning ways."

I'm stunned silent. How can anyone talk about their child that way? He also hasn't asked what his son did, all but confirming he knows what has been happening. Actually, he wants to stand here and make it out to be her fault. My hand tightens on the door frame, the wood creaking under the pressure.

"You make me sick." I shake my head at him, I don't know how a woman as amazing as my darlin' came from a man like this. "Lyndsey is a blessing, the best thing that has happened in my life, and I'm going to show her every day what it means to be loved unconditionally the way you should have. I would walk through hell to make her smile and the fact you are going to miss out on her life is your own fault. You have no one to blame but yourself."

"You can have her. She has no value to me." He rolls his eyes. He rolls his fucking eyes. Like we are talking about a fucking casserole dish and not his own daughter. She isn't a stock in a company, she is his flesh and blood, but somehow that isn't valuable enough for him.

"I'm going to keep her and cherish her and I want you to know that your life will always be meaningless." I want to dig the knife in, cause him even a moment of the pain Lyndsey has suffered since she was kicked out of this very door all those years ago. "Your legacy is a daughter who has prevailed through your bullshit and a son who's drowning in debt. You will be forgotten with nothing but your stupid pride to keep you warm at night."

With that I turn and walk away from him, leaving him shouting obscenities after me before I hear the door slam with enough force for the sound to echo. A neighbour over the road is at his mailbox watching the scene unfold with his jaw hanging open. I hope he tells every other neighbour what he saw. The captain of the Seattle Spears putting Mr Stone in his place.

I hope they all whisper when he walks by, glare at him like gum on their shoes. I nod at the man as though giving him permission to gossip. I doubt Lyndsey's parents will ever feel as shunned as she did but maybe, just maybe, they will feel the same shame they placed on their daughter.

I leave the Stone house without looking back and get into my car. Coach Mitch doesn't have to worry about me not being focused on the ice but the punching bags will be taking a beating. Anyone who is forced to play against me today will be pushed to their limits. I want to skate and I want to skate hard. We have to travel for a game this weekend so I have a target to aim my raging emotions into. By the time I make it home on Sunday I want to put this behind me.

I'm going to move forward with Lyndsey, no longer being tied down by the weight of blackmail or my grief.

Just me and her.

The next step is to make sure it stays that way. We just have to be open to it. I know I'm ready, so she'd better buckle up.

Chapter Thirty-Eight

Lyndsey

Aiden got in late last night. He flew out on Thursday afternoon and I was fast asleep when he got home in the early hours of Sunday morning, meaning I haven't seen him in person for days. We talked on the phone and texted almost constantly but it has nothing on being in his presence. After spending so much time together in Texas it was strange to come back to Seattle and spend so much time apart between working and travelling. Especially since he moved me into the master bedroom, sleeping alone after getting used to being intertwined was a stark feeling. Still, I get to watch his games and I love seeing him on the ice. It is almost artistic to see the way his body moves while balancing on blades. The whole team comes together in a choreographed dance that only they know.

He played hard last night. I watched the game with Liam and Ellis and a few glasses of wine and Liam made sure to tell me that the level of aggression from Aiden isn't normal. He fought and brawled like I've never seen and it was hot. That's probably wrong of me but, damn, seeing him sweaty and panting with blood dripping from his eyebrow... yeah that was sexy.

Now, he looks so at peace. I stand at the side of the bed with a tray of breakfast but I can't find it in me to wake him. There is a small bandage on his eyebrow from where he had to get stitches and I want to kiss it better. He just seems so completely exhausted.

So much has happened over the past few months. We got married. He travelled to Texas. His grandfather died. I was being blackmailed. He moved me in with him. All that while still being the captain of the Spears. I don't know how he hasn't completely snapped. It's too much for one person to handle and yet he has done it with grace. Never taking out his frustrations on me when I know I'm the source of some of the pressure on him.

That is why I wanted to make him breakfast. A deep, quiet part of me wants to prove to him that he needs me around. As if by making a ham omelette and a pot of coffee I can show him that I make his life better. Because he makes mine better. He came clean about confronting my dad. Basically, as soon as he walked through the front door the words and apologies tumbled out. I wasn't angry. I was just tired. He refused to tell me exactly what my dad said but I know it wasn't good. Nothing he ever says is good. He protected my honour and now I want to look after him in return.

That's when I realised, I really do love my husband. The feelings weren't caused by emotion or proximity. I love him because he sees me. He knows me down to my soul and treats every part of it like it is precious. He has my heart in his hands and as scary as that feels I know he will keep it safe. Exactly the same way I'll keep his safe if he wants to give it to me.

My feelings for him could surpass any sonnet or declaration. That's why I haven't said the words. They are too small for what I feel.

I love you.

It seems so easy and nonchalant when what I feel is bigger and brighter than any universe. I remember the letter he wrote for me in Texas. He found a way to share his feelings with me and I need to believe he meant it. Just because my parents didn't mean it when they told me they loved me that doesn't mean that Aiden is lying. He has never lied to me.

From the first time we met he has told me how I wormed my way under his skin. But taking the leap, trusting the words, feels like a canyon I can't cross.

Being in love is unlike anything I could have imagined. My heart is exposed to the elements, ready to be broken, and yet I smile through the pain. So endlessly happy to have ripped it from my chest and given it to him. When I woke up in Vegas wrapped in his arms, I never would have pictured me here. Looking down at him sleeping, still married after all this time. Hell, I wanted an annulment five minutes after I awoke and now the thought of separating myself from him would shred me apart.

My life before Vegas feels like a different woman. In a way she was. I was hiding myself because I wanted to be what everyone wanted instead of just being me. I was so scared that I would never be enough that I created this impenetrable wall to hide behind. All for Aiden to drive a damn wrecking ball right through it. I couldn't keep him from seeing me no matter how hard I tried.

I saw him, the way he puts everybody above himself to feel needed; and he saw me, a woman who needed solid support to fix my crumbling foundations. By marrying me and asking me to stay his wife he started to fill in the holes in my heart.

It hits me now that we didn't have to stay married. After Texas he could have divorced me and still let me live here to keep me safe. Being his wife didn't give me extra protection and yet neither of us brought it up. If anything he acted more like my husband. Bringing me into his home. Bringing me into his bed. Bringing me into his heart.

He has shown me in a million ways that he is serious about this. From that letter to his unwavering protection, and now it is my turn. I'll show him how in this I am. How much I love him. The words might not come yet but he needs to see it. I don't want him to think this is some hero worship, to worry that I love him for helping with my asshole brother.

For a while I thought his affection was because of his grief. Then I thought it was because of the fact I was in his house. But I can't deny myself any more. I know Aiden loves me. I'm his wife because we both want me to be. He is my husband because I never want to lose him. Because I love him.

I love him because of the way he makes us breakfast.

I love him because of the way he holds me in his arms like I might disappear.

I love him because of the way he treats his sisters.

I love him because of the strength he leads his team with.

I love him because he loves me.

Chapter Thirty-Nine

Lyndsey

I decide not to wake him up, I can't bring myself to disturb him. Instead, I get ready in silence and order a taxi to Bloom and Blossom. By the time I make it to work I'm filled with determination. I have never been the type of woman to tiptoe around things. Yes, I like to be independent, but I know that I want Aiden and I know deep down that he wants me too. No matter what those anxious thoughts try to tell me. If he wanted a divorce, we would be divorced by now. I have to trust my own intuition and look at all of the things he has done for me. He has protected me and let me into his house – hell, into his bed. He has shown me grace but most of all he has let me in. He has let me see the real him. Not the captain of the Spears, but the man. Aiden Anders, brother and protector, with a huge heart that I own a part of.

Peter scared me, I'm not too weak to admit that he had me on edge, made me feel like I was still a teenager and he still had power over me. I felt myself regressing back to that scared girl who couldn't believe that anyone would love me for me. But I have friends who care about me, people to lean on and a husband who will go to war for me. I won't let him win by breaking me and Aiden. I'm stronger than what he threw at me. I won't sit around and wait for things to happen to me. I want my husband despite how unconventional our beginning was and I'm going to show him that I'm all in.

"Ellis... can I ask a huge favour?" I yell to where she is in the back office ordering some gerberas. We don't have any consultations today so I know I won't be leaving her in the lurch.

"Sure thing, what's up?" She comes to join me behind the front desk, slapping the order forms down and putting her weight on her hands so she is almost down to my height. I have known her for long enough to know that her hips must be aching. Her fibromyalgia is a struggle for her but she never complains. Always just chipping away at the day, doing what she needs to do so she can make money and go home healthy to her kids.

"Can I leave?" I ask, biting my lip. A part of me wishes she had stayed in the back room so I wouldn't have to see the way her eyes widen when they snap to me. Her mouth opens slightly.

"What?" She laughs, shocked. I never say no to working extra hours. I know what it is like to not know when you are going to be able to pay the bills, I never just give up a shift.

"I want to surprise Aiden." I can hear the hesitance in my words but she doesn't comment on it. I don't want to share the whole plan that is forming. I want to keep that close to my chest.

"Aw, Lyndsey, yes of course you can go. I like seeing you happy." She puts her hand on my shoulder, her eyes glistening with tears. A few years ago she would never have been this open with her emotions, but since she has fallen in love with Liam again her emotional walls are a lot thinner.

"Don't be sappy," I say with a roll of my eyes, but I can't smother the wide grin splitting my face.

"Oh, get out." She pushes me, still laughing. I have her to thank for my happiness. If it wasn't for her and Liam then I never would have met Aiden, never mind married him. He was just a celebrity athlete I had a crush on and now I share his bed.

"I'm going, I'm going. Thank you!" I know she won't change her mind but still I grab my bag and hustle out of the shop without looking back.

My mind runs with ideas of how I can show Aiden exactly how much he means to me. We have never even been on a date. I have met his family and, unfortunately, he has met some of mine, but we have never got dressed to the nines and hit the town for a real date. I'm going to change that. But I want more than just a nice meal, especially because I know he will pay even if I demand that it is my treat. Plus it feels too easy, not "us" enough. Aiden deserves to feel cared for and seen, the way he has made me feel. That is why I'm going to do more.

My plan forms. Clues around the city. Places that remind me of him. Clues for him to solve with the prize at the end being me in a pretty dress ready for a romantic meal with my husband. Now I just need to figure out how the hell to do all of that in the few hours before he comes home from the gym and watching game clips with Coach Mitch.

Hours later I sit in Il Moroso, a restaurant I could never get a reservation at, especially on such short notice – but I had a trump card. Cassie. She was more than happy to throw the Spears name around to get me a table and it worked a treat. The lights in the restaurant are low and sultry and quiet orchestral music flows around the room.

It is the type of restaurant that somehow is quiet no matter how many people are inside. Hushed voices, the sound of forks on plates, but that is it. There are no arguments or rambunctious kids running around. Definitely not my usual scene but it felt the most romantic place I could find. The Italian food is apparently super authentic and tasty.

Now I just need to wait for Aiden. Every second that I sit here alone I think he isn't going to make it. What if I made the clues too complicated? What if he doesn't want to come on a date with me in case we get hounded by fans? My anxiety climbs by the second and I wish I had a stiff drink to take the edge off. But no. I want to seem classy so I sip at my glass of red wine, picking my fingernails. I know that he will come. He always shows up for me and I need to remember that. I'm his wife and he is my husband, we chose each other and I know in my heart he will be on his way. I push down the niggling anxieties that feel almost built into my DNA as I picture how his eyes will light up when they see me.

My dress is a lush velvet in a dark blue shade, so dark that in certain lights it appears black. My hair is twisted in a messy updo and my make-up is layered to perfection. When I was getting ready, I imagined Aiden's eyes when he saw me, the heat that would flash there, but as I sit here alone I wish I blended in with the wall. I know that I'm here early, Aiden isn't due to be here for another few minutes, but with every glance around the room it feels smaller. As if every other person here pities me, looking like I have been stood up at the most romantic restaurant in all of Seattle.

They know I'm not supposed to be here. I feel so judged but the more I look around the more I see that nobody is paying me a lick of attention. All too wrapped up in their own date nights. It's my own doubt scaring me. All of my internalised homophobia and my low confidence. I deserve to be here just as much as anyone else. My parents made me feel so small that sometimes I still find it hard to take up space. Instead of my parents' voices, it's Aiden's that pulls me out of my head. Every time he has called me beautiful. Every time he has caressed my skin. I don't need to be worried about him not showing because he loves me. I know that I'm worthy of his love even if we haven't actually said the words.

The bell above the entrance chimes; my eyes dart to the door. Aiden stands in the entrance in a crisp suit with a huge bouquet of flowers filling his arms. Once he spots me across the room his eyes sparkle, darting all over my face as though I'm a sunrise, filled with beauty.

Not wasting a second, his long legs cross the room and I find myself standing to greet him. Every moment of anxiety I have felt melts away when he drops the flowers on the table and pulls me into his arms. My hands grip at the lapel of his suit jacket as he kisses me. It is an appropriate kiss, nothing super long or steamy, but it is everything. I can feel the curve of his lips smiling against mine. His hands settle on my hips when I pull away from the kiss, not letting me go too far.

He looks down at me smiling and I know mine matches his. I feel almost giddy in his arms as we stare in silence, just enjoying each other's space. Blinking rapidly as though coming out of a trance, Aiden shakes his head.

"You're incredible," he tells me, his voice low. Dropping another light kiss on my lips, he pulls out my chair.

Based on the heated look in his eyes and the way he refuses to drop my hand, I think I have been successful. I'm on a date with my husband and I'm the luckiest girl in Seattle.

Chapter Forty

Aiden

It's late in the morning by the time I wake up. When my arm stretches across the bed, I feel the cold sheets where Lyndsey should be. I hate that she didn't wake me. I feel like I haven't seen her in such a long time between travelling and needing sleep. I want to spend every minute with her but I know she has her own life. Still, when I grab my phone to send her a good morning text my face breaks into a huge smile when I see she has already sent me a message.

> Morning Cowboy, I think you should go look in your car... there might be a little gift there for you

My heart starts to pound as I jump from the bed, not bothering to throw on any warmer clothes. Just wearing my boxers and a pair of slippers, I slide into the garage and fling open the driver's-side door to find a small white envelope waiting there. What is she up to? Not being gentle, in my impatience I rip it open, pulling out the small card inside.

> *The smell of food and sunshine was the backdrop of the first place I met you. Do you remember where?*

Of course I remember. That barbeque where Ruin introduced us to Ellis for the first time and the moment I realised her best friend Lyndsey was the most beautiful woman I had ever seen. Quickly I jog back inside and upstairs, throwing on the first clothes I find. A pair of jeans and an old T-shirt that has seen better days, but I don't waste time finding something better. I need to know what she has in store for me.

It takes every part of my restraint to not break any laws as I zoom the few minutes to Ruin's house. His modern home is littered with proof of his family. Jack, his stepson, has left his bike on the grass out front and there is a basketball hoop and small hockey net near the garage. Knocking on the door I rock from one foot to the other as I wait for him to open it.

I hear Charlotte squeal from behind the wood and let out a deep breath as the door swings open, revealing my old teammate and his daughter strapped to his chest.

"Here he is!" he laughs. Charlotte reaches out for me and I take her. She puts her little hands on my face, squishing my cheeks together.

"Hi!" she yells right in my face, making me laugh, and Ruin steps out of the way so I can bring her inside.

"Hey, Char, how is my best girl?" I tickle her little belly and she howls out laughter, trying to wiggle out of my arms again for her dad to save her. Seeing him as a dad is amazing to me but I always knew he would take to it like a duck to water. He is naturally one of the most caring men I know and any kid would be lucky to have him as a dad. Still, I want to know what he has for me more than I want to chill with Charlotte.

Without saying anything he pulls an envelope out of his back pocket, identical to the first one. I rip it open just the same.

I like it when you are looking fresh, don't be late.

"I don't know what this means?" I tell him, panicked. The first clue had so much more information.

"I do. We're going on a trip, aren't we, baby?" And Charlotte nods like she is in on this plan.

The two of them put on their coats and we get into our cars. It's easier if I just follow him that way, we don't need to move the car seat over. Plus Ruin is a bad liar so I think he wants me to be in my own car so I can't question him. After a few minutes, when I don't bother to even turn on the radio, we pull into a parking lot I recognise. Stopping the car in the spot beside his we get out of our cars and head to the shop our barber owns.

I don't know how Lyndsey knows where I get my hair done but I could do with a cut. A lot of players don't cut their hair or shave when they are in season, so worried about their superstitions, but I have always felt like I play better when I feel fresh. And if Lyndsey is wanting me to look my best I won't complain, especially with how tired I have been.

Edge is waiting inside the shop for me. Ruin slaps my back and Charlotte waves as they call out their goodbyes. I'm whipped into a chair as soon as I'm inside and my barber starts working on my usual cut. Short but not to the skin on the sides and enough on top for Lyndsey to pull on.

My day seems to be flying by. By the time my hair is finished, Edge is waiting outside for me and, when I walk out, he hands me another envelope.

> *I have spoken to Coach Mitch, you can watch tapes another day. My favourite hockey to watch is our smallest hockey player where you spilled the beans about our marriage. What could be waiting there for you?*

I know what this one means luckily. The rink where Jack plays with his kids' league. I smile at Edge, but he is looking at me with a crinkle between his brows.

"What's wrong?" I ask, even though I want to get in my car and speed off again.

"You will figure it out. Your wife is something else." He laughs now. Whatever had him troubled disappears. Just as Ruin did, Edge pats me on the shoulder, sending me on my way again.

When my car pulls into the rink's lot, I realise what had Edge frowning. Rook is waiting for me, his eyes widening in excitement when my car pulls up. Instead of waiting for me to get out he comes over and climbs in, bringing a big clothing bag with him.

"This is so fucking cool, eh!" He is bouncing in the seat, looking so much lighter than he did at the end of last season. We didn't make it to the playoffs last year, his rookie season, and he took it out on himself, but this year there has been a change in him. He is as bouncy and childlike as he always is but I can see in his eyes that there is something more relaxed about him.

"You have a note for me?" I ask because he isn't as quick on the draw as the other two were.

"Oh shit, yeah. I have it somewhere." He starts rustling through his pockets until he finds an envelope tucked in his jeans back pocket. It's a little bent where he has sat on it but I'm no less excited. "Wait, before I give this to you, have this first." He hands me the garment bag and I pull the zip down a bit to peek inside and see a full suit.

"Jesus, how did she plan all of this?" I ask, but it is rhetorical. I'm just so blown away with her clear display of affection.

"All of us had a part. Mine was obviously the suit and Cassie got a reservation. Wait, shit, I wasn't supposed to tell you anything. Fuck!" He slaps his hand over his mouth. His eyes are wide, scared I'm going to be mad at him, but it just makes me laugh.

"Give me the envelope, Rook." I take pity on him. I'm too excited and happy by how my day has unfolded that I couldn't be mad at him even if he had actually done something bad.

I had already assumed this day was going somewhere and a restaurant makes the most sense. And besides he didn't tell me where it is so he hasn't ruined any clues.

"Yep, I'm leaving before I say anything else. Have a good night." He winks, his words filled with innuendo and absolutely no subtlety, and I roll my eyes. He jumps out of the car with a small salute and ambles off towards his car.

I don't tell him but I think this night is going to be amazing. Setting all of this up is the most romantic thing anyone has ever done for me. Hell, I have never had a real partner before and, when I thought about it, I always assumed it would be me planning all of the dates.

> *I am a simple girl, I love flowers. Even if someone tried to ruin this place for us, they couldn't succeed. One final stop before you find me.*

The memory of Kayla warning me away from Lyndsey isn't a great one but we do have a lot of good memories of Bloom and Blossom. It is where I would visit her with coffee when Ellis was on bed rest. It is where I held her in my arms for the first time – yes, she was crying, but it is still nice to me. Plus, after all of this, I know Ellis would have been angry if she didn't get to be involved.

She might be Lyndsey's boss but they are each other's best friend. They found each other when the other was at rock bottom and I'm thankful that Ellis took Lyndsey into her heart because if she hadn't then I never would have met her. Never would have fallen in love.

The drive to the shop is a familiar one. I have done this drive most mornings I have been able to since we came back from Texas to take her to work. For the first time my hands start to sweat against the wheel. The road outside of the shop is filled with cars so I park a few blocks away and walk down to cool my hammering heart.

Before I even make it to the shop the door swings open and Jack's head pokes out, looking up and down the street, and when he sees me he darts out, running to me.

"Anders! Come on, quick, you have to hurry!" he yells, bouncing at my feet, grabbing my hand and tugging me with all of his might.

"Okay, bud, let's go," I laugh, letting him pull me along, and when we get inside Ellis is stood with her arms crossed, clearly mad.

"Jack, you can't just run out!" she admonishes him, but he doesn't seem fazed as he runs over to her, pulling the next white envelope out of her apron and handing it to me.

"But I found him!" he tells her as though she hasn't noticed me. She just rolls her eyes at him, clearly a little excited but not wanting to let him off with being reckless.

"I'll deal with you later. Hey, Aiden." She smiles, nodding at Jack as he hands the card to me.

I open it to find one final message.

Come find me husband. Il Moroso 6pm

It is already after five so I understand why Jack was so rushed. Knowing that after one last drive I'm going to see her makes my heart soar. After the day I have had there is nothing I want more than to kiss the hell out of her and see her green eyes shine up at me.

"Is this what I think it is?" I ask Ellis, noting the "husband" part of Lyndsey's message. I don't want to get my hopes up but all this fanfare must mean something.

"That depends, if you think it is Lyndsey showing you that she wants to be your wife for real then yes. If that's not what you think then… no, it's not what you think." She grimaces but I just burst out into excited laughter. She is finally ready. After all this time my darlin' is ready to admit that she was always supposed to be mine.

"I love her," I say to nobody in particular, I just like saying the words out loud.

"I know you do. Here, take these with you." She hands over the giant bouquet of flowers that is on the front counter. It is filled with flowers of all colours. Red roses and bright yellow sunflowers. Baby's breath in different colours and lush green leaves fill the gaps. There are flowers I don't know the names of but they look so beautiful that I know this must cost a lot of money.

"Wait, she didn't prepay for this, did she? She can't buy her own flowers." I start digging for my wallet but Ellis slaps my hand away when I try to hand her my card.

"No, she didn't. It's on me," she tells me with a smile, her eyes flicking between me and the garment bag that Rook gave me slung over my arm.

"No, Ellis." I try to protest but she gives me the mom glare I haven't seen since my own mom died. Still, it has the same effect now that it did then. I don't try to argue further, knowing it would be futile.

"Go in the back room and get dressed and get out of my store, Anders, we don't have time to argue! She is waiting for you," she tells me, pointing towards the back.

Jack claps from beside me, hooting and hollering in excitement. I leave them behind to get dressed, throwing my jeans and old shirt in the bag. I look damn good. The suit fits perfectly and I don't know how Rook knew what sizes to get but I don't even care because with my hair and this suit I'm going to be Lyndsey's Prince Charming on my way to a date with my princess.

-

I make it to Il Moroso just in time and my heart skips a beat knowing she is only a few feet away from me. I can't see her through the large windows but I know she is inside. As soon as the door opens my eyes scan around and I freeze when I see her. My smile almost hurts as I look at her draped in blue velvet, her ginger hair tied up on the top of her head, leaving the pale skin of her neck on display, and I want to kiss every inch of her skin.

Ignoring the maître d', I walk towards my wife with large strides, dropping the flowers on the table in my haste to take her into my arms. I have so many things to say but none of them seem big enough for this moment. Instead I kiss her. I pour every ounce of love and admiration I have for her into the kiss while also trying to keep it appropriate for the public. Though it is a real struggle.

I'm hypnotised by her beauty. I don't know how I got lucky enough for her to give me a chance. Especially when I thought there would be no way she would date me. And yet now here we are. I shake my head, blinking away the thoughts of where we would be if Vegas hadn't happened. I don't want to even imagine my life without her.

"You're incredible," I tell her. It feels so insignificant but I have to remember where we are, I can't exactly start yelling from the rooftops how in love with her I am.

Once we are both sitting, I take her hand in mine. I know I won't be able to get through this date without telling her exactly how I feel. She has done so much for me today, to show me how she cares about me. I know it must have been hard putting herself out here like this, offering me her heart on a silver platter.

"I love you." The words slip out but I don't regret saying them. She deserves the words.

"Aiden." She sucks in a breath, her hands starting to shake in mine, and I tighten my hold on her, knowing she will need a minute to process. "Do you know why I did all this?" she asks. Her voice is heavy with emotion but she looks at me with stars in her eyes.

"Because we have never been on a date?" I ask with a laugh, trying to take the pressure off. And it works, she smiles at me, lightly taking a deep breath, trying to soothe the anxiety that I can see pulses through her.

"That's what it started as but…" She pauses again, lifting my hand up to kiss my fingers where they are interlocked with hers. "Aiden, I love you too. Will you marry me?" This time I'm stunned into silence.

"What?" I ask, my jaw hanging open. I must have heard her wrong. There is no way she asked me to marry her. When I went to sleep last night, I thought I still had a lot of fighting to do to prove what she means to me, but she knows.

"Stay married to me?" She stands from her chair, walking around the table until she is beside me. I push my chair out and she settles onto my lap sideways. "Be my husband for real? Have a real wedding with our friends and your family. Our family."

"Fuck me, Lyndsey." I hold her face in my hands, only now noticing how they are shaking. "Of course I'll marry you again." The smile she gives me could stop time. I'm so lost in her orbit that I almost miss her quiet words.

"You may now kiss the bride."

And I do. I pull her closer, locking our lips in a kiss worthy of this moment. I no longer care that we are in public, I need the taste of her lips on mine. It's something I could never replicate. The delicate flavour of her lip gloss and her mint toothpaste. She tastes like mine.

She is going to be my bride and this time I vow to remember every minute of it. This time I'll remember her walking down the aisle towards me. I'll remember her wrapped in white fabric. Our friends will get to stand by our side while we remember saying our vows. We will have a first dance and will share a slice of cake. Have hundreds of pictures just in case my memories start to fade as we grow old together. I'll always have proof of how much I love her.

Lyndsey Anders.

Epilogue

Aiden

The first time I did this there were no wedding-day jitters. Probably because I didn't know it was going to be my wedding day. By the time any nerves could have come up I was drunk enough to not remember. This morning there are still no nerves. All I feel is excitement. I have more adrenalin now than I do when I am on the ice. I want to be standing at the aisle waiting for Lyndsey more than I need air.

Technically this is just a vows renewal, but I'll always think of this as our wedding day. We are surrounded by our family – well, not Lyndsey's family. It was not even a question whether or not they would be invited, there was no chance. We wouldn't let their judgement affect our day. Plus they might be her blood but they haven't been her family for a long time. Her brother has been let out on bail pending his harassment charges but he has kept his distance. The restraining order is ironclad but I know that when he is desperate enough, he will crop back up.

I won't think about that today. I'll only think about what I think Lyndsey's dress will be like when Ruin walks her down the aisle. He was so honoured when she asked him that I saw him blinking back some tears. I love that my teammates are her family. Even if something ever happened between us, I know they would support her and I couldn't ask for anything more.

I'm alone pacing the room where my groomsmen and I got ready. They are out greeting guests and doing any last-minute things Lyndsey needs, giving me a moment to myself. A knock at the door makes me jump, but Alice doesn't wait for me to answer before she strolls in.

"Last chance to run." She hands me a glass with two fingers of whisky.

"I'm good." I laugh, knowing that she knows good and well there is no force that could pull me away from today.

"She looks amazing." She wiggles her eyebrows at me and I want to ask questions about every detail, but she won't give me anything.

We fall into silence, me sipping at my whisky and her sipping at the bubbling glass of champagne. I'm glad for the company but I know my twin well enough to know there is another reason she is here. She knows I wouldn't want to run so why would she bother coming to see me? Not to stand in silence.

"What's wrong?" I ask, taking her empty glass out of her hand, guiding her to the sofa in the middle of the room.

"Nothing bad, but I have something to tell you and I know you are probably super uptight right now so I thought I'd give you something else to think about," she rambles. It is so unlike my sister to not say what she is thinking. She isn't the type of woman who beats around the bush.

"Okay?" I'm worried but I don't think it can be bad news. She wouldn't start off what is supposed to be the best day of my life by giving me some terrible news. I don't think she would anyway.

"I'm moving to Seattle." She smiles and I just blink at her. Her words sound foreign to my ears.

"What?" I cough, not wanting to get my hopes up. She might mean she is coming to visit.

"You are looking at the Spears newest rink-side photographer." She laughs at my shocked face and I start to laugh too. So completely blown away by this wedding gift. My damn sister is coming to work with me.

"Alice! Why didn't you tell me?" I ask, jumping to my feet, so filled with excitement that sitting still feels impossible.

"I wanted to wait until I knew for sure." She bites her bottom lip, this must have been a hard decision for her. Her coming here means the girls will be in Texas alone but they are adults. They can look after themselves. "Now that I don't have Pops keeping me home, the girls told me I had to go for it while I had the chance."

"I'm so happy for you, come here." I tug at her arm until she is standing, pulling her into my arms. We aren't always the most physically affectionate siblings but with the way she wraps her arms around me I know she needed this. To know I'm proud of her. "Come on, I want to introduce you to everyone you will be working with. You will love Cassie." I guide her towards the door but she lets out a nervous laugh, pulling back on my arm and stopping me.

"I already love Cassie." She grimaces at my confused face. "She helped me keep it from you while I was interviewing."

"Jesus, does everyone know except me?" I ask, a little offended. I understand why she wouldn't want to tell me. She wanted this job because of her talent and not because I put in a good word for her with the Spears management.

Plus if I had known I would have got my hopes up and it could have been for nothing.

"No. Just most people." She shrugs, walking out of the room herself. I follow her, it's almost time for the ceremony to start anyway.

—

Edge stands beside me at the front of the room. I feel my hands shaking so I try putting them in my pockets just to pull them out again a second later. Every minute that I stand here feels an hour long as I wait for the doors at the other end of the room to open and Lyndsey to walk through.

"Take a breath." Edge leans forward to whisper and I suck in a staggering lungful of air, nodding at him in thanks.

I want to remember every minute of this day. Every little feeling. Every sound in the room. I want to remember the smell of the flowers and the looks in the eyes of our friends and family.

We are having a small wedding – still, it's bigger than the last one. There are only around fifty guests so we decided to hold it at a hotel in the centre of Seattle. We hired out a few floors so everyone can spend the night and everyone has somewhere to relax for a few days. I'm glad we waited until the off-season so there wouldn't be any injuries in our wedding pictures.

The music changes in the room and everyone stands up as the door at the back creaks open. Then I see my wife.

Lyndsey is wearing a fitted white dress that gleams in the sunlight through the windows. The light behind her makes her an angel-like mirage coming to bring me salvation. When her eyes meet mine the smile she gives me makes everyone else in the room disappear, it is just me and her. Slowly she walks towards me, her arm in Liam's and a bouquet of pale pink flowers matching the bridesmaids' dresses of Ellis and my sisters.

I have to hold myself back from walking down the aisle to kiss her. I have to wait for her to come to me and the walk feels miles long, like she will never make it. After what feels like half an hour, she is in front of me. Ruin hugs her tightly before giving me a wink as he walks to the front row where Ellis, Jack and Charlotte are sat waiting for him.

"Hey, cowboy." She smiles a soft, contented smile up at me.

"Well hi, darlin'." I take her hands in mine, trying to pay attention as the celebrant talks to the room. My eyes are on her. They are always on her.

-

We have done our first dance.

We have cut the cake.

Now we are sitting at the sweetheart table watching our guests drink and dance and generally have a good time. It is amazing. She has been my wife on paper for a long time but now Lyndsey is my wife in the eyes of our nearest and dearest too. I can't keep my hands off her. If I'm not kissing her then I'm holding her hand. If I'm not holding her hand I have her pulled into my side. When she isn't close to me? I'm watching her with a smile.

"What is he doing?" she asks from beside me, nodding towards where Rook is talking to Alice. He'd better not be doing what I think he is doing. My sister should be off limits.

I'm about to stand when Cassie appears over my shoulder, putting her hand on the back of my neck. "We have a problem." Her voice is low enough that Lyndsey won't hear but she is still looking between Cassie and me, confused.

"What?" I ask, but instead of answering she shakes her head, almost imperceptibly darting her eyes towards the main door. I stand up, leaving a light kiss on my wife's head before following after Cassie.

With quick steps she walks me over to where Ruin is waiting, pacing back and forward with his phone pressed to his ear.

"I have to leave," she tells me when we are far enough away from the rest of the wedding party to be heard.

"Why? What's wrong?" I ask, my eyes darting around looking for any clues of why someone I consider a good friend is dipping out of my wedding.

"Edge has been arrested," she says, rocking back and forth on the balls of her feet as she grimaces.

"What?" I yell. I walk over to Liam where he has stopped talking on his phone and is instead pinching the bridge of his nose.

"Peter was here, he was yelling for you and Lyndsey and basically causing a scene. Edge caught him before he could get in and there was an incident," she tells me, and when I hear Peter's name, I stop short of spinning around to see if she is making some ill-timed joke. Because I can't think of another reason why she would be talking about that asshole on my damn wedding day.

"Fuck, is he still here?" I want to give that son of a bitch a piece of my mind. How dare he turn up today and try to make it about him? He has ruined Lyndsey's happiness enough this year.

"No, he was taken in a police car too, as soon as I knew he was here I called the police, with the restraining order and everything they took him but not before Edge tried to knock him out." Cassie fills me in but before I can ask any follow-up questions Ruin butts in.

"It was amazing." He smiles, shaking his head and acting out a punch. He takes his right arm and swings it as though he is going to hit himself before staggering back a few steps, clutching his nose in what I think is a bad re-enactment of Peter.

"Liam!" Cassie chastises as I laugh.

"What? He was asking for it, yelling for his bitch sister and the man fucking her, if Edge hadn't hit him I would've. Fuck him," he spits out, not hiding his distaste for my brother-in-law.

"This is a mess." I sigh, throwing my head back, thinking about how I'm going to tell Lyndsey about all of this. I wanted today to be a happy day, not shadowed by her brother or all the bad she has overcome in the last few months.

"I'm going to sort it out, I'm waiting for a car to take me to the station to get Edge out. Just enjoy the rest of your wedding day, okay? I'm so sorry." She looks as worked up as I feel. Cassie is the woman who keeps us in line, she is used to control and there is nothing she can control about this. For someone always so put together she looks one wrong move away from falling apart.

"You have nothing to apologise for, go get our boy, okay?" I tell her, hoping I can give her a little boost of confidence.

Instead of replying she just nods, pulling her phone out of her small purse. Before she leaves, I pull her into my side in a small hug to show her that I don't blame her for this. Knowing her, she will be kicking herself for calling the police in the first place, but it was the right thing to do. If Edge had a hold on his anger, he would still be here right now despite her calling the police.

Ruin pulls her out of my arms and into his own. He whispers something in her ear, making her nod. Then as quickly as she came to get me, she is gone again. Like a whirlwind she takes off down the front steps and into a car without looking back.

As soon as I walk through the door Lyndsey runs up to me with Ellis behind her. The two of them look between Liam and me but instead of telling Lyndsey what is happening I take her hand in mine, bringing her onto the dance floor. I settle my hands on the small of her back. The ribbon of the corset back of the dress is soft between my fingertips and I'm glad it wasn't me that hit Peter. I want to use my hands to make her happy, to bring her pleasure, not for hitting her brother. No matter how much of a dick he is.

"Aiden?" She looks up at me with furrowed brows, wanting to know what is happening, but I refuse to darken her day with everything.

"Not right now, darlin'. I'll tell you everything tomorrow but let us just enjoy tonight, okay?" I wouldn't keep it from her if I didn't think it was best. I don't want to start our married life with lies but I also don't want to start it in a jail. If I told her that Edge has been arrested, she would demand to go see him and make sure he is okay. I have to trust that Cassie has it handled for now and by tomorrow Edge will be in his own house where Lyndsey can go and yell at him for rising to Peter's bait.

"Fine, but don't think your off the hook." She is still worried but I think I'm keeping calm enough that it placates her. I feel her muscles relax as we sway together. She looks so beautiful under the lights of the chandelier casting rainbows over the white satin of her dress. The flare of white tulle is hard to dance around so we keep our feet planted, just swaying to the beat of the big band music playing around us.

Off to the side I see my sisters dancing together and Rook trying to join them. Alice rolls her eyes before letting him into their dance circle. Felix, the Spears goalie, has his wife wrapped in his arms and Ruin is dipping Ellis. His parents, Tracy and Alek, came up from Florida so they could look after the kids for the night, plus they want to help them plan their own wedding. They keep putting it off because they want to wait until Charlotte is old enough to be their flower girl. Though I know Liam is desperate for Ellis to have his surname.

Lyndsey pushes up on her tiptoes to kiss me lightly. When I try to deepen it, she pulls away with a sly smile.

"Want to get out of here, husband?" she whispers against the shell of my ear. Her warm breath causes goosebumps to flare down my neck under the collar of my suit.

"I'll go anywhere with you, wife," I tell her truthfully, and she takes my hand in hers, pulling me out of the reception hall, not bothering to say goodbye to anyone. They can entertain themselves with the DJ and open bar.

As soon as the elevator door shuts behind us, I pull her to me, kissing her hard. Now that we have some privacy, I show her exactly how crazy she has made me today. I have wanted to take her from the minute the doors opened revealing her to me and I'm not going to waste any more time.

We don't even make it to the bridal suite before I'm pulling pins out of her hair, desperate to run my hands through her rose-gold locks. I want to mess her up. She looks so perfect, her make-up still intact and her dress perfectly ironed. I want to kiss her until her lips are swollen and her lipstick has smudged. I want to run my fingers through her hair and wrap it around my fist pulling her to me. I want her dress forgotten in a rumpled pile on the floor.

She scrambles to the bed, throwing herself down on the rose-covered sheets, laughing when I pull her down the bed by her heel-clad feet. I lean my body down over her, covering every part of her with me. Her chest heaves and her eyes are blown wide as she smiles at me, her hair fanned around just as wild as I pictured it.

"You get naked, I'm going to run us a bubble bath." I kiss her lightly as she hums.

On my way to the bathroom I pick up the ice bucket and bottle of champagne, leaving it next to the sink. The claw-foot tub will take a little while to fill but it will be worth it to have her soaped up in my arms. I pour a healthy measure of the complimentary bath stuff under the streak of water, watching steam curl around the room. I take my time lighting candles and opening the bottle of champagne, pouring us two glasses.

I stop the water with enough room to make sure it won't overflow when we both get in the water and walk back into the bedroom. What I find halts my plans.

Lyndsey is in nothing but crisp white lingerie on the petal-covered sheets, her make-up wiped bare, meaning my plan to make mascara run down her cheeks is foiled, but she is basically glowing as she lies there. A lacy bra and a scrap of lace between her legs that leaves nothing to the imagination. She looks like a vision. The only problem is the quiet snores that puff between her lips.

My wife is asleep.

I guess the tub took longer to fill than I thought. Today has been a long and exciting day. She told me she had been up since five a.m. this morning getting ready, it shouldn't be a surprise that she is exhausted. I don't bother emptying the tub. It can wait. Instead, I quietly strip out of my suit until I'm just as naked as her, nothing but my boxers. Then I pull back the covers, sliding her from atop the sheet to under it. I worry she will wake but she just lets out a contented sigh, pushing her face further into the pillow.

I slide under the covers beside her, lifting her head to rest on my chest. This isn't how I imagined this night going but it's probably better. I get to look as my wife relaxes in my arms and wraps a hand around my waist. Her skin is warm against mine and I can't help but kiss her head. Even in sleep she must feel it because a small smile flits across her face before I turn out the light, blanketing us in darkness.

I fall asleep knowing everything is exactly as it was always supposed to be. Lyndsey in my arms and my heart filled with love.

My dad was right after all: having a woman by your side does make life better.